The doglike creature that
stopped abruptly now that
feet. It drew back, and ev
mistaking the meaning of

'My God, it's a child,' s
more clearly.

Encrusted with dirt and covered with innumerable scars, his hair a dense matted ball concealing much of his face, the boy remained where he was, ignoring Turk's waving tail and excited yelps. The child was completely naked but seemed unaware of this as he arched his back menacingly and moved his head from side to side, occasionally panting as he watched her standing on the terrace . . .

JAMES FARBER

Nightmare's Child

PANTHER
Granada Publishing

Panther Books
Granada Publishing Ltd
8 Grafton Street, London W1X 3LA

This revised edition published by Panther Books 1985

ISBN 0-586-06422-2

Printed and bound in Great Britain by
Collins, Glasgow

Set in Bembo

For Stephen Lewis –
you will be missed

Birth

In the wet, fragrant darkness the companion stirs, uncoiling like a serpent. The steady, rhythmic thumping of his mother's heart awakens him, and though he cannot see it, beyond his tightly shuttered lids a frightened world awaits his birth. Conceived of doubt, he listens for a sign, while floating beside him another small wet shape embarks on its own journey of awareness. This is Ohrmazd, his twin brother, stirring as Ahriman stirs, awakening to the promise of birth.

Is that a voice he hears beyond the soft, palpitating walls of his prison? Ahriman strains to hear the words his father speaks. The first to emerge will be king, he thinks again. He stretches mightily, pressing his fingers against the sides of his mother's womb, seeking to escape. The firstborn shall be king. It is a challenge he is determined to meet. With a snarl of frustration that causes his brother to float away from him in fear, Ahriman tears at the moist fleshy walls of the cavity, desperate to free himself and claim his father's throne.

'Whichever of my sons will come to me first, to him I shall grant the kingdom.'

It is his father's voice, ordering him forth. Ahriman groans with excitement, knowing he is stronger than his brother, that evil must always be victorious. A salty spray of blood drenches his cheeks. The heartbeat quickens, racing along in maddened haste as the layers of flesh are torn as easily as blades of grass. Although his eyes are sealed, he feels the light like a glowing weight against his lids.

Clad in the stench of human misery, the foul odor of poverty and despair, Ahriman struggles forth, hearing his father weep that Ohrmazd is not first. Behind him the fragrant twin gently slips through the torn and mutilated opening, as if fearing to inflict further damage, stepping forth lightly like a wind-borne seed.

Ahriman grows stronger, and when he opens his eyes he cries out, 'I am your son, Ohrmazd!'

'My son is light and fragrant,' replies his father, 'but you are dark and stinking.'

Ohrmazd tumbles free, washed with the blood of sacrifice. Ahriman stands between him and his father. 'Did you not vow that whichever of your sons would come to you first, to him you would grant the kingdom?'

And still his father weeps, saying, 'O false and wicked one, the kingdom shall be granted you for nine thousand years, but Ohrmazd I have made a king above you, and after nine thousand years he will reign and do everything according to his good pleasure.'

Ahriman raises his shrill, howling voice. In a single instant he creates all that is evil and perverse, and for nine thousand years he rules supreme. But now he stirs anew, a prisoner of another's mind, a 'companion,' if you will. He cannot escape, and so night after night he sends his dreams shrieking through the other's mind, repeating the images of his bloody birth, and the fierce, unending battle he has fought all the days of his evil and deceitful life.

1

San Bernardino Freeway, Sunday, 22 October 1978

All her life Kathleen Duffy had taken chances. Even when people stopped calling her Kathy and knew her only as Amber Cloud, she still took risks, saying that life wasn't worth a rat's ass unless you were willing to skate on thin ice. But on this unseasonably warm Sunday afternoon the ice seemed to have given way beneath her feet.

As she stood along the Citrus Avenue on-ramp of the freeway, a crudely scrawled sign propped against her battered suitcase, she kept her thumb in readiness, hating the sons of bitches who drove right past her. Playing in the dust at her feet was a little boy with corn-silk hair and almost colorless blue eyes, intent on the anthill into which he was poking a stick.

The sign Amber had scratched on a piece of cardboard read DAYTON IF YOU DARE. If she dared. Would her parents welcome her with open arms? After all, she hadn't seen them in seven years, not since she was thirteen. Only once or twice in all that time had she thought of calling them. Even when Blue was born, she didn't phone, but sent a postcard instead, telling them to open themselves a bottle of Cold Duck, they had a grandson whether they liked it or not.

Only problem, now she saw herself going back to everything she'd always hated. The ugly little house on Hazel Street, the fights that went on from morning till night, her father's big beefy hand coming out of thin air to slap her silly. Mom cried all the time before she left, and probably cried a hell of a lot more once she was gone.

She'd told the driver of the Trailways she was fifteen and off to see her Aunt Barbara in Chicago. From there it got easy, at least for a while. She met her first old man cruising Michigan Avenue one night when she was down to her last fifty cents. He was a real sharp dude who knew all the angles, telling johns she was still cherry just to up the ante. Those days she had more money than she knew what to do with. And when they headed west to LA, it seemed to her that Dayton was just some place she'd been passing through, thirteen crummy years on the way to the big time.

When she finally decided to split he beat the shit out of her, and for a couple of weeks she toyed with the idea of giving it all up and heading home. But then she met a drummer with a vision of the good life, and for almost a year it was party party party, everything soft and mellow in a nonstop druggy haze. Only when she had her kid did it start to sour.

She named her son Blue after his strange icy eyes. Even as an infant he'd sometimes look at her so strangely she wondered if he wasn't a little old man hiding out from Father Time. Six years later and he still had that same spooky glance, like he knew lots of things he wasn't telling her about. 'Course, the kid had seen a lot, too, done things most six-year-olds couldn't even imagine if they tried. Still, there were times when he gave her the creeps, the way he'd stare and stare with his cold fishy eyes, like he was looking right through her and seeing her for what she really was.

'D'you love Mama best of all?' Amber said as she stood at the edge of the freeway, waiting for the ride that still hadn't come.

The little boy looked up and smiled crookedly, as if to say that was a question she shouldn't have bothered to ask.

'Don't play in the dust, you'll get dirty,' Amber told him.

She reached down and jerked him to his feet, giving him a good shaking just so he'd remember who was boss.

'If you act like that Grandma'll hate you for sure, Bluie. So don't start forgetting what's right and what's wrong, you hear me?'

The youngster nodded obediently. Then he crouched down and jabbed the twig into the anthill, having long since learned that silence was the best way to answer whenever his mama raised her voice.

'Dumb shits,' she said when a whole mess of cars drove by, a real slutty-looking cunt with a bubble hairdo giving her a look that could have killed. 'You'd think we had the clap or something the way they act.'

But finally a chrome bulldog chugged up the curving on-ramp, and behind the wheel of the Mack truck a nice-looking guy eyed her for a moment and then pulled over to the shoulder and asked her how far she was going.

'All the way,' she said with a laugh, already pushing Bluie onto the metal step just in case the truck driver decided to change his mind.

He reached out and lifted the boy up in his arms, depositing him on the front seat. Amber scooted inside the cab and slammed the door behind her, wedging her suitcase in the narrow space at her feet. Then she flashed her best-behavior smile, all wide-eyed innocence and ain't I just the cutest thing you've ever seen. The truck driver took the bait, grinning back at her as if they were friends of long standing.

'Jess,' he said, extending a big, bearlike hand.

'Amber Cloud.'

'Amber who?'

'Cloud, and don't go making jokes, neither.' She grinned just so he wouldn't think she had a flashy mouth. She nudged the kid with her elbow. 'Say hello to the nice man, Bluie.'

The little boy looked up, as solemn as a Sunday preacher.

'Don't talk much, does he?' Jess said as he rolled down the on-ramp and out into the middle of east-bound traffic.

Amber sat back, eying the driver and wondering if he liked what he saw. She didn't have much bread, and it might pay to turn a quick trick so she and the kid would have enough to keep going until they reached Ohio.

'Dayton's a long way from here, ain't it?'

Amber shrugged, then flashed a wan smile. It didn't seem to matter how long it took, so long as she put the miles between her and her old man. He'd come back tonight and find her gone and then all hell would break loose, 'specially when he discovered she'd ripped off whatever bread he had around the house.

'You from LA?' she asked, trying to make conversation while Blue sat stiffly in his seat, making engine sounds as he turned an imaginary steering wheel from one side to the other.

'San Diego.'

'I've never been there.'

'You mean you never took your kid to the zoo?' Jess said with surprise.

What was he trying to do, make her feel guilty or something? With a rough edge to her voice, she said, 'No, I never been there. Sorry.'

Jess smiled lamely. 'No big deal. It's an all-right place. Weather's nice. How come you're going back to Ohio?'

Amber rolled her eyes: like, man, it was a real long story, so why go into it?

It was at that point that Jess reached out, his big hairy hand like a mitt as he squeezed her shoulder. ''S okay, kiddo. I get the message. Hard times, ain't that what it's all about? Shit, I've had my share . . . more than my share, if you catch my drift. So now you figure home-sweet-home can't be all that bad, now, can it?'

'It can.' She wondered why it bothered her to hear him

trying to psych her out. 'Look, if you want to know the truth, my old man was a fucking creep. Used to slap me and the kid around for no goddamn reason.'

'Grr,' went the boy. 'Puff-puff-puff.'

'That's right, Bluie. You call 'em like you see 'em.'

Amber turned her head to the side and glanced out the window. They were driving past what looked like an enormous industrial park, with neat little nothing houses with neat little shingle roofs surrounding it on all four sides.

'I ain't been out here but once, and that was years ago. You been driving this thing long?'

'Honey, I drive my thing as hard as I can,' Jess said with a grin.

Amber returned his smirky smile. 'You married?'

It was Jess's turn to roll his eyes. 'That sure came out of left field, didn't it?'

'Don't mean to pry,' she said hurriedly.

'You didn't. And the answer's no.' He glanced down at Blue, who was still driving an invisible car. 'How old's the kid?'

'Six.'

'Pretty big for his age. Your old man must've been a hell of a bruiser.'

'Yeah, he was big, all right. Real big.' She left the rest unsaid, eying the front of his greasy jeans and wondering if his big hairy hands were indicative of what the rest of him was like. 'Bluie, honey, why don't you switch places with Mama? That way you can look out the window.'

'Grr,' whispered the boy. 'Suckit, suckit.'

'What'd he say?' said Jess.

'Nothin'.'

She helped her son change seats, hoping Jess would appreciate all the trouble she was going through. Then she swiveled around, turning to the side so that her knee accidentally-on-purpose brushed against his leg. Jess let one hand drop off the steering wheel, his long, callused fingers sliding back and forth along her knee. Slowly they began to inch their way higher, disappearing under the hem of her denim skirt.

Amber closed her eyes for a moment and squeezed her legs together, trapping his hand. Johns were all the same, she couldn't help but think. Give them an inch and they take a mile. But this jerk wasn't half bad. He had a nice smile and a nice way with words.

It felt good too, the way he stroked her, ever so gently, like he was in no big hurry. But when she reached over, figuring it was her turn now to return the favor, Jess lifted her hand off his crotch and put it back in her lap.

'The kid,' he said, half under his breath.

She wanted to tell him the kid was cool, but figured there'd be time enough to get into that. So for now she just sat back while they drove through the smoggy San Gabriel Valley, heading in the direction of San Bernardino, Palm Springs, and then God knows where.

Amber must have dozed off, because the next thing she knew it was dark out and Blue lay next to her, his head on her lap and his legs tucked under him.

She shook her head and looked over at the truck driver's hard, chiseled profile. 'Jeez, I really konked out, didn't I? Sorry.'

'How does something to eat sound? I bet the boy's hungry.'

Amber eyed the sleeping child, Bluie's golden hair like the halo around an angel, like pictures she'd seen when she went to a museum once.

'You hungry, baby?' she whispered.

Blue stirred in his sleep, warming his hands between his legs. Then he opened his eyes, looking up at her with a blank expression, as if she were a stranger.

'Did Bluie have a nice little nap?' She figured it made her look good if she played attentive mommy.

The child nodded. 'I was in the room again. The one with the pipes.'

'That's nice,' she said quickly. 'Jess here is gonna spring for burgers and fries. Would you like that?'

Twenty minutes later they were sitting in a tacky truck stop near the town of Barstow, halfway on the road to nowhere. She'd hoped they might be passing through Palm Springs so she could see where all the millionaires lived. But while she slept Jess had turned north onto I–15, heading in the direction of Vegas.

'Look,' he said, sounding so earnest she had a sinking feeling he was going to tell her the free ride was over, 'I'm taking this load all the way to Chicago. And to tell you the truth, I kind of like your company, if you don't mind my saying.'

'I don't mind.'

'So what do you think? Can you put up with me? I ain't such a great talker and all. But I got some good moves, if you know what I mean.'

Amber knew exactly. She'd seen that hungry, wide-eyed look so many times before that now it almost came as a disappointment when she realized he was just like all the other horny johns she'd serviced in the past. But at least he wasn't a fat slob, or one of those uptight button-down businessmen types who acted like they were afraid the FBI was gonna bust them for entertaining trade.

Relieved, she said, 'That sounds great, real good, Jess. But I gotta be straight with you. Me and the kid don't have much bread. I don't want you to think you have to be obligated or anything.'

'Hell, it'll be my pleasure,' the truck driver said with a big, easygoing grin, all nice white teeth like he was vain about his smile. ''Sides, a big strong feller like Blue here needs his nourishment. Ain't that right, champ?'

Blue raised his pale icy eyes. 'I like fries and ketchup,' he said. 'Are you like the man who – '

Amber put her hand over his mouth, smiling nervously. 'Now, you mustn't talk with your mouth full, honey. We get the message, don't we, Jess?'

The truck driver looked a little confused. But once they checked into a motel, so much fucking knotty pine she thought she was holding court in someone's finished basement, he stopped worrying about what the boy was trying to tell him, more concerned about what would happen once they got between the sheets.

Amber looked in the direction of the bed, knowing that once you'd seen one, you'd seen 'em all. She had her suitcase open and her nightie on the bedspread before the trucker had time to kick off his boots. But when she started to make up a bed for Blue, pushing two chairs together and folding a blanket over them to keep him warm, Jess walked back and forth like he'd lost something but couldn't remember what it was.

'Anything wrong?' she asked as she helped Blue out of his clothes.

Jess motioned with his cleft chin, gesturing at the boy.

'So?'

'So what are we gonna do with the kid around?'

Amber knelt before her son, unbuttoning his flannel shirt. 'You hear that, Bluie?'

'What?' asked the child.

'Tell Uncle Jess that it's cool.'

'What?' the boy said again.

'Shit, what kind of talk is that, Amber? He's a six-year-old kid, for Christ's sake.'

'What are you getting so hassled about? I'm telling you,

the kid's seen it all. Hell, he even likes to watch. Don'tcha, Bluie?'

Blue stepped out of his jeans, nodding vigorously. 'Watch what?' he said as he toddled into the bathroom to brush his teeth.

'Like when I took you to the room with the pipes on the ceiling,' she called after him.

'Oh, that,' he said with another nod. 'That was fun.'

'What room are you talking about?' asked Jess.

Amber lit a cigarette, blowing smoke rings into the air. She wasn't sure if she felt bored, or annoyed at being given the third degree. 'We did a little porno on the side,' she admitted, refusing to flinch when he looked at her in surprise. 'Shit, man, the kid and I gotta eat, don't we? My old man was a real wheeler-dealer, only he wheeled more than he dealed, if you get my meaning. Hated working more than anything. So if we had a chance to make a couple of bucks, what's the big deal?'

'You and the kid . . . the both of you?' Jess said, still looking at her as if she were a freak.

She shrugged. 'Takes all kinds,' she said, not about to lose her cool when he was holding out the promise of a free ride all the way to the Windy City. 'Bluie here's a real deep sleeper. Once he closes his eyes he's out like a shot.'

But she could see he wasn't taking it so well, and so she unzipped her skirt and let it drop to the floor. 'Now you just relax and let Amber take care of you,' she said in that saccharine voice she used whenever she turned a trick.

Jess had brought along a fifth, and now she unscrewed the top and poured them each a double. A couple of stiff belts later and he was finally loosening up. Blue was stretched out between the two chairs, and even if he wasn't asleep, at least his eyes were closed. Amber turned on the radio, then slipped out of her blouse and sat down on the edge of the bed, one hand snaking up and down Jess's hard-muscled thigh.

'It's a long ways to Chicago,' she reminded him. 'No reason we can't make it worth each other's while.'

Amber eased him back onto the bed, tasting the whiskey on his lips and struggling to get the buttons open on his jeans. It didn't take much to convince him that he should cooperate, and she had him all primed when he suddenly staggered off the bed, pausing to pour himself another Scotch before taking off the rest of his clothes. Naked, he looked real good, almost as good as the son of a bitch she'd left behind in LA.

'So you've done porno films, eh?' Jess said as he scooted back onto the bed, kneeling between her legs and liking what he saw.

'A couple,' she said dreamily. 'Pays the bills.'

'You ever do this?'

He had her legs up in the air so fast she hardly knew what was happening. But the moment she felt the head of his cock pressing against her ass she pulled back.

'No, thanks.'

'What d'you mean?'

'I mean no, thanks. It's not my thing. I don't get off on it.'

'Sorry, but I do,' Jess said.

'The answer's no. Now why don't you just lie back, honey, and let Amber's magic fingers take your mind off your problems?'

Jess glared at her sullenly. 'I don't get off on it,' he said in a mocking tone of voice.

Amber tried to ignore his sarcasm. 'I got lips too, honey, if that's what you mean.'

'That's not what I mean,' he said, raising his voice.

'Well, shit, you don't have to get so uptight. What's the big deal, anyway? I don't like being cornholed, d'you mind?'

'You're damn right I do.'

Before she could stop him he twisted her over onto her

stomach, pressing her mouth into the pillows so she couldn't scream.

'Now you be good, little girl, and do what you're told, and Jess'll be real nice to you, d'you hear?'

Amber struggled to cry out. But each time she managed to turn her head to the side, trying to attract Blue's attention, Jess slammed her face into the pillows. If he kept it up much longer she wouldn't even be able to breathe, and so she shoved back as hard as she could, trying to get him to let go.

That was probably her biggest mistake, because the moment she got violent on him he seemed to go beserk. Even as he kept her head against the pillows and she gurgled helplessly, unable to understand what she'd done wrong, his other hand helped guide his penis into place. The more she resisted, tightening her muscles and trying to prevent entry, the more aroused he seemed to become.

Use some goddamn spit, for Christ's sake! she wanted to scream when she realized there was nothing she could do to stop him.

But by then he'd already gotten his way. As the pain erupted she cried out, pushing herself back again and again. Yet no matter how hard she tried, she still couldn't get air into her lungs.

Just let me breathe, you bastard!

The words raced frantically through her mind while he kept pounding into her. The bedsprings were creaking so loudly she couldn't understand why Blue hadn't woken up.

Please, Bluie, just open your eyes and see what he's doing and make him stop. Please, baby, just do this one thing for Mama and I'll never hit you again, I promise.

She felt his sweaty thighs clamped around her legs, felt the pain like a red-hot poker. But most of all she felt the hot damp pillow against her lips; she was gasping now and wondering how such a thing could be possible. He was a sick freak, that's what he was. He was one of those weirdos you were always warned about but never dreamed you'd end up meeting.

Please, just let me breathe!

The words were trapped behind her lips. She could barely feel him now, and everything seemed to be slowing down so that it seemed as if she were moving underwater, a thick layer of ice preventing her from reaching the surface.

With a strangled cry he fell against her, thick ropy saliva trickling down his chin, his body shuddering violently as if he had the chills. Then slowly everything began to come back into focus.

He rolled over onto his back, satisfied now and thinking that women were all the same. They said one thing and meant another.

'Now, was that so bad?' he said, prodding her with his elbow. 'I bet you loved it, didn't you?'

Amber didn't answer. She lay there with her face buried in the pillows, the dark roots of her platinum hair spreading out like an ink stain across the top of her head. He ran his hand over the rounded swell of her ass, then gave her a playful little slap.

'Hey, come on, babe. It wasn't so bad. Come on, now, little girl, snuggle up to Jess here and everything'll be fine.'

He pushed her over onto her side, ready to wipe the tears from her eyes.

'Christ, I'll pay, if that's what's bugging you.'

The girl stared at him with dead fish eyes, her lips parted and the tip of her tongue trapped between her teeth. He reached over and shook her. Whatever game she was playing was making him very nervous. But the more he shook her, trying to get her to say something, to stop staring at him like that, the more frightened he became.

When he let go of her she rolled back, one arm falling limply over the side of the bed. Jess turned his eyes away, glancing at the boy. The kid was still asleep, out like a light just like she'd said.

'Amber, honey, give me a break,' he whispered. 'Stop playing this game, 'cause it gives me the creeps.'

He put his ear to her chest. When he couldn't hear anything he lifted one limp arm, trying to find her pulse. But all he heard was the blood pounding in his ears, a terrified jarring sound that made him begin to tremble. He shook his head, refusing to believe this could have happened.

How? he kept asking himself, while his eyes darted nervously over at the boy. We were having a good time. I don't understand.

The girl was dead. She'd suffocated or had a heart attack or something. He still didn't know how it was possible, but now he had worse problems on his hands. He'd registered under his own name, and how the hell was he going to start explaining that here they were having themselves a party, and the next thing he knows he's got a fucking corpse on his hands?

Jess slipped out of bed, turning Amber onto her side so that if the boy should wake up, he wouldn't see her lying there with her cold staring eyes and her swollen pink tongue sticking out like a piece of raw meat between her lips. Then he hurriedly dried himself off and pulled on his clothes.

When he was dressed and his kit was packed, he carefully opened the door. At the far end of the parking lot a neon sign shone with a bloody NO VACANCY. He could see his rig waiting there like some oversized coffin, and he closed the door again and went over to the bed.

'I didn't mean nothin', honest,' he said aloud. Then he began to wrap the blanket around Amber's lifeless body, pausing a moment to pull her eyelids down before lifting her up in his arms.

Across the room the little boy turned over, whispering in his sleep. Jess waited until he'd settled down again before tiptoeing from the room. Fortunately, it was situated around the corner from the front office, and so he didn't worry that the owner would see him carrying something to his rig. As soon as he propped her up in the cab, he locked the door and hurried back to the room.

Blue was sitting up now, rubbing his eyes with the backs of his hands. 'Where's my mama?' he said when Jess returned.

'In the truck, asleep. We wanted to get an early start. You know, before folks start going to work and all.'

He stuffed Amber's clothes into her suitcase, then helped the boy get dressed.

'Are you gonna be my new poppy now?' Blue said, still half asleep.

'Sure, champ, whatever you like.'

The child reached for Jess's hand. 'I watched before,' he said shyly. 'I like to watch.'

Jess could barely keep his voice from cracking. 'What are you talking about, champ?'

'You and Mama playing horsie. Giddyup!' he cried out. 'Whoa, boy, suckit, suckit.'

Jess didn't know what the kid was talking about. But as soon as he hustled Blue into the cab and swung onto the driver's seat, the boy quieted down, looking at his mother as if he didn't even recognize her.

Halfway between Barstow and Baker, Jess stopped the rig and pulled over to the side of the deserted highway, trying to stifle the waves of panic that kept rising in his chest.

Blue looked at him curiously. 'I don't have to make yet,' the little boy said.

Instead of answering, Jess got down and went around to the other side of the cab. He unlocked the door, catching Amber's body just as it began to tumble out.

'You take the suitcase, champ. We're going for a little walk.'

'Where?' asked Blue.

'You just follow me, you hear? Your mama's not feeling well, and she needs to lie down.'

He waited until the child was standing beside him, dragging the battered suitcase in the dust. The youngster's eyes seemed to glow, and when Jess looked down at him he had this real spooky feeling, like the kid knew exactly what was going on, even if he wasn't saying a word.

Jess started out across the desert, barely able to see in front of him. A cool, dry breeze swept across his cheeks. If only the bitch had cooperated, he kept thinking. If only she hadn't played hard to get.

He clocked himself for fifteen minutes, keeping up a brisk pace so that Blue fell farther and farther behind. Only when he felt confident he'd gone far enough did he stop, lowering Amber's body onto the rubble-strewn ground and waiting for her kid to catch up to him.

'Now, you stay here with your mama till she wakes up,' he instructed the child.

'Where are we, Uncle Jess?'

'We're going camping, champ. Only I'm going back to the truck to get us some sleeping bags. So you stay right here and don't get yourself lost.'

'It's dark,' the boy whispered in a frightened voice.

'A big strong feller like you shouldn't be afraid of the dark. Nothing's out here, anyway.' He took a hesitant step back, hating himself for what he was about to do, yet unable to see any other way out of it. Maybe the kid would be all right. Maybe when it got light out and he saw his mother wasn't going to wake up he'd head back to the highway, and someone would pick him up and take care of him.

I'm sorry, Bluie, he thought, really I am. But I just can't help it. 'You just stay here. I'll be right back.'

Jess turned, breaking into a run. When he got back to the truck he noticed Amber's sign lying crumpled on the floor of the cab. Who the hell wants to go back to Dayton, anyway? he thought. He tossed it out the window, and by the time the sun came up he was already in Utah.

The she-wolf pricked up her ears, listening to the wind and tasting the air. The message was very clear. There was food out there, perhaps no more than a short distance away. A faint man-smell made her mane bristle with excitement. Her tail stiffened and she lifted her narrow muzzle, trying to determine from which direction the scent was coming.

'Soon,' whispered the voice she had learned to obey, the voice that saw to her needs, just as the pack leader had once done. 'Yes, very soon and we won't be hungry.'

2

Tehran, Iran, Monday, 21 August 1978

Two months earlier, and many thousands of miles from where the boy had been led into the desert, Gasem Zahedi awakened with a start. The night was dark and stinking, and as he sat up in bed he listened carefully, as if searching for a sign. But the close, muggy air carried no clue. Everything seemed as it should be, even the nightmare of something clawing its way free of a womb, a vision he had not been able to shake for so many years now he'd long since forgotten what it was to dream of anything else.

He closed his eyes again, pressing his lips into the pillows. Sleep gradually overcame him, but outside the gates of his compound his guards were being overpowered. The three intruders then moved as furtively as shadows, eager to crush the monster who slept within.

The youngest of the three was a student enrolled at UCLA, the son of solid upper-middle-class Iranians, grown wealthy and complacent in the years of the Shah's reign. Amir Farsian had been recruited into the Ayatollah Khomeini's secret army several months before, when he returned from the United States to spend his summer holiday with his family.

Now his task was to avenge the deaths of more than four hundred men, women, and children, all of whom had lost their lives as a result of decisions made by one man – Gasem Zahedi, a high-ranking officer in SAVAK, the Shah's dreaded secret police.

Zahedi's guards lay where they had fallen. In the darkness their blood ran black as Iran's precious oil, trickling from their slashed throats and forming tarlike puddles at their feet. The bodies were dragged into the bushes, Farsian and the two others then moving up the stairs like cats, light on their feet, through the palatial rooms to Zahedi's bedroom.

With a brief nod Farsian moved forward, and he was halfway to Zahedi's bed when suddenly the officer cried out in alarm and sat bolt upright, reaching in the direction of the nightstand.

But he had no time to grab his service revolver, the three men pinning him down just seconds after he opened his eyes. As Amir listened to the colonel's muffled shouts he drew a slim, gleaming knife from his pocket. One glance at the weapon and Zahedi's struggles grew more heated. But though he tried to speak, the hand over his mouth made his words unintelligible, a pitiful bleating like the cry of a frightened sheep.

'Surely you know why we're here,' Farsian said at last. He leaned over his victim, relishing the way Gasem Zahedi's almost colorless blue eyes opened wide in terror. 'We know all about you, Colonel. Four hundred dead, and hundreds more if we did not stop you. Our party is Allah's party, and our leader is Khomeini.'

Having said these words in a hoarse whisper, Amir Farsian held the knife before Colonel Zahedi's panic-stricken eyes, forcing him to stare at the sliver of reflection captured in the gleaming length of blade. An instant later he brought the knife down in a single unflinching arc, slamming the tip of the blade directly below Zahedi's rib cage.

The SAVAK officer stiffened, propelling himself half off the bed as if trying to meet the powerful thrust of the weapon. As the flesh tore like a strip of moist, pink lamb and Amir Farsian felt the jets of blood drenching his fingers, something began to stab at the nape of his neck.

He dropped the knife and staggered back, blood-stained fingers clamped to his temples as he swayed from side to side, unable to overcome the monstrous pain. It started like the sting of an insect at the back of his head and kept mounting in intensity until it felt as if his skull would explode, shattering at his feet like so much broken glass.

Colonel Zahedi fell back against the bed, a dry, rattling sound escaping from his lips. At that exact moment the pain vanished.

Amir shook his head, as if trying to clear away the cobwebs. He was still dazed, unable to explain to himself what had happened. But now, in retrospect, the pain seemed inconsequential, something that had already passed, and perhaps had existed solely in his imagination. Putting all thoughts of it aside, he looked down at the dead man, weeping for Zahedi's victims, and exulting that their murderer had died as painfully and sadistically as they.

Los Angeles, Monday, 9 October 1978

'Come in, Amir. Please, make yourself comfortable.'

Dr Browning rose halfway from his seat and motioned him to a leather chair positioned directly in front of his desk. He was a youngish-looking man with a thick, drooping mustache and thin straight hair that fell halfway over his ears. Amir wanted to like him, but the voice in his head, the mocking voice that gave him no peace, warned him to be on guard, that Dr Browning was not to be trusted.

The Student Health Service had arranged this appointment for him more than two weeks before. But Amir had found numerous excuses not to keep it, each time postponing the session to a later date. He had shown up this afternoon only because Dr Browning had gotten on the telephone, urging Amir to give him a try.

The psychiatrist studied his new patient for a thoughtful

moment, then leaned forward in his chair, trying to elicit Amir's confidence with a smile.

'Do you want to tell me what's been bothering you?' the doctor began.

Ever since the night he had soaked his hands in Gasem Zahedi's blood, a voice had begun to speak to him, a taunting, jeering voice that lacked both shape and substance. It was as if Amir were talking to himself, except that he knew such conversations weren't the product of his own disordered mind. They couldn't be, for the things he heard in his thoughts he would never have dreamed of, they seemed so alien to his nature.

'Terrible dreams,' he whispered, fearful the voice would immediately interfere. 'It's like I'm being split in half. I can't sleep. I can't think straight. I don't know what's happening to me, Doctor, but it's terrifying.'

'Please, tell me more,' Browning said in a neutral tone of voice, refusing to make any judgments until he had been told the entire story.

Amir listened carefully. The side of himself he didn't understand, the frightening evil side that told him things he knew could not possibly be true, was strangely silent. All morning it had mocked him, telling him that if he kept his appointment the doctor would never let him leave his office. Men in white coats would arrive, and he'd be judged insane by the courts, committed to a mental hospital where he would be forced to remain for the rest of his life.

But now the silence was reassuring, and, responding to Dr Browning's concerned and gentle manner, he hurriedly began to explain what he'd been going through.

'And you never know when you're going to hear it?' Browning asked.

Amir shook his head.

'Can you hear it now?'

Of course you can, you little fool. Can't you see how he's trying to trap you, Amir?

Amir stiffened, clutching the arms of the chair.

His look of panic didn't go unnoticed, for Browning gazed at him in alarm. 'What is it, Amir?'

You didn't think I'd gone away, did you, Amir?

'You're not there,' he whispered.

Oh, but I am, Amir. I'll always be here, as long as you live, my friend.

Amir groaned in terror and clapped his hands over his ears, hoping to blot out the sounds.

'Is it talking to you, is that what's happening?' the doctor asked, speaking so loudly that Amir couldn't help but hear.

He knows you're crazy, Amir. Dangerous. I warned you not to come here, but you wouldn't listen. You'd better leave before he tries to stop you. See how he's looking at the telephone? He's thinking of calling the police. We can't have that happen. We can't let ourselves be locked away when there's still so much more to be done.

'I have to leave now,' Amir said. He came abruptly to his feet, trying to sound as calm as he could. 'I . . . I promised my roommate I'd bring back his car.'

The psychiatrist ran his fingers through his thinning hair. 'Is it making you do this, run away from me?'

'No, of course not,' Amir blurted out. But even then he was already halfway to the door, afraid of what the voice might do to him if he continued to oppose its will.

'Will you come and see me again tomorrow? I think it would be very helpful, Amir.'

'What if it won't let me?' he wanted to say. Instead, he nodded, his fingers tightening around the doorknob.

Only when he was safely past Dr Browning's receptionist did he breathe more easily. As he rode the elevator down to the basement garage he strained to hear the voice.

But though he even tried to talk to it, there was absolutely nothing there, just a dead space between his ears, a vacuum waiting to be filled.

That night, Amir lay awake as the voice moved desperately through his thoughts, creating panic and despair. Finally he threw his legs over the side of the bed and came shakily to his feet. The shadows of cars moving out on the street drifted restlessly across the ceiling. He pulled on his clothes, then stuffed his wallet and checkbook into his back pocket. But when it came time to leave the bedroom he hesitated.

What good would it do to run away? The voice would always be there, just as it claimed. He could go halfway around the world and he still wouldn't lose it.

Take the keys, Amir, or else they'll lock us away before my work is done.

'I can't,' he whispered.

Take the keys, Amir!

A knifelike pain shot through his chest. He gasped, and for a moment, it felt as if his heart had stopped.

I can make it much worse. I can rip you apart and still leave you whole.

The voice pounded against his temples, throbbing feverishly. When he closed his eyes and tried to shut it out it only grew stronger, louder too, an angry howling like the wind off the desert, like wolves closing in on their prey.

Amir found his roommate's car keys on the table near the front door. He stuffed them into his pocket, then let himself out as silently as he could. He had no idea where he was going, or what he would do once he got there.

Las Vegas, Tuesday, 10 October 1978

The Wolfman couldn't have been happier. After nearly five years of dreary gigs, playing third-rate carnies and two-bit country fairs, Danny Riggs had finally clicked into a semiclass act in Vegas, home of the hot showgirl tush and the one-arm bandit.

Circus Circus wasn't world renowned for animal acts, and it took a little doing to convince the management he had something the yokels would get off on.

'Just give me a little space to strut my stuff and, I'm tellin' you, people are gonna go bananas. My puppies do things you won't believe. Ever see trained wolves? Sure you haven't, and neither have your customers.'

The bimbos from Yonkers, Butte, and all points east really got their jollies off when the ringmaster cried out, 'And now, di-rect from a record-breaking engagement with the Circus de Paree, Mr Danny Riggs, better known as "The Wolfman".'

Let's hear it for him, folks. Yea, hooray . . .

Six weeks later and Riggs knew he was on a winning streak. One night after he put his puppies to sleep a real smooth talker rang him up and said, 'Why don't we sit down and talk business, Mr Riggs?' Turned out this guy with the gift of gab was the talent scout for Ringling Brothers, the classiest outfit in the country. He'd been snooping the act and liked what he saw, so much so that he was ready to have Riggs sign his John Hancock, nice and neat on the dotted line.

Circus Circus was pretty decent about it too, when it came time to give them notice. 'On to the bigger and better,' said the talent booker with a sweaty handshake, a decal of zinc oxide covering the third-degree sunburn on his nose.

Packed and ready to go, Riggs made sure his puppies were happy. There were eight wolves in the act – in the *pack*, as he liked to call it – all of them hand-raised since they were pups. When he traveled they were crated separately, because there was less chance of their hurting themselves if they were kept in a small, confined space.

As soon as everything was secure, and the kennels wouldn't go bouncing around the back of the van the first time they went over a bump, Riggs climbed behind the wheel and drove down the Strip in the direction of McCarran Airport and I–15.

Amir Farsian kept both hands on the wheel, staring straight ahead and wondering why he was running and how long he'd have to keep it up. He'd driven half the night, finally checking into a motel near Crestline, at the foot of the San Bernardinos. Morning, and he was on the road again, winding his way up into the mountains, still not sure where he was heading.

On the other side of El Cajon Pass the timberline retreated, and stretching before him lay the flat vista of the Mojave like a pale smudge of indeterminate color.

The blank eroded landscape seemed to calm his companion. For the next half hour the only sound Amir heard was the air conditioner, chugging along as it tried to keep up with the rising temperature. Then, as he drove into the town of Barstow to stop for gas, thinking that he'd better call his roommate and tell him where he was and what had happened, a surge of such incredible rage poured over him that he could barely keep his eyes on the road.

There were no words now, only feelings, emotions of such overpowering intensity that Amir knew if he didn't pull over to the side he'd lose control of the car.

'Who are you?' he screamed as he swerved onto the shoulder, jamming his foot down on the brake. He was thrown forward in his seat, narrowly avoiding hitting his head against the windshield.

'Haven't you guessed by now?' the voice whispered in his ear as the waves of hatred and violence continued to pound against his brain.

Amir saw his mother, her mouth like a great gaping

sore, her body covered with flies as she lay rotting in the dust. He saw his father screaming in pain, a vise tightening around his scrotum as agents of SAVAK kept up their torture, accusing him of conspiring against the Shah. His sister was being passed from one man to the next, thick rivulets of blood and semen oozing down her thighs. She looked at him with haunted eyes, begging him to save her.

Amir kept screaming, hoping the visions would pass, that once again he would see nothing but the emptiness of the desert, the skeletal buff-colored hills rising like sentinels in the distance. But still it showed him things he could not bear to watch.

And you dare to disobey? Haven't you guessed who I am, Amir? Don't you know what you've become?

Amir rubbed his hands across his eyes, brushing aside the tears. His fingers felt numb as he turned the key in the ignition and pulled back onto the road. Although he was down to less than a quarter of a tank of gas, he was too afraid to stop, not knowing what it would make him do. Life itself seemed to be its enemy; it fed on hatred and despair as maggots feed on carrion.

But if I die, it dies with me, Amir thought. It can't survive without its host.

Amir pressed his foot down on the accelerator, speeding through Barstow's dusty main street and on into the desert. Had he a map, he would have had no trouble deciding on a destination, for the vast alkali sink known as the Devil's Playground lay straight ahead.

Riggs could have kicked himself, he felt like such a horse's ass. Didn't the kid at the gas station tell him his tire was bald? So why the fuck didn't he listen? He was lucky he had a spare, though it wasn't much better than the one that had just suffered a blowout. Here he was, practically stranded in the middle of nowhere, the pack panting to beat the band though he'd opened the back doors of the van, hoping they'd be able to get enough air.

'Just keep cool, boys and girls,' he said, ''cause I'm doin' the best I can.'

Lucky we didn't all get killed, Riggs thought as he got the jack and went to work changing the tire.

Inside the van, the pack breathed heavily. It was ninety-seven degrees out, and the sun was still climbing.

Amir tried not to listen to the chilling laughter echoing in his ears, his foot flat against the accelerator, his hands as rigid as iron bars as he gripped the steering wheel.

'What is it you want from me?' he pleaded.

Your obedience. Your blind devotion. There's much to be done. And with you I'll be able to accomplish it.

'What?'

My work. The work that never ends. The work for which I was born, cast into your world like an afterthought. But you mustn't drive so fast, my friend. You might hurt yourself.

Massive stone outcroppings rose up in the distance. An occasional stunted paloverde grew along the dry washes on either side of the road. There was little traffic, and certainly no sign of life. He thought of turning off the highway and heading out across the desert until he ran out of gas. But death would come slowly that way, painfully too.

You must rid your mind of such thoughts, Amir. You're young and healthy, a perfect host. You have many years ahead of you. But if you fight me like this you will only suffer needlessly, I'm afraid.

Off to his right lay a jumble of granitelike boulders. If he could only steer his way toward them he'd never again have to listen to the voice or suffer its presence. It would die when he died, and Amir Farsian tried desperately to turn the wheel, knowing then what must be done.

But as he tried to steer the car off the road he began to

tremble as if he were cold, his body vibrating painfully against the seat.

You dare to disobey! the voice shrieked in his ear.

The car began to sway from side to side. Each time he tried to turn off the road his hands locked tight and the wheel spun in the opposite direction. Up ahead he saw something else, a disabled car perhaps. He was still too far away to make it out, but as he floored the accelerator a van began to take shape, a wiggly line of metallic-red letters catching the rays of the midday sun and scattering them like a burst of fireworks.

Danny Riggs heard the overheated whine of the engine just as he was tightening the last of the lug nuts. For a moment he thought it was an ambulance, or a squad car engaged in a high-speed pursuit. But as he straightened up, cupping his hand over his eyes like a visor, the distant speck of a dusty automobile began to grow steadily larger.

'Hell if I know what it's all about,' he said when the pack began to whine, moving restlessly in their cages.

He started back to the driver's seat, only to stop suddenly short. The car was weaving from one side of the highway to the other, for by then Amir Farsian was battling for control not only of the vehicle but of himself.

He was intent upon taking his life, crashing into the rocky outcropping several hundred yards beyond the shoulder, but the voice screamed in his ear, demanding his obedience. Unable to pull his hands free of the wheel, Amir saw the van parked at the side of the highway. But as he tried to turn away from it the car spun out of control.

Riggs never knew what hit him.

He was behind the wheel of his van when the car came at him at what must have been close to ninety miles per hour. He saw the chrome of its bumper flashing in the sun, saw the shadowy stick figure at the wheel, and threw up his hands as if he were about to witness an explosion.

At the moment of impact, when a wall of flame shot into the air and the windshield shattered, bits of molten glass slicing Riggs like a thousand razors, two of the cages near the rear of the van were thrown free. One broke apart, spilling its contents into the sand. The other, though twisted out of shape, remained intact, and the wolf that was trapped inside began to howl in pain as the fire rapidly engulfed it.

As she dragged herself to her feet, whining and sniffing at the ground, the lone survivor of the pack tried to approach the burning wreckage. The she-wolf was able to hear the anguished cries of her packmates, but each time she attempted to get closer, the hot lashing flames held her back, forcing her to keep her distance.

One of her pads had been ripped when she was thrown clear of the van. Now she paid little attention to the wound, hopping on three legs as she moved in an ever-widening circle around the wreck, desperate to get nearer. The smoke drifted toward her, stinging her eyes. A last feeble cry, and then all she heard was the crackle of flames.

The air was filled with a suffocating stench. She pawed at her muzzle, rubbing it against the ground to rid herself of the odor of burning meat. Behind her, at the nape of her neck, something clung tightly to her fur. Unable to see what it was, she twisted her head back, snapping futilely. Agonized now, she rolled on the ground, trying to dislodge it. But as hard as she worked to free herself, it rode her still harder, slowly burrowing its way down until she could feel it piercing her skin like a needle.

Then, just as quickly, she was no longer afraid. A new leader was with her, sharing her thoughts, telling her she would never be alone. Once again, there was someone she could follow. When she saw a car draw near, slowing down as it approached the burning wreckage, she turned and made her way across the desert, limping and trying not to put pressure on her wounded pad.

The pack was no more. But soon, the voice promised, he would find her a companion, and together they would run free, ever watchful for that hated creature known as man.

3

Mojave Desert, Monday, 23 October 1978

Blue sat up all night, forcing himself to keep his eyes open even though he was very sleepy. Once or twice he tried to get his mother to wake up. But each time he touched her, he pulled his hand back, afraid she'd be angry at him for bothering her.

By the time it got light and he knew that Jess wasn't coming back, he decided to risk a licking and began to shake her as hard as he could.

'Come on, Mama, wake up,' he said, first softly, to ease her out of her dreams, then louder and more frantic when she failed to respond.

Why was she so cold? he wondered. He touched himself and then touched her. He was warm, but she was like cold water.

'Mama, please, it's time to get up,' he begged.

But she didn't move. She just lay there on the ground, so still and silent that he didn't know what to do. Something was wrong, wasn't it? Something was very bad, worse than the things Poppy did to him, worse than when Mama got mad at him for making potty in his pants even though he was a big boy and knew better.

'I'll be good,' he promised. 'I'll do tricks for you and everything.'

Mama didn't answer. She lay there in the dirt, her mouth hanging open so he could see something gold and shiny flashing on one of her teeth. But what if she never got up? What would happen to him then? The man named Jess must have done something bad to her. But what?

What could he do that would make her so cold and still, refusing to talk to him?

'Mama? It's time to wake up, Mama, it's time.'

Blue pulled himself to his feet. He was stiff all over, and he ached like he did when Poppy did mean things to him. There wasn't anything here. Just rocks and dirt. He looked all around, turning in a circle, wondering where the people were, and the cars and the houses and the trucks.

On the other side of a jumble of rocks he heard a sound he didn't recognize. It was low and sad, scary too. Yet somehow he wasn't afraid. Maybe someone was coming to wake up Mama, and then everything would be all right.

Again he heard the sound, almost like a dog now, a deep, drawn-out howling that made him turn expectantly in the direction from which it was coming.

'Can't you wake up?' he cried out to his mother, who still lay there on the ground where the man named Jess had left her.

A shaggy head appeared over the top of the rocks. Two luminous golden eyes peered down at him.

Maybe the doggy would know where Jess had gone, Blue thought. He watched the animal approach, wagging its big bushy tail just like the dog Poppy used to keep before it ran away.

'Puppy, c'mere, puppy,' he called out, glancing anxiously at his mother. He didn't know if she'd like it, the way he wanted to play with a strange dog. But he couldn't get her to wake up, so even if he was doing something wrong, it didn't seem to matter anymore.

'Puppy, nice puppy,' babbled the little boy.

He toddled over to the wolf, throwing one arm over her bushy mane even as she growled softly, not certain if this was a threat or a way of expressing friendliness such as her old pack leader used to do. But the child's touch was soft and gentle, and instinctively she knew he didn't mean to harm her.

'A friend,' said the voice of the leader, a voice she understood not as words spoken out loud, the way the man-child spoke, but as signals in her brain, a kind of communication she had once had with the other members of her pack. 'I promised you a companion, a pup, and now you have one.'

The she-wolf nuzzled the child, her long raspy tongue licking its cheeks. The little boy made a laughing face, then looked back at the figure lying on the ground.

'Mama, come see the nice doggy.'

Your mama's dead, Bluie.

Blue whirled around in surprise, wondering where the voice was coming from. 'Is that you, Uncle Jess?' he called out.

Your mama's dead, Bluie, and now Az will take care of you.

'Who?' he asked. He started to the rocks, the she-wolf trotting along after him.

Jess is gone, Bluie. I sent Az to find you. She'll take care of you now.

'Where are you?' he said when he didn't find anyone hiding behind the rocks. 'I can't see where you are, and Mama won't wake up.'

Mama's dead. Do you know what that means, Blue? It means she's sleeping for all time, because the man you call Jess didn't want her to live. One day we'll find him and punish him for being bad.

Tears filled his eyes. 'She won't wake up again? Not ever?'

That's what death is, Blue.

'But who are you?' he asked, frightened that he could hear the voice very clearly but still couldn't see who was there. 'How do you know my name? What's yours?'

In time you'll know everything you have to, Blue. But now you must go with Az. If you don't, bad people like Jess will come and take you away. They'll hurt you like Poppy did.

The she-wolf nudged him with her muzzle, trying to get him to follow her.

Do you want them to hurt you, Blue?

'No,' he whispered.

Then let Az take care of you. She knows where there's food, and water to drink. It'll be very different now, Blue. But if you do as I ask, no one will ever hurt you again. Because if they try, Az will kill them, just like Jess did to your mama.

The she-wolf turned away, lifting her bushy tail in the air and waving it from side to side. Blue fell in step alongside her. She didn't go fast like Jess did. She wouldn't let him get lost or leave him all by himself. And whenever he felt scared the nice man would always be there to talk to, telling jokes and secrets, playing games, whispering to him and him alone.

Morongo Valley, Saturday, 10 April 1982

Off in the distance a coyote howled mournfully. Eileen Dembart, a biology teacher from Encino, edged closer to the fire, not at all sure if she liked what she heard. In the reddish glow of the flames she could see her roommate looking at her with laughing eyes.

'Did I miss a joke or something?' she asked, immediately defensive.

'You look like a little kid who's afraid of the boogeyman,' replied her roommate.

Only last week Eileen had read about two campers who were attacked by a gang of bikers, but she figured that as long as she stuck with the group, she wouldn't have anything to worry about. Not for the first time this weekend she wondered why she'd agreed to go on this Audubon birding expedition with her roommate. But now that she was here in the middle of the desert, having second thoughts about it wouldn't do her any good. So when it was time to go owling, she gathered up her flashlight and field glasses and, with a weary sigh, followed the group's leader, Kimball McPhee, into the night.

Somewhere in the grove of fan palms figures moved in the darkness, whispering and shuffling their feet. Bright yellow lights swung to and fro, and the boy darted back into the shadows, warning Az to stick close, the man-smell was getting stronger. There were at least six of them, any one of whom could provide them with more than enough meat to take back to the den.

Az made a snuffling sound, swinging her head from side to side, alert and on her guard. The boy responded in kind, growling softly and then leaning over to rub his face against the wolf's cold wet nose. It had been two days since they'd fed, and now his stomach tightened in anticipation. But first they must be patient, tracking their prey as silently and skilfully as possible.

The yellow lights flickered like fireflies, moving off in the direction of the damp streambed where he sometimes went to drink. The boy waited for Mr Harriman to tell him it was safe. Then, as soon as permission was granted, he began to follow after the prey, Az moving like a shadow right alongside him.

Kimball McPhee, a stocky, bearded young man who could spot a distant speck in the sky and know exactly what bird it was, turned on the recording and waited patiently for the elf owl to respond to its call. The group held its breath as the rapid *whi-whi-whi-whi-whi-whi* echoed through the darkness.

Eileen bent down to tie her shoe, wondering why everyone was standing there as if they expected the Second

Coming. She was tired and her feet hurt and enough was enough.

'Wait,' whispered McPhee. 'Listen carefully now.'

Sure enough, from somewhere in the oasis the high-pitched chattering of an elf owl responded to the call.

'Don't use your flashlights yet,' he cautioned as he played the recording over again, hoping to bring the bird in closer so that everyone would have a chance to see it.

Eileen straightened up. Suddenly she stiffened and turned slowly around. She thought she'd heard something, like a twig snapping underfoot. But there was nothing there, just the shadows of the palms, the faint whispery sound of the fronds as a breeze blew down from the mountains.

'This way, guys,' McPhee whispered. 'I think we've got it now.'

'Eileen, are you coming or aren't you?' her roommate said impatiently.

'Yes, I'm right here.'

She followed after the others, wondering why she couldn't get excited about a ridiculous little owl. So what if they finally saw it? So what if she could add another bird to her life list? It was late and she was dead on her feet. Only a bunch of fanatics went birding at eleven o'clock at night, and in the middle of the desert, to boot.

Behind her another twig snapped, and now she knew it wasn't her imagination.

'Carole, there's someone following us,' she called out. But her roommate was more interested in following McPhee, hurrying down the narrow trail that wound its way between the palms.

Promising herself she'd never do this again, Eileen swung around and aimed her flashlight into the darkness. A pair of glowing eyes sent her rushing down the trail. But when she caught up to the group, they had finally sighted the elf owl and everyone was too excited to pay her much attention.

'Must've been a ringtail cat,' said McPhee.

'What's that?' she asked. She glanced nervously over her shoulder, but the eyes were nowhere to be seen.

'Kind of like a raccoon, only smaller.'

Something flew overhead, cackling loudly.

'There it is, guys,' McPhee cried out. He aimed the beam of his flashlight through the trees. 'That's it, all right. Six o'clock in that mesquite over there.'

'Where? Which is the mesquite? I still can't see it,' everyone was saying at once.

'Six o'clock,' McPhee said again. 'The mesquite's the low one over . . . wait . . . nope, now, it's gone.'

'It's over here now. I have it in my glasses,' Eileen's roommate called out, and the birders rushed down the trail in hot pursuit.

Fanatics, Eileen thought again. She started after them when something slammed into her back, throwing her down to the ground. Her flashlight went flying, and the next thing she knew she was sprawled in the dust, her field glasses trapped under her chest, digging painfully into her collarbone.

For a moment she was certain she'd tripped over a shoelace. But then she felt a hand pressing her face down into the ground. When she tried to cry out the fingers tightened around the back of her neck, squeezing so hard it felt as if her spine would be crushed from the terrible pressure.

'Let me go!' she screamed. But her mouth was already filled with dirt, and she knew no one would hear her.

Eileen tried desperately to pull herself free. She clawed at the ground, sending up little clouds of dust which stung her eyes. Each time she moved, the pain grew more intense, as if her attacker had no intention of ever letting her go.

'Help me, someone!' Eileen screamed into the gravel covering the trail.

Whoever had knocked her down now grabbed her by the back of the head, tearing at her scalp as he forced her over onto her back. Eileen looked up, and as her eyes opened wide and a terrified shriek erupted from her lips he fell against her, snarling and tearing at her throat.

A pair of glowing golden eyes drifted into view. Eileen whimpered in fear, unable to escape. Far away, on the other side of the world perhaps, a faint crunching sound reached her ears.

Dear God in heaven, it's . . . eating . . . me.

Her mind went blank as Az tore a long ragged strip of muscle off the inside of her leg. With a pitiful gurgling sound, Eileen Dembart went into shock. Moments later her body stiffened convulsively, her shoulders rattling against the ground.

The boy and the wolf continued to feed, while off in the distance the elf owl flew from tree to tree, certain it had finally found a mate.

4

Palm Springs, Sunday, 18 April 1982

Everything was perfect, and perfect was the way everything was supposed to be. What could be nicer than driving home to someone she loved? Janet Kaufman smiled to herself and glanced over at the safety seat where three-year-old Matthew slept with his head to one side, as if he were listening to everything she was thinking, and only pretending to be asleep.

'What's my little Matt dreaming of?' she said aloud.

She reached over and ran her fingers through his hair. So soft and baby-fine, as pale as corn silk. Then she turned her eyes back on the freeway. The traffic was thickening like oatmeal in the bottom of a bowl.

Now eat it all up, Matt. That's a good boy. Can you see whose picture's on the bottom? That's R2D2, remember him?

Janet kept smiling. How different her life was now that she and Neil had Matt. It seemed to her that before the baby was born they were always searching for projects, ways to get closer to each other. When they bought the house up in the hills, that became project number one, and a day didn't go by when her husband wouldn't walk from one end of the property to the other, telling her how it would look when they could afford to take out a second and really do a job of renovation.

But the step-down dining room, the greenhouse windows in the remodeled kitchen with the built-in wok, the skylights and the sybaritic bath, were all put aside when the baby was born. The project that was the house, the ideal environment they would create for each other, seemed secondary then, for all of their attention was devoted to the helpless gurgling infant their love had given to each other.

'How can you write and still take care of the baby?' her husband Neil would say when he came home from school and found her hunched over the typewriter in the den, the baby making cooing sounds as he lay in his carry-cot.

Janet would shrug. Matt was such an easy child that it never occurred to her she might have difficulty working. If anything, the steady clickety-clack of the typewriter keys always seemed to quiet him down, as if he were listening to a strange, percussive kind of music.

That afternoon she'd gone to give a reading at a junior high in Costa Mesa, ninety minutes or so from home. Her second young-adult novel had just been published, and according to all the reviews, she was well on her way to establishing herself as a writer who seemed to know instinctively how to communicate with young people. *Matthew Bender's on a Bummer* was the title of her new work, and the kids who filled the auditorium of the Costa Mesa Junior High School had given her the same attention they paid to the *Star Wars* saga.

Matt, however, had slept through it all, and he was still sleeping when Janet began to maneuver over to the right-hand lane, knowing she'd be getting off the freeway in just another few minutes. A car suddenly shot in front of her, and as she slammed her foot down on the brakes a sickening crunch told her what her eyes refused to believe. Her car shimmied violently, weaving from one lane to the next and colliding with two other vehicles as she fought to regain control of the wheel.

Matt woke up and began to cry, flailing his pudgy little hands in the air as Janet saw the freeway spinning around like a ride at Disneyland. The center divider reared up before her, and as she hit her head against the windshield all she kept hearing was Matt, crying, 'Mommy, Mommy, Mommy . . .'

What do you mean he didn't make it? What are you talking about? No, I don't believe you, I don't. I'll never believe you, never.

Janet punched the sodden pillows with her fists, gasping and trying to get air into her lungs. She raised her head and looked up. Neil was still lying there sound asleep, unaware that she'd just had another nightmare.

'How come I'm the only one who has bad dreams around here?' she said aloud, trying to make a joke of it. Yet she knew in her heart there would never be anything even remotely humorous about what had happened.

Nearly a year ago a car had cut her off while driving on the San Diego Freeway. By the time the paramedics managed to pull her free of the wreckage, Matt had suffered irreparable brain damage. Less than twenty-four hours later, all the happiness she had made for herself was consigned to a small black casket, the repository of a life that had scarcely had a chance to blossom.

The nightmares began shortly after the funeral, though in recent months they came with both less frequency and less severity than in the past. Perhaps, as she had confided to the psychiatrist with whom she'd consulted for several rather unproductive sessions, the nightmares were her only link to her son. She was secretly afraid that if they stopped, all memory of Matt would vanish.

Whatever the reasons, the nightmares were real, something she would just have to learn to live with. Neil certainly wasn't having any problems with them, for he slept on as Janet slipped into her robe and went outside.

How still it was. The desert sky was cloudless, suffused with red as the sun rose slowly above the distant line of hills at the horizon. The sparkling blue of the pool and the pale ocher of the desert floor made an oddly pleasing contrast, and she understood why her brother Andy had always found Palm Springs such a special place to live.

She and Neil had come down for the weekend. It had gone by all too quickly, and in just another few hours they would have to start heading back to LA. She glanced behind her at the long expanse of glass, the blinds uniformly drawn from one end of the house to the other. Everyone was still asleep, and so Janet threw her robe down on a chaise and gently lowered herself into the pool.

The water was warmer than the air. She dove down, trying to put the nightmare aside as she swam to the far end of the pool and came up for air.

A pair of glowing yellow eyes confronted her when she reached for the tiled coping. For a moment she didn't know quite what to make of them and even gasped, about to cry out. But just as quickly she realized it was Turk, their golden retriever, who hadn't been too happy about being put outside when everyone had gone to bed.

'Poor little pup, all alone,' Janet said. She tickled Turk behind his ears, and the retriever's tail semaphored instant gratification. 'Bet you're hungry too, aren't you, boy? Would Turk like a biscuit?'

Turk sat back on his hind legs, raising one of his paws to be shook. Far off across the desert a coyote began to howl. Turk came to his feet in a flash and started pacing along the edge of the terrace, whining softly and then barking a challenge to the unseen intruder.

'It's no one, no one at all,' Janet told him. She climbed out of the pool, shaking her head to get the water out of her ears. 'How's about a biscuit?'

Turk looked back at her. Then, when Janet clapped her hands, the retriever trotted obediently after her. Soon he was stretched out on the kitchen floor, watching her with soulful eyes as she went about preparing breakfast.

* * *

Less than a mile away, on the other side of Highway 111, a dense grove of date palms gave shelter to two fugitives. The boy and the wolf had been running for nearly a week, the den they had made for themselves some twenty miles to the north no longer a safe haven.

The boy still could not understand what had happened. They had done what they always did, bringing down prey so they would be able to survive. But this time something had gone wrong.

The morning after their last successful hunt the man-smell was everywhere, and shouts ran through the chaparral. Mr Harriman told them not to be afraid, that if they stayed in their cave until it got dark, they would be all right. When at last the sun went down they slipped out of the den, staying upwind of the man-smell that filled the valley with its stink. North there was only desert and badlands, with little game and less in the way of natural shelter. South, and the cars traveled like shooting stars down the highways. There were towns there, houses and barking dogs, the man-smell covering everything like a thick layer of dust.

Now they waited in the shadows, feeling hunger's sharp, gnawing pain. They had caught nothing for three days, and as he crouched on all fours, peering through the tangled mat of hair which half obscured his face, Blue thought he smelled food. His ears quivered in anticipation and he turned to Az, seeking confirmation of the tantalizing message carried on the air.

A group of trailers was clustered together at the far side of the grove. It was here that Blue caught the scent of food. Drawing himself half erect, he slowly made his way forward, Az padding silently after him. He had seen those long boxes where people lived many times before but had only been inside them once.

Hunger, however, made him bold, and so he crept

through the grove of date palms, steadily advancing to the edge of the trailer camp. Although the man-smell kept getting stronger, there weren't any sounds coming from the long boxes. The sun had risen just a short while before, and he guessed that the Jesses inside were still asleep.

When he stepped out from the shadows, Blue dropped down onto all fours. Bounding along with surprising agility, he reached the nearest of the trailers and hauled himself up onto two feet, his long curving fingernails clicking against each other as he tried to grasp the doorknob. It had been hot and dry and then cool and wet since he had last been so close to a place where Jesses lived. But the pain in his stomach couldn't be ignored much longer. Mr Harriman wasn't telling him to rush away and hide, and so Blue tugged at the doorknob, raising his lips in a smile when the door swung open.

A sweet floral scent made his nostrils flare in disgust. He knew right away that a woman lived here, though why the weak two-legged creature hadn't bothered to lock the door was something he barely took time to consider. He was too hungry, and as he slipped into the darkened trailer the faint yet unmistakable aroma of food made his stomach clench even harder, reminding him how long it had been since he had fed.

Before they came to the valley, before they found their den, he and Az had foraged as best they could, sometimes raiding houses if there weren't dogs around to try to stop them. Thinking of that now, Blue recalled the shiny white boxes that were as cold as the bottom of a stream, boxes filled with many good things to eat. He began to search for one, leaving the man-smell at his back as he made his way into the trailer's narrow kitchen.

The cold yellow light streamed over him when he opened the refrigerator and saw the food that he and Az needed so desperately. He began to grab whatever he could, trying to hold on to as much as possible. A bottle of something thick and red that he remembered liking very much slipped from his fingers, shattering at his feet.

'Who's in there? That you, kitty?' a voice called out, sending him rushing back to the door.

An old woman in a faded nightgown shuffled out of the bedroom. Blue was trying to open the door when she caught sight of him. For a second she didn't say anything, too astonished even to breathe. Then she opened her toothless mouth and began screaming at the top of her lungs.

Az barked a frantic warning, but by then it was already too late. Dropping half the food on the floor, Blue clawed at the slippery knob. The old woman continued to stand her ground, and though he would have liked to tear her throat out, there was no longer any time to spare. He flung the door open and leaped outside, where the man-smell seemed to be coming from everywhere at once.

The long boxes that were trailers were now filled with a bewildering array of sounds as the old woman's neighbors awoke to her terrified cries. A man with an enormous belly waddled outside. Catching sight of Blue and the wolf, whose hackles were raised the instant he appeared, he rushed back into his trailer.

'Help! Murderers! Rape!' the old woman kept screaming.

Still carrying some of the food, and thus forced to remain upright rather than lope along on all fours, Blue started off to the grove of date palms, hoping to lose his pursuers. Az was right beside him when he heard a shot ring out, followed by a man's victorious cry.

He glanced back. A thick stain of blood like the ketchup which had spilled all over the floor now began to spread over Az's flank. The she-wolf faltered for a moment, losing her stride.

Mr Harriman, help us! Blue shouted when he heard the Jesses giving chase. He darted into the grove, slowing down so that Az could catch up to him.

Keep running! said the voice which rang in his ears.

But where? Where can I go? The Jesses'll hurt me, you know they will.

Run before they catch you, Bluie! Az can make it, I know she can.

But she's hurt real bad.

You will do as I say! Now run, and don't look back.

Behind them the brittle palm fronds crackled like fire. Az was still limping, but when Blue broke into a run, the she-wolf bounded along after him, leaving a trail of blood to mark her flight.

By the time they reached the opposite end of the grove the Jesses were still giving chase. Before them Highway 111 cut a narrow swath through the desert.

Run, or they'll lock us up!

Mr Harriman sounded so angry now that Blue didn't dare disobey. With a final glance behind him he shot across the road, the muscles in his legs aching from having remained upright for so long.

The sloping sides of a flood-control channel sent him tumbling head over heels to the bottom, where a trickle of slow-moving water met his fall with a splash. For a moment it looked as if Az were afraid to chance it. But then the she-wolf slid down along the steep concrete embankment as if someone were pushing her from behind.

With no time to think of anything but escape, Blue began to make his way down the channel, urging Az to follow. But by now the she-wolf had lost a considerable amount of blood, and if it weren't for Mr Harriman she would have already dropped in her tracks.

The man-made gully veered off to the left at nearly a right angle. It was here that they stopped, Blue leaning back against the wall of the channel and trying to catch his breath.

Food, I have food for us! he thought excitedly. Food will make you strong again.

Az sank down onto her side, too weak even to reach back and lick her wound.

Tell her I have food, Mr Harriman. Tell her the Jesses won't find us. We'll look for a new den and go hunting and everything will be right again.

But instead of answering, Mr Harriman held his tongue. He was silent for the first time in so long that Blue was suddenly afraid he'd be left all alone, and just like a little boy he began to cry.

At breakfast, the talk turned to real estate, a subject that, along with cars, was as intrinsically Californian as the Hollywood sign.

'I don't know why you're so afraid of a second, Neil. Believe me, it's the only sensible way to go. You'll use the money for your down on a condo – they're only asking ten percent out here – sell it a year later, and start pyramiding.'

'Buying up is what he's saying,' said Andy's roommate Mike. The two of them were partners in one of the more successful realty firms in the area. Every time the Kaufmans came down for a weekend that's all they heard, how it was so easy to make a killing it was just a shame they didn't give it a try.

'I don't want to take out a second mortgage,' Neil said between mouthfuls of ham and eggs. 'Besides, we can barely afford our first.'

Neil Kaufman was a big beefy man in his early thirties, with a thick shock of curly brown hair and the look of an athlete who was just starting to go to seed. Neil's favorite line was 'I'm joining a gym just as soon as I get my act together,' and periodically he would come home at the end of the day, stretch out on the living-room sofa, and bemoan his lost youth.

'You look fine, terrific,' Janet would tell him. 'But if you really think you're out of shape, then do something about it. Start jogging or play tennis or swim every day. There's a pool at school, isn't there?'

Neil taught biology at the Benedict Canyon Day School, where he occasionally filled in for the lacrosse coach. He had taken his master's in zoology only after failing to gain admission to a medical school. That rejection was still a thorn in his side, particularly now that Janet's career was beginning to take off, critically as well as financially.

'We're just lucky we bought the house when we did,' he announced as he scraped up the last of his breakfast, then looked expectantly at his wife.

With a sigh that was meant to be heard by everyone, Janet came to her feet, snatching his empty plate off the table. 'He loves to be waited on,' she said.

'It's my mother's training, what can I tell you?'

'Here, eat yourself silly,' said Janet, winking slyly at her brother. Neil looked up with a wounded expression, but she still kept a straight face. 'You don't see Andy and Mike asking for seconds.'

'They didn't have a Jewish mother. Besides, they're gay, and gay guys worry about their bods more than anyone.'

Andy Hilliard grinned and started to clear away the dishes. 'Not a bad habit to get into, Neil, all things considered.'

'Come on, I'm not fat,' said Neil as he loaded his fork with more ham and eggs. 'I was always big-boned, even as a kid. And Janet likes me that way. Isn't that so, honey?'

'Whatever you say, dear.' But then she had to smile, swooping down and wrapping her arms around his neck. 'Did you ever see such a big teddy bear in all your life?' she went on, when Turk suddenly shot out of the kitchen as if his tail were on fire.

'What the – ?' Andy looked out onto the terrace just as the retriever leaped over the low brick wall which encircled the property.

Before anyone could stop him, Turk was heading across the desert, racing flat out so that by the time Janet tried to call him back, he was already too far away to hear.

'Probably gone after a rabbit.' Neil pushed his plate aside and smiled contentedly.

Mike was riffling through the Sunday paper, trying to find the real-estate section. But something else caught his eye, and when he looked up he shook his head.

'Here's something creepy.' He glanced at Neil. 'You guys hear about that murder in Morongo Valley?'

'Where's that?' asked Janet.

'Oh, 'bout a half hour from here. Some people from LA were camping out and one of them was attacked.'

'By whom?' said Neil.

Mike shrugged. 'That's the creepy part. It looked like she'd been eaten.'

'Nice talk at breakfast,' Andy said with a frown.

'Don't look at me, kiddo, that's what the paper says. Parts of the body haven't even been recovered yet. Sheriff's office thinks it was a rabid dog, maybe even a coyote. Hell of a way to go, any way you slice it . . . no pun intended, of course.'

Janet pretended to smile. She suddenly felt very uneasy, though she wasn't sure why.

Mr Harriman, where are you?

Blue waited for an answer, and finally he heard his friend whispering in his ear. He sounded weak and tired, and Blue clung to Az even tighter, bending down to lick her wound. But as fast as he lapped up the blood, more trickled out, the she-wolf panting feebly now as she lay stretched out on the bottom of the channel, water flowing around her in a slow, meandering stream.

It was then that Blue heard the dog, and when he raised his eyes and looked up, Turk was already trying to make his way down the steep side of the flood-control channel. Immediately on his guard, Blue crouched on all fours, snarling and warning the dog to keep its distance. He and Az knew what these creatures were like. They went around on all fours, but they still smelled of man, the foul stink of Jess clinging to their fur and the leather collars they wore around their necks to prove they weren't wild.

Even Az tried to raise her head, growling at the big yellow dog who kept wagging his tail as he slowly drew near. Blue's upper lip lifted clear of his teeth and he bristled with mounting rage, daring the dog to come any closer.

Turk backed off, lowering his ears and tail. Whining softly, the retriever showed them his side rather than approaching head-on. Then, to prove further he meant them no harm, Turk suddenly rolled over and urinated, grinning submissively.

Rarely if ever had they met a dog who acted like this. Confused by Turk's behavior, Blue stopped snarling. But he still remained in a crouch, ready to spring at the least provocation.

A friend, whispered Mr Harriman. *A new friend for you.*

But Az –

Az is dying, Blue. There's nothing we can do to help her.

Blue didn't want to believe this was so, even though he knew Mr Harriman had never lied to him before. Only the Jesses lied, but when he looked down at the wolf her eyes were glazed and half closed, and she was breathing so slowly now it was as if she were already asleep. He put his head against the thick ruff of fur around her cheeks and neck. Az still carried the scent of the den, a safe musky smell that made Blue whimper fearfully, knowing he would never be able to find his way back there again. And even if he did, Az wouldn't be able to follow him.

This is the dog they call Turk. I've summoned him for you, Blue. But things will be very different now. You will have to return to your own kind, relearn your old ways. Do you remember the night Jess left you in the desert?

Yes.

Do you remember that you were just a little boy, afraid of the dark? Now you mustn't be afraid anymore. I'm going to stay with you, so you needn't ever worry about being alone.

The she-wolf closed her eyes, her hind legs kicking spasmodically. Even as Blue watched her dying, shaking her and getting no response, something began to bury its way into the base of his skull. He reached back, swatting futilely and unable to pry the insect free. But it wasn't a tick that clung fiercely to the back of his neck.

We'll be together for all time, Blue.

It was Mr Harriman talking, only his voice was louder and clearer than ever before.

Now that Az is dead we can finally be together. You are my host now, Blue, and I am your companion. Together we will find the man you call Jess. Together we will tear him apart and make a feast of him.

Saliva trickled down a corner of Blue's mouth. He ran his fingers over Az's thick reddish coat, remembering death as if it were someone he hadn't seen in a very long time. His mama had died and now Az. A tear dripped slowly down his cheek. Brushing it aside with the back of his hand, he sat back on his haunches, staring warily at the yellow dog Mr Harriman had summoned to his aid.

How could he go back to being a two-legged Jess when they were the creatures Mr Harriman hated above all others? If he became one of them again, wouldn't Mr Harriman begin to hate him too?

You will always be different, Blue. Special. We will make a game of it, you and I. We will fool them, then punish them for their treachery. But come, it is time we went home.

Home? he thought in confusion, wondering if Mr Harriman was referring to the den.

Mr Harriman was now so close to him that each time he took a breath it felt as if his friend were breathing too. He was still hungry, but though there was food scattered about where he had dropped it, Mr Harriman told him there would be better things to eat at home.

What kind of place is it? he asked.

Turk will take us there, and then you will be able to see for yourself.

It hurt too much to straighten up, and so Blue began to slowly follow the yellow dog, moving on all fours. When he looked back, flies were already swarming over Az.

One day we'll get even with them for killing Az. But first we must trick them, Bluie.

But how?

You must never tell them about us. If they knew I was with you, they would lock you away and never let you out. But when you've learned their ways again, when you've become as much a Jess as Jess himself, then we will begin to punish them for what they have done.

And you won't go away and leave me alone like Jess did?

I will be with you forever, Blue, for as long as you live. We are as one now, and nothing they can do will ever separate us.

5

It was Janet who first saw him.

She was sitting out by the pool, trying to take notes for her new novel, when she heard Turk's familiar bark. When she looked up, it was with a gasp that was as much of fear as of surprise. She jumped to her feet, shouting at Neil. Her husband lay stretched out on a nearby chaise, too busy examining his thickening waistline to pay her much attention.

'It has to be my metabolism, that's all it is. A man reaches his thirties and there's nothing he can do about it.'

'Neil, don't say anything, please,' she whispered urgently.

'What?' He screwed up his face and looked at her in confusion.

'Just sit up and look out there.' She was afraid to point lest she scare it away, and so she gestured first with her eyes and then with her chin.

Neil's mouth dropped open and he was on his feet before she could stop him.

'Don't, you'll scare it!' she warned.

'What in the name of – ?' Neil couldn't even finish the sentence and just stood there transfixed.

The doglike creature that was tagging along after Turk stopped abruptly now that the Kaufmans had come to their feet. It drew back, and even from a distance there was no mistaking the meaning of its snarl.

'My God, it's a child,' she said now that she could see it more clearly.

Encrusted with dirt and covered with innumerable scars,

his hair a dense matted ball concealing much of his face, the boy remained where he was, ignoring Turk's waving tail and excited yelps. The child was completely naked but seemed unaware of this as he arched his back menacingly and moved his head from side to side, occasionally panting as he watched her standing on the terrace.

Turk bounded over the low brick enclosure, jumping up to try to lick Janet's face. Then he raced back to the child, who remained on all fours, resting on his knees and the palms of his hands.

'What are we supposed to do?' she said.

She was still feeling shock, but the more she looked at the youngster, the less frightened she became. Fear gave way to pity. Convinced the boy had been terribly abused and then abandoned in the desert – for what other explanation could there be? – she now made her way to the wrought-iron gate at the far end of the patio.

'What the hell do you think you're doing?' Neil said with alarm when she opened the gate, taking the first hesitant steps in the direction of the child.

'What do you think? He needs us.'

Turk was beside her now, wagging his tail, acting delighted by all that was happening. As for the boy, the instant she approached he backed off, and she could see his upper lip quivering as he bared his teeth. Many of them appeared to be either cracked or broken, though they were all remarkably white.

'It's all right. I won't hurt you,' she kept saying in a low, soothing tone of voice.

Janet crouched down as she might have done were she approaching a strange dog, but the boy still kept his distance. His eyes glimmered faintly behind the course, tangled mat of hair which hung over his forehead. Yet there was a strange, almost teasing delicacy about his features than even the layers of filth could not obscure, and

Janet was even more determined than ever to communicate with him.

Still remaining in a crouch so as to ensure maximum eye contact, she edged forward. But each step she took resulted in the boy's stepping back, as if to maintain an exact distance between them. Only Turk was able to approach him, though the boy hardly paid any attention to the retriever. His eyes focused on Janet now, occasionally darting up to the terrace where Neil was still standing, watching them with mounting disbelief.

'It's all right,' she said softly. 'I'm a friend. I won't hurt you.'

As she slowly rose to her feet the boy growled so savagely that for a moment she was taken aback. Just as quickly her fears passed. No, this child couldn't hurt her, despite whatever mistreatment he'd suffered. He was just a little boy, terrified that she meant to harm him.

Neil called out, warning her to keep her distance. 'I'm calling the police,' he shouted.

'Don't . . . not yet, anyway. If he runs away before they get here they may not ever find him again.'

'Then what do you suggest we do, Janet?' he said, sounding annoyed.

Didn't he understand this was a child, a little boy? Didn't he realize something monstrous had happened to him, and that if they turned their backs on him now he might be lost forever?

'Don't call them yet,' she pleaded. 'Wait until we can get him into the house.'

'The house? What are you, out of your mind? The boy's disturbed. He must've escaped from – '

'From where?' she snapped. 'A zoo?'

'Okay, okay, I didn't mean it that way. But there's no telling what he'll do. And I don't want you taking chances.'

Neil opened the gate, but the moment he started toward her the boy began to snarl, his entire body quivering as if he intended to attack.

'He knows. See, he knows what you said.'

'He doesn't know. I'm calling the cops.'

'Stop being so goddamn stubborn, Neil.' Then she remembered there were leftovers in the fridge. 'Bring me some of the fried chicken we had last night. If he takes food from us, then he'll know for sure we don't mean to hurt him.'

She edged back to the gate, hoping the boy would follow. Turk was still romping between them, acting as if this were all a game. By the time she reached the terrace, each step she'd taken slow and deliberate so as not to frighten the youngster, Neil had returned with the chicken.

'Andy's calling the police,' he said. 'Here, I'll do it.'

But the boy would have none of it, acting as if he couldn't tolerate Neil's presence.

'They didn't believe me, but they're coming anyway,' Andy called out.

He and Mike came out of the house. When they caught their first glimpse of the boy, they reacted in much the same way the Kaufmans had. Both of them just stood there, helplessly shaking their heads.

Janet held out a drumstick to the boy. 'It's food. It's good for you. See, we won't hurt you. We want to give you something to eat.'

Once again she slowly tried to approach, waving the piece of fried chicken before the youngster's wary eyes. When she was perhaps no more than a yard away, the child's smell became almost overpowering. Her stomach recoiled, and she gagged and put her hand over her mouth.

'Take it,' she whispered. She turned her head to the side and tried breathing through her mouth. 'Please, I know you're hungry, so take it.'

But the boy still refused to come any closer. Suddenly Turk snatched the drumstick from her hand. Before she could scold him he trotted over to the child and dropped it at his feet. The boy grabbed the piece of chicken between his jaws and backed off. Then he crouched down, holding it against the ground as he tore at the meat, snarling between bites.

'Bring me some more. And a bowl of water. I don't think he's had anything to eat in days.'

Judging from the size of the calluses on his knees and elbows and the heels of his hands, whatever had happened to the boy hadn't taken place yesterday, or even the week before. He had probably been out in the desert for at least a month, if not longer. Again she held out a piece of chicken, determined to have the youngster take it from her directly, rather than using Turk as a go-between.

'I won't hurt you. I promise.'

Janet squatted before him, hoping that was the proper kind of body language. She didn't want the boy to think she posed a threat as she held out the chicken, trying to entice him closer. The stench he gave off was sickening. She swallowed hard, trying to stop her breakfast from rising in her throat.

With a sharp little bark that sounded like a warning, the boy leaped forward, grabbing the chicken out of her hand.

'Come on, Janet. Leave the food where it is and get your ass back here.'

'Do you believe him?' she called to her brother, annoyed that Neil was being so unsympathetic. 'He works with kids five days a week, but as soon as he meets one that isn't a Beverly Hills brat he's ready to throw up his hands and chuck the whole thing.'

'I just don't want you getting hurt,' Neil replied. 'It's obvious to all of us the kid's very disturbed, maybe diseased for all we know. There's just no telling what he might do.'

'And when the police arrive with their sirens wailing you know damn well he's not going to stick around to say hello, either.'

'What about the garage?' Mike suggested.

'What about it?' she said while the boy bent over the bowl of water, lapping it up with his tongue just the way Turk drank.

'We'll get him inside and lock the door. When the cops come let them deal with it.'

Andy brought out the last of the chicken. Holding it out as bait, Janet began to make her way around to the front of the house, where Mike had already opened the sliding door that led into the garage. The more the boy ate, the less frightened he seemed to become. By the time they reached the garage he was actually trotting along after her, moving so effortlessly on all fours that Janet had to keep reminding herself he wasn't a dog but a human being who had obviously been horribly mistreated.

'There isn't any chicken left,' she said when the boy had devoured the last piece, standing awkwardly for a moment and using one hand to reach out and grab it.

'I have some hamburger in the fridge. Do you think he'll eat it?' Andy asked.

It was certainly worth a try, and as Janet backed into the garage the boy followed after her, lured on by the smell of raw meat.

'Drop it on the floor, Janet, and get the hell out of there,' Neil shouted. He was holding the automatic garage-door opener, ready to activate it as soon as she rushed outside.

The moment she flung the hamburger meat on the floor, the boy pounced on it as if it were alive. Lifting chunks of it off the floor with his teeth, he didn't even take the time to chew as he gulped it down.

Janet edged away from him. When she stepped outside, Neil pressed the button on the door opener and the heavy wooden door began to swing out and down to seal off the garage. But even before it was halfway down she suddenly changed her mind and slipped back inside.

'My wife the fearless white hunter. Son of a bitch,' Neil swore from the other side of the door.

The naked bulb burning overhead made the boy's eyes glow like an animal's. The moment he realized he was trapped, he rushed from one end of the garage to the other, looking for a means of escape.

Janet remained where she was, calling out to Neil and warning him not to open the door until the police arrived. By then, she hoped, the boy would have had a chance to calm down, making it easier for the police to capture him.

The youngster backed into a corner, snarling so angrily that for a moment she felt fear again, not knowing how she could defend herself if he decided to attack.

'We're your friends,' she kept repeating. 'No one's going to hurt you, I promise. We want to help you.'

Gradually the boy quieted down, until all she could hear was his ragged breathing, the way he panted as if he were overheated. Outside, Turk began to whine, scratching at the edge of the door and trying to get inside.

'It's all right, Turk. Everything's fine,' she called out.

The door that led into the house was suddenly flung open. Before she could warn Neil to get out of the way, the boy lunged forward, leaping into the air and knocking him sideways against the doorframe.

'Don't! He won't hurt you!' Janet cried out as Neil stumbled back, wincing in pain.

With a vicious growl the child backed off, swinging his head from side to side so that he never lost sight of either of them.

'See, Neil, he does understand,' she said excitedly,

convinced the boy's actions were proof that she could communicate with him.

Turk started barking, and a moment later Janet heard the sound of tires on gravel. Rapid footsteps followed, and then her brother began explaining what had happened. Neil remained by the open door, rubbing his shoulder where the youngster had slammed into him.

'I'm opening the door now,' Andy called out.

'Just make sure they don't hurt him. He's only a little boy, Andy.'

'Don't worry, Jan, I've told them everything.'

The door began to swing open, sliding back along its track. As sunlight flooded the garage the boy made his move. He darted outside and was halfway down the gravel drive when one of the policemen managed to tackle him, throwing him down to the ground. Janet rushed down the driveway, but by then the second policeman had already come to the aid of his partner.

'Christ, the little fucker's got teeth like you wouldn't believe,' she heard one of them say.

With a dull, hollow-sounding thud, a nightstick came down across the back of the boy's head. The child's eyes opened wide, as if he couldn't believe what had happened. Then he slumped over, lying there motionless in the middle of the driveway.

'God, how can you bear the stink?' said the cop who'd knocked him down.

Turk suddenly stiffened and bared his teeth, an angry, low-pitched growl rising from the back of his throat. Neil, who'd never known the dog to act like that, grabbed him by the collar, afraid he'd attack the police. The two officers lifted the boy by his arms and legs. Cursing him for all the trouble he'd caused, they carried him back to their squad car.

* * *

At Eisenhower Medical Center, Neil idly turned the pages of a magazine, looking at his watch and telling Janet there wasn't much time.

'For what?' she said distractedly. She kept her eyes on the doorway of the visitors' lounge, where any moment she expected to see the doctor who'd been assigned the child's case.

'If we don't get a move on, hon, we're never going to get home. You know what traffic's like on the freeway. Sunday nights are a killer.'

'I want to stay down here another day or two, Neil.'

Neil looked at her as if that were the last thing he expected to hear. 'What for?'

She gestured helplessly, so unsure of her motives she couldn't even begin to explain what she was feeling.

'It's Matthew, isn't it?'

Janet looked away, unable to bear the reproach she saw in his glance. 'No, of course not,' she said hurriedly. 'I might want to write about it, that's all.'

Neil reached over and put his hand on her arm. 'You heard the police, Janet. They're going to do everything they can to try to locate the kid's parents. Sticking around here and getting in the way isn't going to help things any.'

'Parents?' she said bitterly. 'It was probably his goddamn parents who did this to him in the first place.'

'Maybe he's a runaway; we don't know.'

'Mr Kaufman?'

Neil raised his eyes and came quickly to his feet. A young man wearing horn-rimmed glasses and an earnest expression stood in the doorway. He couldn't have been much older than twenty-five, and for a moment Neil felt a twinge of envy, seeing himself in the doctor's place.

'I'm Dr Feingold, the boy's physician.'

'My wife,' said Neil, motioning to Janet.

'The youngster's suffered a minor concussion, but he's

resting comfortably now and I'm sure there won't be any complications. He's still unconscious, and so we're going to take the opportunity to clean him up as best we can. I don't know if you noticed, but he's infested with lice. Worms too, I wouldn't doubt.'

'How long do you think he was out there?' Janet asked.

'No way of telling,' Dr Feingold replied. 'A month, maybe two. The size of the callosities on his hands and feet might give us a clue, but it's still hard to say. For all we know there could be someone else involved.'

'He was abused first, is that what you're saying?' she asked.

'Abused, battered – it all adds up to the same thing. He might have escaped and . . . well, you know the rest. A child wanders in the desert, no telling what can happen. To tell you the truth, I'm amazed he survived as well as he did.'

'I'd like to see him if that's all right,' she said.

The doctor eyed her curiously, as if trying to fathom her motives. 'I wouldn't advise it, Mrs Kaufman. The youngster's unconscious, as I said. The police report indicates he's capable of extreme violence. I have to be responsible to my staff, you understand. If anyone should get hurt . . .'

He left the rest unsaid, though Janet knew exactly what he meant to imply. The doctor had spoken with so little feeling that she felt anger at his lack of sympathy. Was the child going to be transferred from one institution to another? Was that what everyone was already planning for him?

'Well, there you have it.' Neil sounded relieved, and he put his hand on her shoulder, nodding gratefully at the doctor as he led her to the door.

But she wasn't ready to leave yet, and she slipped free of his grasp and turned back to Dr Feingold. 'I'd still like to see him.'

'But you heard the doctor. The kid's unconscious,' Neil protested.

'I don't care, Neil. I still want to see him.'

'You can't fight with 'em, can you, Doc?' Neil pretended to laugh.

She shot him an angry glance, annoyed at being patronized.

Neil held up his hand to signal a truce. 'I'll wait downstairs. You'll need a lift back to Andy's.'

'Five minutes,' Dr Feingold reminded her as he led her down the corridor to the child's room.

When she was alone with the youngster, the first thing she noticed was the terrible stench he gave off. Yet now that he was resting, the savage in him rested too. Asleep, he looked more like a little boy than ever. He was curled up on his side, his heavily callused knees drawn up to his chest.

But why was she so concerned? Was it because of Matt, as Neil had suggested? Was it possible that she was looking for an outlet for her feelings, a means of expressing that complex web of emotions that fell under the general heading 'maternal instinct'?

After the accident, Neil had wanted to have another child as soon as possible. But Janet didn't feel she was emotionally equipped. If she'd lost one child, what could prevent her from losing another? So in the year since Matthew's death she had avoided getting pregnant.

As she stood near the door and looked over at the boy, she tried to see through the layers of filth encrusting his skin, tried to see what he would look like once his hair was cut. Now it hung down over his eyes like a great shapeless ball, and even from a distance she could see things moving through it, the head lice Dr Feingold had been so scrupulous in reporting.

'Mommy?'

Janet jerked her head over her shoulder. The door was still closed. No one had come into the room, and certainly not a child.

'Mommy, is that you? Don't leave me, I'm afraid,' the pitiful voice whispered in her ear.

Janet shook her head, trying to stop her imagination from playing tricks on her. Too much had happened, that's what it was. She was emotionally exhausted, drained by the day's harrowing events. Besides, it wasn't a voice she'd heard so much as a suggestion of one, as if she were eavesdropping on someone else's thoughts.

She edged closer to the bed, trying her best to ignore the sickening smell of sweat and excrement.

'Talk to me,' she whispered.

But though she strained to hear the tiny childish voice, all she heard was the youngster's breathing, slow and rhythmic.

'I'll be back in the morning,' she said, even though she knew he couldn't possibly hear her.

Then, unable to help herself, and putting aside whatever physical revulsion she might be feeling, Janet bent over and kissed the sleeping child on the cheek.

'Mommy, it's Matthew.'

Janet stumbled back, her eyes wide with fear and confusion. The boy hadn't moved. He lay there sound asleep, his chest rising and falling with each breath he took.

God help me, she thought. She backed out of the room, angry with herself that she still hadn't learned to cope with her loss.

It was a big long room, with pipes running back and forth across the high ceiling, and bright bright lights on big high poles. There were windows at one end, and heavy black shades to keep out the light. In the middle of the room sat an enormous bed, the mattress right against the floor so it wouldn't be hard to crawl on top of it. He had never seen such a big bed, not even in stores when Mama sometimes took him shopping.

'Hey, Amber, honey, what took you so long? We've been standing around with our fingers up our butts for more'n an hour.'

'My old man was giving me a hard time,' his mother said. 'You know the story. Same old shit.'

'You brought your kid with you too?' said a man with a big bushy beard and a loud angry voice.

Blue didn't like him at all. He looked mean like Poppy, and Blue held Mama's hand as tight as he could, afraid to let go.

'Sure. He's cool. He ain't no dope.'

'Okay, then, let's get out asses in gear. We're making a movie, guys,' shouted the man with the beard.

'Okay, okay, we're comin'. You'd think we was making *Gone with the Wind* or something, the way everyone's acting.'

Blue shrank back into a corner while his mother undressed and got into bed. Soon she was joined by a man.

Blue peered out at them, and the big black machine started to go whir-whir-whir, just like a choo-choo train.

'Cute, huh?' The man with the beard laughed. 'Real Cute!'

Blue got more and more confused. The man was hurting his mommy, the camera whirred and the noise was in his head . . .

'Do you believe this kid? Pubic hair at his age . . . Jesus.'

The voice came from far away, not like when Mr Harriman talked, so close it was like someone whispering in his ear. As Blue lay there warm water washed over him. It felt so good he kept pretending to be asleep so it wouldn't stop. He'd been dreaming and dreaming, and now the dreams were becoming real.

Once, after Mama took him to the room with the pipes and the enormous bed and the machine that went whir-whir-whir, they'd taken a bath together. It was like that now, the warm sudsy water washing over him. Mama had pointed to his doodle and said he was going to grow up to be quite a stud, whatever that meant.

Only now he began to feel other things too. What was happening? Where was he? He waited for Mr Harriman to tell him, but Mr Harriman was probably asleep, because he didn't answer. He felt hands over him, touching and rubbing and covering him with soap and warm water.

Maybe it was Mama, taking another bath. But no, he remembered then what the man Jess had done. He remembered everything. How the Jesses had killed Az. How the yellow dog had taken him home. How two Jesses had hit him so hard he didn't know what happened after that. But now it felt good, all this warm water, like he was back in the den snuggling up to Az.

Someone touched him between his legs, and then a lady began to laugh, saying, 'I'd watch where I put my hands if I were you.'

'How long do you think he was out there?' another lady said.

'Couple of weeks.'

'With hair like that? Feingold says they're going to have to worm him too.'

'Thank God I get off in an hour. At least we got the stink off him.'

Like the flies that had swarmed over Az, the voices droned on and on. Where was he? Was it safe here, or would the Jesses come and take him away?

Blue didn't know, and when he asked Mr Harriman, his friend remained silent, so maybe he didn't know, either. The warm water felt so good, though, that he couldn't help but like what they were doing. And when they scrubbed the insides of his legs, when they rubbed a washcloth over his groin and stomach, all he could think of was the room with the pipes and the whir-whir-whir, the Connie with red hair saying, 'Now it's my turn, honey,' as she bent over him, washing his chest with her hair and using her tongue to make him giggle, it felt so nice.

It was like that now. Even though Blue didn't have a word to describe what he was feeling, he wanted to stretch and shiver and ask the ladies to do that for him, to tickle him with their hair and their tongues, their lips and their fingers. He reached out, grabbing the nearest hand and pressing it down against his doodle.

Suddenly he heard one of the two-legged bitches begin to scream. It was a terrible sound, worse than animals made when he used to go hunting. This scream wasn't filled with pain so much as fear. He opened his eyes with a start, and when he saw all those strange faces hovering over him, it was now his turn to be afraid.

With a snarl to warn them he knew how to defend himself, Blue tried to pull away. But he was lying in a tub of hot sudsy water, the bitches in white rushing every which way like the people in the room with the whir-whir-whir.

'Call in some orderlies!' one of the women cried out. 'Feingold's still on the floor.'

Blue looked down at himself, amazed to see he was a different color. His doodle rose straight up in the air, surrounded by skin that was so much lighter than before he thought they'd done something mean to him, and he growled loudly, challenging them now as he tried to climb over the side of the tub. He sniffed anxiously at the air, but all he smelled was flowers, not the comforting and familiar scent of the den.

'Az!' he cried out.

How difficult it was to get his tongue to work. It felt fat

and swollen, lost inside his mouth. And where was Mama? Why had Mama let this happen to him? Why was he a different color and his peepee so hard it hurt and everyone rushing back and forth like big white moths flying in and out of the den?

I'm here, Bluie. I'm with you still.

Yes? he thought with relief. You haven't run away like Jess did?

How can I run when you're my legs now? Understand me, Blue, so that you'll never forget. We are as one. Together. But you must listen to me carefully, do you hear?

Yes, I hear you, but they're screaming.

They don't know any better, the stupid fools.

Mr Harriman sounded so angry that Blue couldn't help himself. As he crouched on the floor with the water dripping down his flanks, he peeled his lips back and howled as loudly as he could, sending several of the cunts in white racing to the door at the end of the room.

They won't hurt you, Blue. They're just afraid because you're so strong. They don't know the things you know. They don't know about the room with the pipes and the man with the beard.

Or Jess.

Yes, Jess too. So you must pretend to be good, and do as they say. Then Matthew's mother will come back and take you with her.

Matthew?

A little boy just like you, explained Mr Harriman.

But then Blue saw the door open wide, and this time two Jesses hurried inside. They were white Jesses, not like the blue ones who had hurt him before.

His eyes darted everywhere at once, trying to find a way to escape. But there was only one door, and even as he started toward it another Jess stepped inside the room.

'Just calm down, feller. It ain't gonna hurt.'

Mr Harriman, what do I do!

The two big Jesses grabbed him, and though he and Az had been the most powerful animals in the valley, he couldn't pull free.

'Just a hypo, kid,' said one of the orderlies as a thorn pricked his arm and the floor suddenly fell out from under him.

You're safe with me, safe . . .

Mr Harriman closed his eyes, and Blue closed his eyes too.

'At least he looks human now,' said the Jess who was trying to keep him on his feet now that they'd taken away the floor.

Blue kept falling, while far away the black machine went whir-whir-whir and the lady with red hair pressed his head down between her legs and held it tight.

6

Neil wasn't happy, and neither were Andy and Mike. They all told Janet she was out of her mind for getting involved. The authorities were doing everything they could. The kid was well looked after. Why did she have to take it on herself to be his unofficial guardian? Neil had called when he'd gotten back to LA, and though he once again tried to convince her that she could do nothing for the boy, Janet refused to get into a discussion.

'It's important to me, Neil. No one cares about him, don't you see?'

'What I see is a woman who's latched on to something she has no way of handling. And if you tell me it's because you've decided to make him the subject of your new book – '

'But that's it, that's it exactly,' she blurted out, trying to put as much conviction into her voice as she could muster.

'I don't believe you, but I won't argue. I just want you home, Janet. Christ, I'm not even here an hour and I already miss you.'

His gentle tone, the effortless way he flattered her, softened her mood. 'I'll be back tomorrow, if not the day after,' she promised. But when she hung up she got the same routine from her brother, who couldn't understand why she felt so responsible for the youngster.

'Someone has to be,' she had said, tired of defending herself.

'But why you?'

'Why anyone, Andy?'

What she didn't tell him was that the boy had spoken to

her, whispering things she herself found difficult to believe. Yet she'd heard the child's voice. Heard *something*, at least. What that something was remained a mystery and no doubt would always be one unless she tried to solve it. And so early the next morning she borrowed her brother's car and drove over to the hospital, eager to be there when the youngster awakened.

It wasn't very comforting to see him strapped into bed, leather bindings securing his arms and legs.

'We had a little difficulty with him last night,' explained the nurse who came into the room. 'You're not his . . .'

'Mother? No, of course not,' she replied, surprised the woman would even think such a thing. Surely the nurse didn't take her for a psychopath. But maybe the boy had been kidnapped; his parents could be desperately trying to find him. Yes, that was a possibility.

Then why do I hope it's not the case?

Confused by her feelings, Janet pulled up a chair and sat down alongside the bed. Now that the boy had been cleaned up she was able to see what he really looked like. Despite all that he'd gone through he was a beautiful child, with fine, delicate features, high cheekbones, and pale, silken lashes. Although his hair had been closely cropped, she could still see how blond it was, like the mane of a palomino.

Would Matt have looked like this? She wondered.

The thought disturbed her, and when she glanced back at the nurse, the woman had already slipped out of the room, leaving her alone with the boy. Janet sat back and folded her hands in her lap, prepared to wait it out as long as necessary until he awoke.

The world was different now. The smell of antiseptic stung Blue's nostrils. Medicine, he dredged up from his memory. He awakened all at once, his eyes flying open to confront a place so different from the den, the valley, that he could do nothing but howl in protest. He tried to jump off the bed, but there were leather belts like Poppy used to hit him with buckled tightly across his chest and legs. His eyes swept frantically from one corner of the hospital room to the other, stopping abruptly when he saw the nice lady who belonged to Turk. She was sitting on the edge of her chair, peering at him as if she knew who he was and what had happened to him.

She'll keep you if you're good, Mr Harriman told him. *That's why she came back, because she needs you as much as you need her.*

I need Az, Az –

Az is dead. You have no one now but Matthew's mother. Look at her, Blue, so you won't forget. She cares about you. She'll keep you safe.

How frightening it all was, all these terrible memories jostling against each other, rushing into his mind until it felt as if they were crammed together, so tight there wasn't room for another thought. The den and the valley, escaping the Jesses. The yellow dog, the gunshot and the blood. It was all there, imprinted on his memory, never to be forgotten.

He screamed in anger, scaring Matthew's mother. She pushed her chair back, and as it scraped along the floor he threw himself against the leather bindings, trying to break free.

'It's all right, I'm here now. I won't let anyone hurt you again,' she said.

I want food. I want Az. I want to find the Jesses who killed her and the Jess who killed Mama. I want . . . I want . . . Mr Harriman? Mr Harriman, I'm afraid they'll hurt me.

They won't, Blue. She'll protect you.

Mr Harriman didn't lie. Yet Blue was frightened all the

same, and he growled that the Jesses had tied him down like this. Now they'd be able to do anything they wanted to him, knowing he couldn't defend himself.

The door swung open and Dr Feingold stepped inside, surprised not only to see Janet, but that the boy was awake and once again violent.

'I've brought him breakfast,' Feingold murmured uneasily. He took a hesitant step toward the bed, stopping abruptly when the youngster drew his lips back and began to snarl, making a sound that was so unlike anything a child could have uttered that even Janet had to keep convincing herself he was just a little boy, terrified now that he was among people again.

'I've brought you something to eat,' the physician said, speaking slowly and loudly, as if he were talking to a foreigner.

After sniffing at it suspiciously, the boy pressed his face into the bowl of oatmeal. For a moment all Janet could hear was the way he gulped down the cereal, emptying the bowl so quickly she could hardly believe her eyes.

When he was finished he raised his head, his pale, almost colorless blue eyes darting between her and the doctor.

'Can't you get him something else?' she asked. 'He's still hungry.'

Dr Feingold rang for a nurse. He eyed the boy with open distrust, as if he were a new species of animal he didn't quite know what to make of.

'He's autistic, no question about it,' he said at last, looking at Janet with a patronizing expression.

'Autistic? You haven't even tested him yet.'

'He'll be tested, all in good time. I've seen to his physical condition, and now it's up to others to attend to the rest.'

'Meaning?'

'The Palm Springs police and the Riverside County sheriff's office have both been contacted. We've also notified LA. They're running it through their computers to see if they can come up with anything. Personally, I doubt it'll do any good. Whoever did this to the boy certainly wouldn't have bothered to report him missing. It's very possible they abandoned him simply because of his autism. These things aren't unheard of.'

There was something so smug about the way he spoke that Janet had to exercise all of her self-control just to remain calm.

'In any event, I've made arrangements for him to be transferred to a state-run facility, one that's better equipped to handle his special needs.'

'And so he'll just be shipped off somewhere and that's the end of it?'

Feingold acted surprised by her tone. 'What more would you like of me, Mrs Kaufman?'

'A little compassion,' she felt like saying. But rather than antagonize him, she said instead, 'And if I wanted to assume responsibility for his care?'

'Pardon?'

'Is it so unheard of, Doctor?'

'I appreciate your good intentions. But for now the boy is a ward of the state. I don't think you realize the depth of his problem. Putting aside all that he's been through – and that in itself is next to impossible – we're still left with his autism. I don't know if you've ever been exposed to an autistic child, but – '

'I don't believe that's the case,' she interrupted.

Dr Feingold shrugged, and he took off his horn-rims and began to polish them on the sleeve of his lab coat.

'Where do you intend to have him transferred?'

'San Andreas State.' The doctor put on his glasses, squinting at her just to make sure they were clean. 'He'll be among his own kind. Really, it's all for the best.' He glanced inquisitively at the youngster, who had remained remarkably calm throughout the exchange, acting as if he'd been paying close attention to everything that was discussed.

Janet waited until she was alone with the boy before she spoke. There was an eagerness, almost a kind of desperation, about the way he looked at her. Pathetic and vulnerable all at once. He followed her with his eyes the way Turk sometimes did.

'On top of everything else, you should've seen Turk,' Neil had said. 'Whined and carried on all the way home, he missed you so.'

Missed me or the boy? she wondered now, remembering what her husband had told her on the phone.

'I'll come and visit you,' she said, knowing that at this point there was little else she could do.

His mouth still smeared with oatmeal, the boy began to shake his head. Then, with a snarl of frustration, he struggled to break free. One violent tremor followed another as his body thumped helplessly against the bed, the leather straps effectively immobilizing him.

'My name is Janet, Janet,' she told him, trying to get him to quiet down. 'Do you have a name?'

Blue, Blue!

But though he tried to get his lips to move, all that came out was a harsh guttural sound, one she couldn't possibly understand.

Don't let her leave! We need her, Blue. Without her the Jesses'll keep us locked up, helpless.

Janet saw the terror in the child's eyes. Sensing the anguish he must be feeling, she reached out, pressing her hand against his shoulder. The skin was hard and leathery to the touch, tanned a deep shade of bronze. The boy turned his head to the side, and like a puppy he began to nuzzle her fingers, licking them with his tongue.

'I'll be back, I promise,' she told him. 'If you can

understand what I'm saying, I intend to do everything I can to help you.'

When she turned away she waited for him to call her back, to cry out, 'Mommy, it's me, Matthew!' But all she heard was a soft mewling sound, a low, broken whimper like that of an animal in pain.

San Andreas State Hospital, Thursday, 3 June 1982

Locked in a room Mr Harriman told him was a cell, a place the Jesses would always put him unless they escaped, Blue moved restlessly on all fours, pacing from one end of the narrow room to the other. Holding his head erect so as not to be caught by surprise, he moved with smooth rhythmic jerks, back and forth on his hands and the soles of his feet. Sometimes he paused, resting on his callused knees, sniffing the air in expectation of freedom, the promise of fresh meat. Prey was scarce here. He and Mr Harriman had captured a mouse, pouncing on it with great delight and tearing it apart before the little furry creature had a chance to scurry to safety. But they had found nothing else to satisfy their constant hunger.

Now he squatted in a corner of the cell, relieving himself as he listened to the sounds carried along by the darkness. All the Jesses were asleep, except the ones who wore white. There were many of them at the hospital, some with dark skin and some with light. When they came into the cell they always kept him at bay with a long heavy stick, setting his food on top of a table so that he was forced to stand up on both feet. Clutching the edge of the table for support, he would seize the food between his teeth and carry it to a corner of the cell. Here he would feed with watchful eyes, alert to the smallest movement, the way their eyes sometimes flickered in fear, the way they would step back to the door, watching him just as anxiously as he watched them.

Raw meat was what he craved, but none was given to him. Instead, everything they set on the table tasted soft and dead. Or else he would have to chew leaves and grasses like he and Az had sometimes been forced to do when game was scarce and there was nothing else to eat.

Every morning while he tried to sleep (for it was rare to hunt by daylight) the Jesses would creep into the cell and prick his arm with a thorn. Then he would be too weak and drowsy to protect himself. Carrying him outside the room, they made him walk back and forth, holding him stiffly erect so that his back and shoulders ached from the strain.

If he crouched and deposited his droppings on the floor they raised their voices at him. Didn't they understand it was better this way, that Az had taught him how important it was to keep the den as clean as possible?

When he walked, back and forth down a long and endless corridor like a narrow canyon trail, he would meet others like himself, crawling about on all fours, and hissing and baring their teeth when he came near. Yet there was something about these others that made him fearful. They were wolves and yet they weren't. It made him wonder if they were merely pretending to be his brothers, and if they meant to harm him once they gained his trust. So Blue kept his distance, growling back at them when they approached.

Sitting alone in the cell, rubbing his buttocks against the floor to keep himself clean, he would stare and stare at the door until it began to blur. Perhaps if he stared hard enough it would melt like snow, and the Janet would stand in the doorway, holding out her arms to him.

But tonight the waiting was like a wound that burned and festered and wouldn't heal. Mr Harriman told him that he mustn't lose hope. But *hope* was something that had a sound but not a meaning.

Was it hope to think the woman named Janet would come back? Was it hope to wait and wait even when the Jesses did mean things to him, using their long sticks and sharp thorns to keep him under control? If that was what hope meant, Blue wanted no part of it.

Can't we get away? Can't we find our way back to the den? If Az is dead, there must be someone else to hunt with.

The Jesses would capture you and bring you back, Mr Harriman replied.

But I'm faster than they are.

You must be patient, Blue. Matthew's mother will come, just as I've promised.

And if she doesn't? he said defiantly.

Anger rippled through his mind. Oh, it was terrible to feel Mr Harriman's rage, and he clamped his hands to the sides of his head and rocked back and forth, stunned by the force of his friend's temper.

So you don't want to trust me anymore, is that it?

No, I'll be good, I promise! he cried out, rolling on the floor now and trying to stop the pain.

Then let the Jesses come, my little friend. We shall see what a great hunter you are!

Silence where there had been thunder. Numbness where there had been pain. Blue pulled himself back into a crouch, resting on his knees and the palms of his hands. From outside the cell came the distant tapping of footsteps.

We'll wait for the Jesses to come and pay us a visit, whispered Mr Harriman. *Then you can show me how brave you are.*

The footsteps grew louder: one of the white Jesses making his rounds, spying on everyone and poking at them with his heavy stick. Blue could smell him long before he reached the door. When keys jangled loudly through the darkness he moved swiftly to the doorway, waiting for Mr Harriman to tell him what to do.

Remember when the little girl banged her head against the wall and you lapped up the blood? Did it taste good, my friend?

That had been just a few days before. Remembering it as if it had just taken place, Blue nodded emphatically.

It was warm and salty, like fresh meat. Then do it again, Blue. Show the Jesses you haven't forgotten what they did to your mama, what they did to Az.

If Mr Harriman was still angry at him it was an anger Blue couldn't understand. The voice in his head, the voice that he alone could hear, was urging him to do what he had wanted ever since he was taken here, thrown into the narrow white cell that reeked of medicine and fear.

The man-smell was almost on top of him now. The lock turned and then the door swung open. As the orderly peered curiously inside, Blue jumped out of hiding with a snarl of excitement. His teeth caught the two-legged Jess around the ankle. His jaws snapped shut and blood spurted hot and salty over his lips and tongue. Yes, this was what he was born for, the challenge of the hunt, pinning down his prey and feeding as was his right.

But the Jess was very strong, and he had his heavy stick to use for protection. He swung the bat down against Blue's shoulder. But even the pain didn't stop Blue from holding on, trying to tear through the Jess's pants so he could reach the warm flesh of his calf.

Kill, kill, kill, kill!

Mr Harriman was screaming as loudly as the Jess. Wanting desperately to please his friend and knowing how important it was to obey, Blue let go of the guard's leg and hurtled straight up in the air. His hands fastened around the Jess's neck, and together the two of them went crashing to the floor.

Remember what Az taught you. His throat, strike at his throat, Blue! Then tear it out and feed, feed!

The Jess was strong, but now that he'd lost his stick he

also seemed to have lost his nerve. He kept screaming as Blue tore at his neck, digging his fingers into the man's terrified eyes and pushing his head back so that his Adam's apple bobbed up and down like something floating right beneath his skin.

Footsteps raced down the corridor. The man-smell made him gag. Out of the corner of his eye he saw another Jess rush inside, holding his bat in both hands. It came down so quickly that Blue didn't have time to jump out of the way. The blow sent him staggering back, reeling from the pain that shot up and down his leg.

'You fucking freak!' shouted the guard. Again he slammed the club down, hitting Blue across the stomach.

Then, as his fists descended, striking Blue across the face with one ferocious blow after another, his knee came up, and the dead things they had fed him, the foul-tasting leaves and grasses, all rose up in Blue's throat, filling his mouth before spilling down his chin.

'Puke all you want, you little shit.' The guard held his hand to his neck, and blood dripped over his fingers. Not content to leave it at that, he rammed his knee into Blue's groin, forcing him to double up in pain.

As Blue slid down along the wall, falling in a wounded heap on the cold cement floor, he couldn't help himself, and a stream of urine flowed down his leg. The other guard hauled his friend back, warning him they'd have hell to pay if they didn't leave the kid alone.

'What kid? The little animal gives me the creeps. They should stick him in a fucking cage and never let him out.'

By then it didn't matter. One eye already swollen shut, the other drooping like a leaf deprived of water, Blue just sat there, watching the pool of steaming urine spread out across the floor.

* * *

Driving west along the Ventura Freeway, June's smog following them all the way up the San Andreas State, Janet hugged her side of the front seat, excited and yet anxious, all at once.

It was nearly two months since she had seen the boy, although she'd been in regular contact with the chief psychiatrist at the hospital. The doctor had insisted she postpone her visit until the boy was adjusted to his new surroundings. But though she expected to hear optimistic reports, for she still refused to accept the diagnosis of autism, none were forthcoming.

If anything, the youngster's behavior was even more antisocial than when he was first admitted. The psychiatrist had already indicated that he saw little chance of improvement. Children suffering from infantile autism, he had explained, were governed by basically one principle – an obsessive need to maintain absolute sameness in their environment. Completely unable to relate to others, autistic children retreated into a world of their own devising, one which effectively shielded them from outside stimuli.

It was the psychiatrist's belief that the behavior of so-called feral children – children supposedly raised by animals in the wild – was actually the result of having been raised by a parent who behaved like an animal, and certainly not the result of an animal who behaved like a parent. The boy's violent defensiveness was a shield that protected him from the sort of destructive experiences he'd suffered in the past. To hope for improvement was, at best, unfair to herself as well as to the child.

Yet Janet was unable to ignore the memory of hearing a pleading voice, a little boy fearfully whispering to her and begging for help. Who that child might be she still didn't know. She was convinced that the boy was ultimately as sane as anyone else, his problems stemming not from autism but from neglect and physical abuse.

To tear down that wall of defenses would require a great deal of patience and compassion. Yet that was precisely what she was willing to offer him, even without Neil's enthusiastic support.

'There it is,' she called out, breaking the silence that had fallen between her and Neil for the past twenty minutes.

She continued to hug her side of the seat as Neil followed her directions once they got off the freeway. Soon a high chain-link fence reared up alongside the road, and she realized that for all her brave talk and good intentions, she was suddenly frightened beyond reason.

What if he really is autistic? And why have I taken this on myself, like some sort of sacred cause, a crusade? she wondered. If I knew that, we probably wouldn't even be here. Or would we?

The green-and-white sign read SAN ANDREAS STATE HOSPITALITY, the last three letters pulsating in day-glo orange. The same unknown artist had used his spray can to wreathe the sign in a rippling circle of color that vibrated painfully against the back of her eyes. She looked away, Neil pausing at the gate while the security guard got clearance to let them in.

It was just like a prison, and that alone reaffirmed Janet's determination. Turk had brought the boy to her for a reason. And she could not pretend otherwise. Besides, there were so many unanswered mysteries in the world that what was another, especially in the person of one small boy.

The visitors' parking lot was nearly deserted. When she got out and stretched her legs she could hear voices murmuring like wind in the distance. The grounds were flat and dusty, the main building sending its shadow across the brown parched grass. There were bars over all the windows, and metal screens over the bars.

Once they were inside the building, her resolve began to

crumble, giving way to dismay. She hung on to Neil's arm, listening to the babble of voices echoing down the hallways. A young Chicano nurse got up from behind the information desk and asked if she could be of help.

'We're looking for the children's ward,' Janet explained.

'Your name?'

'Kaufman, Mr and Mrs Kaufman. Dr Abernathy's expecting us.'

'That would be the third floor, west wing.' She motioned to the bank of elevators at the far end of the starkly decorated lobby. 'There are signs. You'll know if you're lost.'

When they got off the elevator on the third floor, the signs were plastered everywhere, and you had to be blind to miss them. HOSPITAL PERSONNEL ONLY . . . SEE NURSE FOR ESCORT . . . NO UNAUTHORIZED ADMITTANCE . . .

'Where's "proceed at your own risk"?' Neil joked.

It wasn't funny, and yet that's just what it felt like.

At the nurses' station they were told to wait until Dr Abernathy was paged. Janet tried not to stare too hard at the barred doorways, while again there came back to her the whisper of seemingly countless voices, then a long, drawn-out howl as if someone were being tortured.

Quick, purposeful footsteps reached her ears. She looked up to see a white-coated figure striding resolutely down the hallway, where he paused to confer with a burly, muscle-bound orderly before proceeding in their direction.

'You must be the Kaufmans,' he said, his handshake as rough-hewn as his features. 'Lynn Abernathy. Nice to meet you. How was the ride up?'

'Fine,' she replied, hoping that would be the extent of the small talk, since she was anxious to hear about the boy. 'How is he, Doctor?'

'Well, he's been confined to his room this last week or so,' Abernathy said slowly.

'Why?' she asked.

The doctor looked pained and explained about the attack on the orderly, that it took three men just to subdue him. 'Of course, autistic children can be very violent, as I'm sure you're well aware.'

She hadn't been aware of that, but she still refused to believe the boy was autistic. 'How have you made that determination, Dr Abernathy?' she asked as the psychiatrist led them down the corridor, unlocking a door that opened into a large, sunny dayroom.

Before he could answer, Janet stopped short, reacting with both fear and surprise. When her initial shock wore off she began to shake her head, having never been exposed to a roomful of autistic children. It was a pathetic sight, and she instinctively reached for Neil's hand, holding it tight.

In one corner of the room a little girl with lank blond hair sat on the floor, rocking back and forth, staring vacantly into space. Here and there were collections of cardboard boxes, sheets, and tattered blankets, under which she could make out an occasional arm or leg, once a face that peered through the opening of the homemade cave with a gaze that saw absolutely nothing but the reflection of its own malaise.

'Dens,' explained Abernathy. 'Many of these youngsters find comfort in darkness, though we've discovered it has nothing to do with light-sensitivity, as was first thought.'

Janet nodded dumbly. A teenage boy crawled along the floor on all fours, pausing to wash himself. He reminded her of a cat, the way he applied saliva to the outside of his hand, then rubbed it over his face. Another child sat forlornly along the wall, picking at her face with bandaged fingers. There were numerous scars and fresh scabs on her cheeks, and Abernathy told them this kind of self-destructive behavior was also quite common, and that some autistics had even been know to bite off their own fingers.

'That's why we try to keep them bandaged if we see they're attacking themselves.'

'How long have they been here?' Neil asked, moving away from a boy who seemed particularly upset by his presence and had to be led out of the room by an orderly.

'Depends on the child. Most of these youngsters are mentally retarded, and many of them have known no other home but this one. Occasionally we're able to get through to them. Then, by the use of traditional behavior-modification techniques, rewarding them whenever they show improvement, they can be toilet-trained and taught to dress themselves, sometimes even to communicate in primitive grunts. But that's usually the exception.'

'So there's no cure?' said Neil.

'Not in the convential sense. You can ask five specialists about infantile autism and get five different explanations. Some believe it's a chemical imbalance, a kind of biological disorder. Others insist it's solely the result of a specific kind of upbringing, usually by a parent who, for reasons of his or her own, is unable to relate to the child in what we consider a normal manner. Still others claim autism is just another way of describing schizophrenia.'

'And our child . . . I mean . . .' The words dwindled away. The boy *wasn't* their child, and yet Janet couldn't help but think of him that way. Why? Again and again she'd asked herself that question. Again and again she'd shied away from an answer.

From the dayroom they headed down another corridor, with rooms on either side. Once she regained her composure, she again asked Dr Abernathy how he'd concluded that the boy was autistic.

'I think it's rather obvious, Mrs Kaufman. There's nothing he does that we haven't seen before. The crawling on all fours – regression to the crawling stage in infants. The fact that he prefers raw food and has no control over his bodily functions – again, this is very typical among extremely autistic children. The howling and the animal-like sounds he makes, the refusal to wear clothes, the acute sensitivity to smell. All of these things we've seen before, and unfortunately will probably continue seeing, since I don't believe infantile autism is a disease for which we're going to one day come up with a cure.'

'Do autistic children talk?' she asked.

'Not usually. As I said, they can be taught to communicate, but only on the most rudimentary level. Even those who aren't retarded rarely venture to speak. And when they do it's never much more than a word or two, hardly ever a complete sentence.'

'And yet I've read that on occasion children who appeared to be autistic have gradually come out of their shell. They've become normal again, Doctor.'

Abernathy smiled patiently. 'In the case of this particular youngster, I'm afraid that's highly unlikely.' With these words he fished a key out of his pocket and opened a door at the end of the narrow corridor.

Janet caught the unmistakable odor of excrement even before she stepped inside. But that, she'd already decided was the very least of it.

'Oh, my God,' she whispered when she saw him, crouched in a corner of the cell-like room. 'What have they done to you?'

With an angry glance at Dr Abernathy, and before either he or Neil could stop her, she rushed across the room, taking the youngster in her arms and holding him close. It hadn't occurred to her that he might become violent, and when he cowered in her arms, rubbing his cheek against her hand, she looked up at the psychiatrist and found it difficult to control her temper.

'If the boy's autistic, then how can you justify what you've done?'

One of the youngster's eyes were swollen shut, surrounded by an ugly purplish bruise. The crusty scab of a recent cut inched its way across his forehead. As she rocked him back and forth she noticed the numerous contusions and black-and-blue marks on his arms and legs. The child had been severely beaten, and nothing he might have done could excuse that kind of physical abuse.

For a moment Dr Abernathy seemed at a loss for words. Then he stiffened defensively. 'I assure you whatever happened was as necessary as it was regrettable,' he replied.

'Necessary?' It came out a shout, and Neil's eyes flickered a warning, as if to say it wouldn't help things any getting into an argument.

'The boy attacked an orderly. The man was severely wounded. In attempting to subdue him, the staff may have been a bit overzealous, but you have no idea how strong he is.'

'That's why he's holding on to me for dear life, because he's so big and strong,' Janet said contemptuously. She looked down at the boy, kissing the top of his head. His blond hair was coming in even lighter than expected. 'It's all right now,' she whispered. 'I promised I'd come, and here I am. I haven't forgotten you, not for a minute.'

'I'm rather surprised,' she heard Dr Abernathy admit, keeping his distance from across the room. 'He's not even medicated – we haven't been able to get that close – and yet there's no doubt he trusts you, Mrs Kaufman.'

'He recognizes me too,' she said.

The child looked up at her, the eye that wasn't closed so pale and nearly colorless it was like a bit of ice floating in an arctic sea. Yet Janet felt warmth in his gaze and knew there would never be a moment when he would try to harm her.

How thin he felt, snuggled up in her arms. The shapeless

white hospital gown made him look oddly like a doll, covered up for modesty's sake until a more appropriate costume could be found. He was much paler than when she'd first seen him in Palm Springs, when his leathery skin had borne the full brunt of God knows how many weeks, or even months, out in the desert sun. A faint peach fuzz covered his sallow cheeks, stippling his upper lip. But then Dr Abernathy made a move to approach him, and the boy suddenly pulled free of her embrace and scampered back.

Crouching on all fours, he raised his head stiffly, his upper lip trembling violently as he began to snarl. But even the coarse, guttural sounds he made weren't nearly as frightening as they once were.

'See?' said Abernathy, as if the point he'd made was perfectly clear.

'See what? He's afraid of you, as well he should be. But I bet he's not afraid of my husband. Come closer, Neil. Let him know that you don't mean to hurt him.'

An obsession, Neil was thinking, a goddamn fullblown out-and-out obsession. And I'm in the fucking middle of it, whether I like it or not.

The boy continued to growl, occasionally making a sound that was very much like the way Turk barked whenever strangers came to the house. Neil took a single faltering step forward.

It wasn't their child. Why was she making herself suffer like this, when they both knew what would happen in the end? The visits would become fewer and fewer. The boy would wander around in a Thorazine haze. Soon she wouldn't come at all. Soon the memory of what had happened at her brother's house would be grist for her typewriter, another chapter in another book, sanitized for the benefit of her preteen audience.

Yet it shocked him all the same, not the boy's wolfish

behavior so much as the way Dr Abernathy had clinically dissected the child's condition, serving it up in as inoffensive a package as he could manage.

Another form of whitewash, Neil thought, when there's no denying they've beaten the shit out of the poor kid.

He dropped down into a crouch, squatting several yards away from the boy, the better to maintain eye contact. 'I'm not going to hurt you,' he said slowly and distinctly, enunciating each word as if the boy were a lip-reader.

'There's really no point in – ' Abernathy began.

'Let me be the judge of that,' Neil said sharply. 'For once, I agree with my wife. I don't see any indication the boy's retarded. And in a place like this, one doesn't come away feeling satisfied he's getting the best care money can buy, either.'

'The boy is a ward of the state, Mr Kaufman. Our budget is limited. We're given just so much money per patient.'

'I don't think that has anything to do with it. He's been here two months now, and as far as I can tell the only progress he's made is that he's learned to be afraid.'

Neil looked back at the child, who seemed to be frozen like a rabbit in the glare of headlights. Only his ears twitched as he returned Neil's stare, occasionally turning his eyes away, no doubt so as not to appear too threatening.

'My name is Neil. My wife's name is Janet. Do you remember us? You came to our friend's house. Our dog took you there. Turk. Do you remember Turk?'

If only the child would nod. If only he'd say something, just a single word, a faint but audible yes. But he remained silent, quivering now as if he were cold.

'Talk to us,' whispered Janet. 'We're here to help you.'

Dr Abernathy took another step forward. 'As you can see – '

'Daddy, it's Matthew. I've come back.'

Neil jerked his eyes away in confusion. The boy hadn't spoken, hadn't moved his lips at all. Then whose voice was it, whispering in his ear?

He came to his feet, searching Dr Abernathy's face for a clue. 'What did you say?' he asked.

'Excuse me?'

'You said something to me just then, didn't you?'

'I'm sorry, but I haven't said a word.' The psychiatrist glanced at Janet. 'Did you hear me say anything, Mrs Kaufman?'

She was sitting on the floor now, one arm draped over the boy's shoulders. 'Is anything wrong, Neil?'

The psychiatrist's censuring expression, the way he eyed Neil as if he were prospective patient, made him hold his tongue. He looked down at the boy thoughtfully. Janet was right. This wasn't a hospital. It was a prison; the children had been locked away, abandoned. This was society's garbage dump, its most recent addition a silent little boy with coldly searching eyes and delicate faunlike features.

Who were the child's parents? What had they done to him? Perhaps if they knew that, they could unlock the door and lead the boy back out into the sunshine.

But what about the voice? Neil thought again. Am I catching her obsession, is that it? Infectious madness, is that what the good doctor would call it?

'See? I won't hurt you, young feller,' Dr Abernathy was saying.

The psychiatrist moved closer. All at once the boy sprang to his feet, swaying as he struggled to maintain his balance. Neil could swear he saw the short blond hairs at the nape of the child's neck rise stiffly in the air, and a chill passed through him, nameless dread of something he didn't understand.

'Don't frighten him!' he suddenly cried out, stepping between Abernathy and the child. Janet also came to her feet, ready to protect the boy.

The child staggered back, falling into Janet's arms. 'There, there,' she whispered. 'He won't hurt you again. We won't let anyone hurt you.'

'Seen enough?' Abernathy said.

'No, not quite,' he replied. 'Could you give us a few minutes alone with the boy?'

'I think you're taking a great risk, Mr Kaufman.'

'That's what life's all about, isn't it?'

Abernathy shrugged. 'As long as you realize we can't be responsible.'

'Oh, you don't have to worry about that. I can see you haven't been responsible in quite some time, Doctor.'

I'm getting as wigged out as Janet, he thought as he waited for the psychiatrist to leave, Abernathy eyeing him distastefully rather than trading barbs. What's this kid got that makes me want to protect him?

The door closed with a clang.

'It's all right now,' he began, slowly making his way toward the boy. 'No one's gonna hurt you.'

'Daddy, it's Matthew. Take me home, Daddy. They hurt me here.'

Gooseflesh erupted up and down his arms. The back of his neck felt ice-cold. Just as quickly he was burning up, rivulets of sweat dripping down his arms and chest, making his shirt stick to his skin.

A son, Janet, we have a son!

He had danced around the hospital room, so filled with joy he didn't know how to contain himself. They had taken Matthew home to the perfect house in the hills, the perfect nursery, and the perfect start of a perfect life. Nothing had been too good for his Matthew. He had had it all worked out. The best schools, the best universities.

Matthew would be a doctor, and Neil would live vicariously through his boy, and his boy would know he had a pal for life.

'Mr Kaufman?' the voice had said on the phone, a bland, anonymous voice without the slightest trace of a regional accent, so that it seemed as if he were listening to a computer. 'Yes, this is Neil Kaufman.' 'Do you own a tan Audi, Mr Kaufman?' 'Yes.' 'Were your wife and son . . . ?'

Were my wife and son, were my wife and son . . .

Tears began to trickle down his cheeks. What the hell is happening to me? he thought. He didn't know, and he shook his head, trying to come to grips with his memories.

'Neil, are you all right?'

He started to answer, when there it was again.

'Daddy, it's me. Matthew!'

The voice cried painfully in his ears. He spun around. There was no one else in the room, unless, of course, he wanted to believe in ghosts. The ghost of a little boy, buried with bitter heartfelt tears a year before? No, it wasn't possible. And yet he'd heard the child speak, heard a whispered voice, begging desperately to be taken home where he belonged.

Again Neil looked down at the child crouched on all fours, the callused knobs of his knees flat against the cement. No one's gonna put you through the wringer anymore, kiddo, he thought. Not with Kaufman around to take care of you.

'He talked to me, Janet. He didn't say anything, but somehow he still talked to me.' He looked at his wife with a mixture of fear and yet relief, glad he was able to be honest with her. 'He said he's Matthew, that he wants us to take him home.'

'Oh, God,' she whispered. 'It happened to me, too, when I was at the hospital. I didn't tell you then because . . . because I was afraid of what you'd think. But how – ?'

'It doesn't matter how.' He reached over, gently running his hand over the child's shoulder. 'I heard you,' he said. 'That's why we're here, because somehow you've come back to us. And if it's really not you, Matt, well . . . that's not the important thing. It's still a part of you, no matter what anyone says.'

Before he realized what he was doing he had the child in his arms. How thin and frail he felt, his bones like wicker. The boy trembled and Neil held him even closer, nuzzling the top of his head.

Our son, he kept thinking. Our boy. A family again.

Pitiful whimpering sounds escaped the youngster's lips. Neil eased back, and in that instant, as he caught Janet's calm and glowing expression, it seemed to him that this was how it always was, that they were meant to be together. Despite what all the Feingolds and Abernathys of the world might say, they were a family now, never to be separated.

The boy's lips began to move. His teeth, chipped though startlingly white, clattered against each other. Neil saw his tongue probing the inside of his mouth, as if he were trying to recall how to speak.

'Hehhh . . .' he said.

Saliva trickled down his chin. Janet wiped his mouth with a tissue.

'Go on,' she said. 'You can do it.'

'Sure you can, Matt. We'll understand.'

Matt, I'm calling him Matt and I'm not even asking myself why, Neil thought. But now he was too involved in watching the boy to start questioning his motives.

'Hehhh . . . hehlll . . .' The child's tongue pressed against the roof of his mouth. That he was even making the effort to speak was convincing proof that he wasn't autistic, at least as far as Neil and Janet were concerned.

They kept nodding and encouraging the boy to try again.

'Hehlll . . .'

'*He'll* what?' asked Janet.

'Not *he'll*.'

'Hell?'

'No, of course not.' And to Matt: 'That's it, take your time. We got all the time in the world, son.'

Son! I'm just as nuts as she is. The two of us, two loonies egging each other on. What's going on here, Kaufman? Your kid is dead, dead and buried with a marker over his grave. MATTHEW DAVID KAUFMAN, 1978–1981.

'Helll . . . hell puh puh . . .'

'What?' Neil said.

'Helll puh . . . helll puh . . .'

'*Help*, is that it?'

'Hellpp,' said the boy, a bubble of saliva breaking across his lips. 'Hellpp . . . mee . . . mee!'

Another chill passed through him, only this time it had nothing to do with fear.

'He does understand,' Janet said excitedly. 'He's not like the others, Neil, I'm sure of it. *Help me.* Yes, of course, Matt, of course we'll help you.'

'Daddy, Daddy, I love you,' the childish voice whispered in Neil's ear.

'I love you, too,' he said aloud, and he and Janet held the boy in their arms, laughing through the tears.

You did well, Matthew, said Mr Harriman.

Not Matthew. Blue. It's Blue!

No, from now on it's Matthew, my little friend. Matthew David Kaufman.

7

After nearly six weeks of red tape it was finally agreed that a psychiatric review board would study the case. If they felt the boy was well enough to leave the hospital, it would then be up to the county Adoptions Department to make the final determination.

'How long do you think that'll take?' Janet asked.

'I suspect you'll be hearing from us sometime next week,' Dr Abernathy replied.

In the interim she had no lack of projects to keep her busy. Her publisher was getting anxious to see her latest proposal for a novel. But when she sat at her desk to write, she didn't have very much to show in the way of inspiration. The notes she'd assembled refused to come together, and she finally put aside her humorous look at first love and instead began doing research on the subject of feral children, 'wolf boys' as the popular literature liked to call them.

Thus, between research at UCLA, redecorating the nursery to make it suitable for Matt, and consultations with their attorney, Janet found she had little time to spare. Each weekend she and Neil drove up to San Andreas State to spend Saturdays with the boy. Occasionally they stayed overnight in a nearby motel, returning to the hospital the next morning. Matt would frolic around them the way Turk did, acting as if he hadn't seen them in months.

The weekend visits only reinforced their determination to take the boy home. For the time being they decided not to mention their plans to anyone, not so much afraid of what their friends might think as they were of being disappointed. If the review board decided against them, their attorney had already cautioned that the adoption process could then go on for months, if not longer.

But when Janet's brother called one afternoon late in July, it didn't occur to her to keep silent on the matter.

'Where've you been?' Andy said as soon as she picked up the phone, having just returned with an armload of books from the research library.

'Today or the last month?'

'Both.'

'UCLA, working. The hospital, visiting.'

'Neil's all right, isn't he?'

She appreciated the concern in his voice. 'Fine. Still battling a midriff bulge, but other than that he's doing great.'

'Then what hospital are you talking about?'

It was too late to change her story now that she realized what she'd started. 'San Andreas State.'

'Christ, what poor soul got stuck up there.'

'Matt.'

'Who?' Andy said, with something very much like fear in his voice.

'The boy. The one Turk brought to your house.'

There was a lengthy pause, as if Andy weren't quite sure what to say. 'Listen,' he finally went on, 'I'm up here on business. Do you think you could squeeze in an evening with your one and only brother? I haven't had decent Chinese food since the last time you cooked for us.'

Janet glanced at the battle-scarred wok that occupied the place of honor on top of the stove. She thought quickly, cataloguing the ingredients she had on hand. There was plenty of roast pork in the freezer, fresh egg noodles, and bean sprouts in the fridge.

Promptly at seven Andy pulled into the drive, his chrome-yellow Mercedes coated with a thin layer of Palm

Springs dust. With his sandy-blond hair and desert tan, his lean and athletic build, her brother resembled a model in a resort ad. He was thirty-seven but didn't look much older than thirty, a fact that never escaped his brother-in-law's eye.

'Flat stomachs. Ugh, who needs the aggravation?' Neil groaned as he poured Andy Hilliard a glass of white wine. But when no one was looking he tightened his belt, just so his lack of willpower wouldn't be too conspicuous.

When dinner was ready, they ate outside where there was plenty of room for a pool but not enough discretionary cash to have one dug. It was still light out, the sun just starting to go down. The opposite rim of the canyon was washed with a soft reddish tint. A flock of mourning doves flew by, their wings whistling loudly.

'So what's the new book about?' Andy asked between mouthfuls of roast pork lo mein, complimenting the chefs on their culinary expertise.

'A feral child.'

'Like – ?'

'Exactly.'

Neil was trying to signal her with his eyes. But if she couldn't be honest with her brother, Janet knew, she was in serious trouble. So she hesitantly told him all about Matt, and how the wheels had been set in motion for adoption.

For a long while Andy didn't say anything. Then he put down his chopsticks, took a sip of wine, and looked at each of them in turn.

'Are you guys putting me on?' he said.

'Not at all,' said Neil.

'But why?'

'Why not?' she said.

'Why not?' repeated her brother with a look of disbelief. 'It's very obvious. The kid's disturbed. I can understand your concern . . . no, maybe I can't, but I'll let it pass. But you can't be serious about wanting to adopt him.'

'We're very serious,' said Neil.

'Don't you think you're jumping into this? I mean, why shackle yourselves with a disadvantaged child? Not disadvantaged even, but emotionally disturbed.'

'He's not,' she insisted. 'He's suffered terribly, that's all too clear. But there's no reason why he can't find himself again.'

Her brother eyed her skeptically. 'Janet, this isn't a book. You can't write *The End* and just put it away on a shelf. This is forever. Maybe he's only going to live with you for the next ten years or so. But he's still going to be a part of your lives until the day you die.'

Janet stared at her plate, no longer hungry. Why couldn't Andy just wish them luck and leave it at that? Why did he suddenly have to resort to playing big brother, when they both knew that was never the role at which he'd excelled?

'I'm only saying this out of love, and concern for the both of you,' Andy went on. 'I don't think you've stopped to consider what this whole thing entails. Come on, guys, it's a little perverse, don't you think? Calling him Matt – that says it right there.'

'I should think you'd be the last person to worry about being perverse,' Neil replied.

Although he was immediately sorry, Neil made no attempt to apologize. What did Andy know about being a parent, anyway? He and Mike had no interest in children. So it was very easy for him to sit back and pass judgement.

Janet hurriedly intervened, knowing Neil hadn't meant to be insulting. 'What Neil's trying to say is that we've thought this out, Andy. We know just what we're getting ourselves in for.'

'I'm sorry, but I don't think you do, Jan. Along comes a stranger, emotionally and maybe even physically scarred, and what do you do? You think of that empty nursery in there' – he pointed in the direction of the house – 'and immediately lose all sense of proportion. Have a child of your own, for God's sake. Visit this boy, sure, that's commendable. But adopt him? And call him Matthew when we all know what that's all about?'

Neil was barely able to keep his voice down. 'What is it all about?'

'It's about not being able to give up the ghost of the past, that's what. Matt's dead, Neil. You lost him. But you can have another child any time you want.'

'We don't need another child,' Janet told him. 'We found who we're looking for, Andy. And nothing you or anyone else can say will make us change our minds.'

'Fine, Jan.' Though there was nothing *fine* in his tone of voice. 'If that's the way you feel, then you do what's best for you. But I'll tell you one thing. I just hope you're not doing something you'll regret one day.'

Mr Harriman had told him it was like a game. Before the Jesses could be punished, Blue-who-was-now-Matt must first learn to imitate them, to copy the way they moved and spoke, even the way they dressed and ate. But Blue-who-must-now-call-himself-Matt didn't like that at all. Whenever the Jesses weren't watching and he was alone in the room that now had a bed and a chair and a table, he would drop down onto all fours, determined never to forget what Az had taught him.

But whenever he refused to stand upright, whenever he made a mess on the floor or wouldn't eat the dead green leaves they kept on feeding him, Mr Harriman went away and wouldn't come back. Blue-now-Matt would call to him with his mind. He didn't like the silence in his head when before there was always a voice to help him decide what to do.

He would reach out with his thoughts, probing the farthest corners of his memory, hoping Mr Harriman was waiting there to remind him of what his life had once been like. But there was emptiness. Instead of the voice he had heard for so long now, there was nothing but silent pictures of Blue and Mama and Blue and Poppy, Blue and Az and the lady with red hair.

Talk to me. Please! he would cry out.

But Mr Harriman pretended not to be there, and Blue-now-Matt was more alone than he had ever been before.

Only when he thought of himself as Matthew, the Janet and the Neil's little boy, did Mr Harriman return to comfort him. Then his friend would urge him to stand up on both feet and practice his walk, to recite words, to eat with a spoon, to use the potty the white-coated Jesses had left in a corner of the room.

What good will it do to be like them? he kept asking.

And always Mr Harriman would tell him the same thing. Only when the Jesses were fooled could he begin to punish them for their treachery.

How?

I'll give you the Janet, promised Mr Harriman. *You can do whatever you want to her.*

The Janet was very gentle and pretty. Her man-smell didn't make him gag. It was more like new grass crunched underfoot, or the tiny blue flowers that dotted the floor of the valley hours after it rained. There was a softness about her too that he liked, not a meaty softness like game but a wet, soft sadness in her eyes. Yet her touch wasn't sad, nor was it like Mama's touch, either.

Mama, he thought. When was that? They don't remember time here by suns moving across the sky, or hot winds blowing over the desert. They have big white-and-black circles on the wall with little twigs moving so slow you can't see what they're doing even if you stop and stare.

Would you like the Janet? Mr Harriman whispered. *Would it please you to have her for your own*?

What would I do with her?

An image of the room with the pipes and the black machine going whir-whir-whir exploded in his mind, so bright and dazzling he had to close his eyes. He felt the strands of red hair brushing across his chest, someone telling him to take off his hospital gown and climb into bed. 'Blue's a good boy,' Mama was saying. 'Bluie's a real good boy.'

And the Janet, does she think I'm good too? he wondered.

The Janet loves you.

Love?

What they did to you in the room with the pipes, explained Mr Harriman.

Yes, that he could understand. Az took care of him, made sure he wasn't hungry. But that wasn't love, that was . . . that was safe, happy. Love was the machine going like a choo-choo through the darkness, and Bluie standing by the bedroom door, watching and watching and never saying a word.

Poppy leaned over Mama, resting on his knees while she lay there without covers to keep her warm. He had hair growing on his back just like Az, just like his teddy bear. Mama was crying and saying, 'Come on, now, what did I do?'

'You know damn well, you ugly bitch,' said Poppy. He did something Bluie couldn't see, and then Mama was making funny gurgly sounds like playing with bubbles in the bathtub. Poppy swayed back and forth, whistling between his teeth.

Bluie watched from the bedroom door, wondering if

they were playing horsie. He never knew if Poppy was glad to see him or if he was angry. When he was glad he picked Blue up and gave him a piggyback ride, tickling him all over like Mama did with towels after a bath. When he was angry he made angry sounds and he got out the belt he called a strap and made Bluie get across his lap, pushing his jeans down and then his underpants.

'Just so you won't ever forget you're a little bastard,' Poppy always said before he used the strap.

The more Bluie cried and tried to wriggle free, the more angry Poppy became, holding him so tight he couldn't breathe. He was on fire then, but Mama didn't say anything when Poppy called him names and used the strap. But afterward she would whisper that one day they'd go away for good and see Grandma.

The strap always burned like fire on the stove. Bluie reached back and touched himself there while Poppy leaned over Mama and made the bed creak.

'Suck it, bitch,' Poppy said. 'Suck it for as long as it takes.'

'Suckit,' Bluie whispered. 'Suckit.'

He must have said it too loud, 'cause suddenly Poppy turned around and stared at him so hard that Bluie wanted to make peepee in his pants. He could feel the strap going whack-whack-whack even though Poppy didn't have anything in his hands but two big fists.

Whack-whack-whack. Suckit, suckit.

'So the little shit wants an education,' Poppy said.

'Leave the kid alone,' Mama said.

'I didn't do nothin',' Bluie whispered. He turned and rushed out of the room even as Poppy jumped off the bed and ran after him.

He hid behind the couch in the living room while Poppy stormed around the apartment, throwing things on the floor and breaking them. 'I'm gonna find you, Bluie,' he kept calling out like he was singing a song. 'I'm gonna find you and teach you good. Now, where's the little spy? I bet he's there behind the couch,' Poppy sang.

Mama couldn't get to him in time. She kept screaming and begging Poppy not to do it, but Poppy wouldn't listen. He threw her down on the floor, then grabbed Bluie by the hair and dragged him away from the couch.

'You gotta learn you can't spy on people, kid.' And as he sang the song he pulled Bluie over his lap. His skin was wet and he was naked like in the bath, like Mama was naked, too.

The burning and the burning and the fire and it hurt.

'Feel it, you little bastard,' Poppy sang. 'You ain't my kid and you never were.'

Don't let him hurt me, Mama! Don't let him hurt me like this!

Mama cried and the burning was like a stick only worse and Poppy laughed and laughed.

Whir-whir-whir. Whack-whack-whack. Suckit, suckit.

Can I do that to the Janet? he asked.

Mr Harriman laughed and laughed, just like Poppy.

8

San Andreas State Hospital, Tuesday, 24 August 1982

Matt-who-was-once-Blue sat on the bed and listened carefully. Mr Harriman told him that today the Janet and the Neil were coming to take him home, just as they had promised. Home wasn't the den and the valley. Home was a place like where he used to live with Mama, only bigger. He mustn't forget about the pretending, and keeping his friendship with Mr Harriman a secret. He must do whatever they asked and try very hard to be good, so that when they learned to trust him, it would be too late.

Too late for what? he asked.

You're getting bigger every day, Matt. Soon you'll be stronger than your new poppy.

And the old poppy? And Jess? And the other Jesses who killed Az? What of them?

Trust me, said Mr Harriman. *You know how bad it hurts when you don't.*

Yes, I know, Matt thought.

He wrapped his arms around himself and rocked back and forth, thinking of the new pain Mr Harriman had begun to use ever since he remembered what Poppy had done to him. It was the burning-hotter-than-fire-on-the-stove-pain, the stick-pain, the wet-bloody-angry-pain. It was the memory of Poppy being mean and hurting that Mr Harriman put to use whenever Matt was foolish enough to think he could disobey.

But this pain didn't make him roll on the floor, pressing his hands to his head as if he were afraid his memories would explode, shattering his skull. No, it was much worse than that, and just thinking of it made him shiver, clenching his buttocks together as tightly as he could.

That's good, that's very good, Mr Harriman said with a snicker. *You remember, Matt, and I like that. The remembering is as important as the pretending.*

Just don't hurt me again, he whimpered.

Hurt you? Mr Harriman began to laugh, and for a moment Matt was certain it was Poppy in his head, trapped there and unable to get out. *Why should I hurt you when you're my legs, my mouth, my heart? Don't you remember what I told you when Az died? We are as one, Matt, and nothing will ever separate us. Besides, you wouldn't want me to leave you, would you?*

No, don't leave, he begged. I'd be too alone.

That's a good boy, said Mr Harriman. *All you have to do is listen to me, and you'll never feel the pain.*

And the Jesses? he asked again. What of them?

We'll find them, but it'll take time, Matt. Until then you must be good and do what you're told. Then I'll give you the Janet.

He thought of the lady with red hair and smiled to himself. It was hard to pretend to be good, but he would try.

The Kaufmans waited in the chief administrator's office, where a caseworker for the Ventura County Adoptions Department handed them one form after another, each requiring both their signatures. Janet was too impatient to read them all, but Neil took his time, asking questions as if that were expected of him.

The first six months would constitute something like a probation period, during which time they could change their minds about keeping the boy, should that unlikely event occur. By the same token, Matthew could also decide to return to San Andreas State if for any reason he was unable to adjust to his new surroundings.

'Not that I anticipate any difficulties,' the caseworker made a point of saying. 'But I think it's wise to warn you of any eventualities.'

Janet was barely paying attention. She had her eyes riveted to the door, where any moment she expected to see Matthew Kaufman waiting to greet her with open arms. When the last of the papers were signed, the door opened as if on cue, and both Janet and Neil jumped to their feet.

That this was the same child who had loped alongside Turk seemed almost impossible to believe. Although he walked with a halting gait, there was nothing to suggest he had once run on all fours. The coarse, leathery look of his skin was gone, and with his neatly combed blond hair and delicate features, there was no reason ever to suspect that just a few months before the boy had acted more like an animal than a human being.

Janet trembled with excitement. After endless bureaucratic hassles, after months of uncertainty, Matt was finally coming home with them. For a moment she was afraid he would drop down onto his hands and knees, or, worse, change his mind and flee down the corridor back to his room. But then he stepped forward, shuffling his feet but remaining upright.

'Hel-lo,' he said, shaping the word carefully to get it right.

Recalling how easily frightened he had been in the past, Janet cautiously approached. She put her hands over his shoulders, then hugged him close. When she felt him reach up, holding her as tightly as she held him, she was so happy that her voice broke and she had to laugh to stop herself from crying.

'We're taking you home today, son,' Neil told the child. 'Would you like to come with us?'

Matt nodded. 'Yess,' he said. 'Turkk?'

Janet laughed, delighted that he remembered. 'Turk's waiting in the car . . . you know what a car is, don't you?'

'Yess.' His head went up and down, his lips shaping a smile with his cracked and broken teeth. Then he reached for Janet's hand, liking the way it felt. It was warm and soft, and he thought of what *love* was and smiled to himself. As for the Neil, well . . . he would just have to wait and see. His new poppy wore a strap like the old one, but maybe he'd never use it. And if he ever tried, Matt knew exactly what he would do, because only Mr Harriman could hurt him now, not anyone else.

But when Neil opened the car door, Matt hesitated, remembering the truck the man called Jess had driven. If he got inside, maybe they'd never let him out again. Or maybe they'd leave him out in the desert, only this time there wouldn't be an Az to find him and keep him safe.

'It's all right, Matt,' said Neil. 'It's only Turk.'

The golden retriever must have caught his scent, for suddenly he bounded out of the car. He began to whine in an oddly subservient way, then started rubbing his head against Matt's leg.

'Turkk,' Matt pronounced.

Janet broke into a grin. 'Yes, Turk. Isn't he a nice dog, Matt? See how he likes you.'

The boy threw his arms over the dog's back, babbling something Janet wasn't able to make out. Turk immediately sat back, cocking his head to one side as if listening attentively.

'Carr,' said Matt, amazing them all the more when he held up his hands, turning them from side to side as if he were holding on to a steering wheel. Then, without having to be prompted, and with Turk quick to follow, the youngster climbed into the back seat and waited for the Kaufmans to join him.

* * *

What a strange and frightening place this world was!

They moved as fast as water rushing down a streambed when the rains came, faster and faster, with nothing to stop them but the force of the wind whipping over the hood of the car. Matt's window was open just a crack, but through that narrow space he caught the man-smell filling every inch of air. No longer did the stink of the two-legged Jesses make him feel ill, like when he sometimes was forced to feed on game that was already dead, the little white crawlies honeycombing their way through the flesh.

The months he had spent in the hospital had taught him at least one thing, if nothing else. This was the smell of their world, and their world was the place he would have to learn to accept. Little boys didn't hide out in caves, or go naked, or run around on all fours.

Beyond the boxlike safety of the car, a den with windows and with wheels that carried it anywhere it wanted to go, were houses and stores and streets and crowds. Jesses, everywhere. Jesses yelling and crying and using their fists. Jesses burning hot as stovetops and cold as mornings when crystals of ice crunched like glass beneath his feet.

All new, every bit of it.

Matt pushed himself down between the seat and door, gazing at the big yellow dog who hadn't taken his eyes off him for even a second. Turk was very quiet, attentive too. The dog watched and watched, and everything Turk saw was captured in his golden eyes, never to be forgotten.

Turk is your protector, your guardian, just as Az was, Mr Harriman explained. *He'll make sure that none of the Jesses ever harm you.*

But how? With his teeth? Az had bigger teeth, and look what happened to her.

Turk is nearly as strong. And if his teeth don't protect you, his understanding will. He knows, Matt. He hears your thoughts, just as I do.

Az understood things too. A thought traveled through the air like a bird flying overhead. Mr Harriman listened to Matt and listened to Az, explaining things to each of them. Would it be the same with the big yellow dog? he wondered.

Matt turned his head to the side, ignoring the Janet and the Neil, who hadn't stopped chattering since getting into the car. They seemed afraid of silence, as if it would swallow them up, bones and all. He looked down at the retriever. Turk's tongue was hanging out of his mouth as he panted softly.

Can you hear me? he asked.

Of course he can, said Mr Harriman.

Will you obey me, always?

In response, Turk backed away, cowering under Matt's unflinching, unrelenting gaze. The retriever began to whine in fear and outright submission, staying as far away from the boy as the length of seat allowed.

Janet glanced back, smiling first at Matt as if needing to reassure him. 'What is it, Turk?' she asked.

Show the bitch how strong you are! Mr Harriman suddenly cried out.

It was like a clap of thunder in his head, like Poppy singing his angry hurting song. Before he had a chance to think about what he was doing, Matt looked down at Turk, a low-pitched growl rising up from the back of his throat. The retriever lunged forward, snarling viciously as he tried to grab Janet's sleeve.

She jerked her hand back. 'Get down!' she shouted. 'Bad dog, get down!'

But Turk refused to listen.

The retriever threw himself against the back of the front seat, trying to climb over it to get to Janet. Neil turned his head back for a moment, wondering what all the commotion was about. Turk snapped at him, narrowly missing Neil's face.

'You do that again – ' he started to say when Matt reached out, grabbing the dog by the collar.

Turk immediately sat back as if nothing had happened. His tongue once again hung out of his mouth, his tail slapping playfully against the seat.

'Something must've spooked him,' Janet said. She glanced at her sleeve. One of the buttons was hanging by a thread. 'He didn't hurt you, did he?' she asked Neil.

He shook his head. 'He must be a little jealous of the boy, though you'd never know it to look at them.'

The retriever had rolled over onto his back, kicking his legs in the air. Matt was rubbing his belly, prattling on in a kind of guttural baby talk.

Janet smiled with relief. 'Guess they've made their peace.'

Neil glanced in the rearview mirror, then raised his voice. 'Just remember one thing, Turk. I'm the guy who keeps you in Milkbones and Kal Kan. So, if I were you, I'd think twice before trying to bite the hand that feeds you.'

In response, Turk began to bark. It didn't sound all that friendly, either.

'This is your room, Matt. Do you like it?'

Janet stood by the door, watching Matt carefully to see how he'd react. The nursery had been completely done over in browns and greens, with a spread over the bed that made it look just like a race car.

'Grr,' said Matt. 'Whack-whack-whack.' He pretended he was driving, turning the steering wheel as he looked inside the room. 'Carr,' he said, pointing to the bedspread.

'Yes, we thought you'd like it. And there are more cars on the wall. See?' She stepped inside and motioned to the wallpaper, which was covered with a pattern of brightly colored sports cars. 'And that big box over there is filled with all sorts of interesting toys, blocks and cars and cowboys. And look at the nice view you have from the window.'

'Grr,' said Matt. 'Suckit, suckit.'

Slug it? she wondered. Well, they'd have him talking complete sentences soon enough. Besides, it seemed very natural for him to progress from baby talk to actual words now that he was once again making the effort to be verbal.

'So what do you think, Matt?' said Neil. 'Pretty nifty room, isn't it?'

'Turkk,' said the boy, his pale blue eyes opened wide.

'Turk can use this room too, if you like,' Janet told him.

The retriever hadn't left the boy's side since arriving home, a few minutes before. Matt reached down, patting him gently on the head. Janet had read that in the few cases of so-called wild children reported in the literature, the youngsters had always responded very well to the presence of animals. Many autistics also shared that trait, and she was glad they had Turk to serve as a kind of intermediary. If the boy already trusted the dog, it seemed likely he would eventually come to trust them, as well.

'Why don't you try out the bed?' Neil suggested. 'See if it's comfortable.'

Matt just stood there, swaying slightly as if it were hard for him to maintain his balance. The orthopedist who examined him advised against surgery, saying the child's bone structure wasn't affected so much as the development of his musculature. That, he assured them, could be corrected with a program of exercises. Of course, it was imperative the youngster continue bipedal locomotion, for once he resorted to getting around on all fours, it would be very difficult to break him of the habit. But so far Matt had made no attempt to get down on his hands and knees, and so Janet reached out, trying to hold him steady.

Neil bounced up and down on the edge of the bed. 'Feels good to me,' he said with a grin. He patted the place alongside him. 'Come on, son, give it a try.'

Matt shuffled slowly across the room, Turk matching his steps as if he were a Seeing Eye dog. 'Carr,' said the boy. 'Turkk. Bedd.'

Suddenly he bounded forward and with a single leap jumped onto the bed. With both hands he began to dig away at the bedspread, just the way Turk sometimes tried to make a nest in the carpet.

Neil started to stop him when Janet shook her head, saying that if it made him feel better, that was the important thing.

Matt gurgled like an infant. Having made a kind of hollow in the middle of the bed, the spread bunched up all around him, he rolled over onto his side, drawing his knees up to his chest.

'Bedd,' he said. 'Bluie doody.'

'Maybe we should show him where the bathroom is,' Neil said.

'Bluie doody,' the boy said again. But then he cried out, 'Matty, Matty,' and began to shake his head. 'No hurt, no hurt.'

'No one's going to hurt you, Matt, no one in the world.' Neil put his arm around the boy, but Matt pulled away, rubbing his backside against the bedspread.

'Doddy, doody,' he kept repeating.

'Come, we'll show you where the potty is,' Janet said. She took him by the hand and led him down the hall to the bathroom. She put down the toilet seat for him and showed him where the roll of paper was. 'Do you want me to help you?'

Don't let her touch you! The less she knows about you, the better.

Although Matt didn't understand what possible harm it could do, especially if the Janet was so determined to be like Mama, he knew better than to argue. Thinking of the stick-pain, he began to shake his head from side to side.

'Do you know how to use the potty?' Janet asked.

'Potty doody,' he said. He reached out and gave her a little push toward the door.

As soon as she stepped into the hall Matt closed the door until he heard it click. Then he tugged at the zipper of his jeans, finally getting it right by the third try. After pushing them all the way down to the tops of his shoes he sat down on the toilet seat. A moment later he jumped to his feet, having forgotten to take off his underpants.

Good, said Mr Harriman as Matt squatted over the seat. *You're learning quickly, my little friend.*

'Doody,' Matt babbled to himself. He looked down between his legs and smiled. He had hair around his doodle, just like Poppy. Soon he wouldn't be a little boy anymore. Soon he'd be like the Neil.

And then? he asked Mr Harriman.

Then you'll be able to do anything you want. Anything at all.

The doorbell rang moments after Matt came out of the bathroom, looking so satisfied with himself that Janet couldn't help but smile.

'Must be Ina,' she said.

But the unexpected sound of the bell caused Matt suddenly to growl, baring his teeth. The sense of complacency that had stolen over Janet quickly vanished. Just because Matt was toilet-trained, just because he stood upright, didn't mean he'd forgotten his ordeal.

'It's all right, Matt. No one's going to hurt you.'

She heard Neil opening the front door. 'Yes,' he was saying, 'we're all together, safe and sound.'

Matt backed away from her, edging toward his room, where Turk had already taken up residence.

'Don't you want to meet your new friends?' she said. 'They live next door, Matt. Ina and her daughter Gillian. I know you'll like them.'

'No hurt,' whispered the boy.

'Of course not. We won't let anyone hurt you, I promise.' She hugged him tightly, kissing the top of his head. 'You're our son now, Matt. We love you.'

Love, Matt thought. Whir-whir-whir.

Then, taking him by the hand, Janet led him into the living room. But the moment he caught sight of Ina Stanton and her fifteen-year-old daughter Gillian, he pulled free and edged back, growling softly.

Ina had already been given a brief history of the boy's past, though the Kaufmans had purposely avoided going into a great deal of detail. Their neighbor knew that the child had been abandoned in the desert, that he'd been forced to fend for himself for an indeterminate period of time. Now both Ina and Gillian came to their feet.

'Hello, Matt,' the woman called out with a beaming smile. 'Welcome home.'

'Oh, he's cute,' said Gillian, and she immediately started toward him.

Matt growled another warning, and Turk came bounding out of the bedroom to stand between Gillian and the boy.

'Well, I can see he's already made one friend,' Ina remarked. She turned to her daughter. 'Let him come to you, Gillie. You don't want to frighten him.'

'He's such a cutie,' Gillian said, as if she were admiring a puppy in a pet-shop window.

As for Matt, he didn't know what to make of either of them. The one who called herself Ina was a big woman with a laughing face, and that, he knew, was good. She had a husky voice and spoke very fast, but he was still able to understand what she was saying. But the smaller one who now crouched down and patted her knee, motioning for him to come closer, wasn't like any Jess he'd met before. She was more like the other ones at the hospital, not yet full-grown.

When he noticed her reddish-brown hair his lips turned up in a smile. His grin delighted the Gillie. She clapped her hands with excitement and said, 'That's a good boy. Come to Gillie, now, come to Gillie.'

Go to her, whispered Mr Harriman.

Matt took a hesitant step forward. Everyone was watching him, the Janet and the Neil, the Ina who was soft and plump and laughing-eyed. Turk glanced back at him, then moved aside as Matt took another step in Gillian Stanton's direction.

'Tell me my kid doesn't have the soft touch,' Ina said with a laugh. ''Cept I thought you graduated from Barbie and Ken a couple of years ago, Gillie.'

'Come on, Mother,' said Gillian, pursing her lips with annoyance. 'What does one thing have to do with another?'

'You'd be surprised.'

'Besides, he's such a sweetie, who can resist?'

The Gillie edged toward him. For a moment he wasn't sure how to react. But then, when she reached out and petted him, gently stroking the top of his head, Matt gurgled happily and pressed his face into her chest. She felt warm and soft. He liked the way she kept touching him, and he liked the way she smelled. And best of all, she had red hair.

'Now, what's your name?' Gillian asked, trying to get him to talk.

He looked up. The Gillie had little red dots all over her face. Her eyes were gray like the fur of a coyote.

'Matt,' he said, as loudly and distinctly as he could.

The Gillie clapped her hands and made a laughing face, just like the plump two-legged Jess standing nearby.

'The kid's got a magic touch,' Ina said. 'You ever need a baby-sitter, Janet, I think I know who you can turn to.'

Am I being good? Am I pretending right? he asked Mr Harriman, even as he wondered what the Gillie looked like when she was wet and naked like Mama in the bath.

Very good, Mr Harriman replied.

Can I have the Gillie too?

When we're ready, when I give permission, you can have anyone you want.

Janet lay in the crook of Neil's arm, so content she couldn't help but feel a little guilty. Maybe it was because things were too good, too right. When life gave you what you wanted, didn't it usually follow that somewhere along the line you'd end up taking a fall? But maybe it wouldn't be like that. Maybe this time nothing would interfere with their happiness.

Even in the few hours Matt had been home, she could see the difference his presence made. Not the obvious difference of having to deal with another person, as opposed to just the two of them. But the difference it made in her relationship with her husband. Suddenly there was something linking them beyond their own feelings for each other. Even though those feelings were potent in their own right, there was something about being responsible for a child, someone utterly dependent upon you for all his needs, that gave added strength to their marriage.

So she lay in the damp hollow of her husband's arm, leaning against him and smiling to herself. Even their lovemaking had taken on a special quality this evening, an intensity of expression that reminded her of when they were first married.

'The forbidden act,' Neil had joked, 'because you know someone's sleeping next door.'

But no, that really wasn't it. After his initial opposition, Neil had come to accept the boy in much the same way she did. That he'd heard an unspoken voice – the past, was it? – whispering in his ear, just as she had, seemed only to confirm the closeness they now shared. And so far it appeared to be working out perfectly. The youngster, alternately shy and endearing, skittish and affectionate, had made remarkable progress in the last few months. Janet had every reason to believe that once he was enrolled in school, it would take no time at all for him to reach his potential.

'Are you having second thoughts, Neil?' she asked, suddenly aware of his silence, the way he just lay there looking up at the ceiling.

He gave her a squeeze, laying his hand gently across her breasts. 'Not a one. I stopped having doubts the day I heard – ' He left the rest unsaid, as if he were afraid to express his feelings.

'Have you heard it again?'

'No, but sometimes I wonder now if I ever did. Maybe it was . . . I don't know. The power of suggestion?' He shrugged and pulled the light summer comforter all the way up to his neck, tightening his hold on her. 'There's that owl again. Hear it?'

But instead of the owl making its nightly reconnaissance of the canyon, Janet heard a peculiar scrabbling sound, like an animal's nails clicking against the floor. Was it Turk, restless and wandering through the darkened house?

'I wonder why he hasn't tried to talk about what happened,' she remarked.

'He's probably blocked it out. If I'd gone through what he did, I wouldn't want to remember it, either. You hear something?'

Janet pushed herself up against the pillows and turned her eyes to the door. Had she seen a shadow pass beneath the threshold? If Turk was so protective of Matt, what was he doing prowling around the house?

'You locked the back door, didn't you?'

Neil said, 'I hope so,' and swung his legs over the side of the bed. He sat there a moment, listening intently.

'I'll go,' she volunteered.

But Neil motioned her to stay put. He stepped lightly across the floor and grabbed his robe from where he'd tossed it over a chair. Then he let himself out of the room and made his way down the hall to Matt's bedroom.

The door was ajar, the race-car bedspread lying like a wreck at the foot of the bed. The room was empty, and he went on into the darkened living room. At the far end, swinging shutter doors hid the kitchen from view.

Even before he pushed them open, he could hear Turk. When he flicked on the overhead lights and the doors swung shut behind him, the retriever let out a sound usually reserved for strangers. But it wasn't the dog who concerned him. Matt was down on all fours, lapping at a puddle of ketchup he had either poured or accidentally spilled onto the floor.

When he looked up, his mouth seemed smeared with blood. Again Turk growled and took a wary step forward, communicating his fear to the boy. Matt froze in his place. Then his head began to move from side to side, reminding Neil of a snake on the verge of striking. The boy's eyes were no wider than slits, and there was something about his expression that was both terrifying and pitiful.

'Hey, Matt, it's okay. I like ketchup too. But you don't have to sneak it. You can have all the ketchup you want. All you have to do is ask.'

Again Turk growled, his muzzle wrinkling as he bared his teeth.

'And as for you,' Neil told the dog, 'you'd better start straightening up your act, Turk. You hear me?' He pointed his finger, but instead of showing submission, a willingness to obey, Turk snapped at the air, glancing at the boy as if to make sure he was still safe.

By then Matt had hauled himself to his feet. 'Daddy,' he said. He lurched forward like a toddler still practicing his walk. He pushed his head up against Neil's stomach, butting him gently, and yawning with a mouthful of chipped and broken teeth.

Turk too began to yawn. He stretched and started wagging his tail, approaching Neil with his ears back and lips retracted in a grin. Matt reached out and put his arm around the dog.

'Dad-dy. Turkk,' he said.

Taking him by the hand, Neil led him back to his room, stopping in the bathroom to wash the boy's face. Matt wasn't taking his eyes off him, though he submitted to the cleanup without a word of protest. Once Neil got him back into bed the child gave out with another sleepy yawn and closed his eyes.

'Sleep tight,' Neil murmured. 'And next time you're hungry, or you want something, all you have to do is ask.'

When he got up to leave, Turk had once again taken up his position at the foot of the bed. Neil decided not to tell Janet what had happened. If she thought Matt was regressing it might alarm her unnecessarily. Let her just think everything was fine, he thought. After all, there wasn't any reason to be unduly concerned. The boy was just starting to get used to his new surroundings. After what he'd gone through, they certainly couldn't expect him to be completely adjusted, not right away.

Give him time, Neil thought, and everything will work out fine.

9

Matt didn't want to go. He huddled in the farthest corner of his room, pressing his back against the wall and stationing Turk directly in front of him. The big yellow dog acted like a shield. If anyone should try to hurt him, Turk would know just what to do.

'Sorry, honey, but I gotta run,' the Neil was saying. He was big like Poppy, but so far he hadn't done anything mean. Even when the Neil found him in the kitchen, that first night home, he hadn't yelled or given him a licking. He'd been so nice that if Mr Harriman hadn't reminded him it was all a trick, Matt would have believed the Neil was different from the other Jesses he'd met in the past.

Now, of course, he knew better.

The Neil was only pretending, just the way Bluie was. If this Jess had his way he'd use the strap and the stick-pain ever day if he could. So Matt was glad when he told the Janet he was late for school, that if he didn't get a move on his principal would raise hell.

'It's the first day, hon. I gotta be there,' the Neil told her. 'You'll be fine.'

The Janet pursed her lips, making a face filled with annoyance. Who was she angry at? Matt wondered. Me or the Neil, or maybe the both of us? But I don't want to go to school, Mr Harriman. I'll stay here with the race-car and Turk, and later if I'm good she'll let me go into the yard, and I can hunt.

When the Neil mowed the grass it smelled so sweet that Matt couldn't help himself. He rolled back and forth on the ground, kicking his legs in the air just the way Turk did.

'A fine pair of mutts I got,' the Neil had said with a laugh. But he was faking it. He wasn't being nice to Matt because he liked him. No, he probably *loved* him, and Matt knew what love was all about, what it meant and how it could hurt.

'Whir-whir-whir,' he whispered to himself. 'Suckit, bitch, suckit.'

The Neil looked at him curiously, wondering what he was saying.

'Babbling,' said Janet. 'Don't you remember, the baby babbled too when he was learning to talk? It's only natural.'

'Gotta run,' he said again. He gave Janet a quick peck on the cheek. 'So long, slugger,' he called out to Matt, then turned and hurried out.

'He's late for work,' Janet explained when she came into the bedroom, where Matt was still crouched on the floor, his fingers hooked under Turk's collar.

The retriever knew better than to bark or show his teeth at her approach, having already been punished for snapping. Mr Harriman had had to warn the dog that the Kaufmans wouldn't put up with that kind of behavior much longer. Even though he had new loyalties, Turk had to learn to pretend as Matt pretended, or else he'd find himself in a kennel at the county pound.

So Turk merely stayed where he was, trying not to growl as Janet approached. She got down in a crouch, sensing that Matt was less intimidated when she made herself as small as possible. Then she began to explain about school, and how important it was that he meet children his own age.

'No, no, no, no, no . . .' Matt whimpered, and he shook his head again and again. 'No go, no go!'

'But no one's going to hurt you there, Matt. The other children are just like you. They've had problems, too;

that's why it's a special school. Why don't we just go down there together and take a look, see how you like it? I won't force you to do anything you don't want.'

Is she lying? he asked Mr Harriman.

No, this time the bitch is telling the truth. But let's test her, just to make sure.

How?

Touch her and see what she does.

Matt did as he was told. Still maintaining his grip on Turk, for he was afraid the retriever might lunge at Janet, he reached out, tracing the lines of her face with the tips of his fingers. It was hard getting used to having such short nails. He couldn't use them to root around in the ground, nor were they very good for scratching himself. But the little itchies that used to bite had all gone away, and so maybe he didn't need long fingernails anymore. Maybe that's why they cut them, first at the hospital, and later at home.

Home.

He hated the word. It was a Jess place. It was all wrong, but he couldn't do anything about it. There was no returning to the valley. Even if he ever found his way back there, guided by landmarks and messages carried on the wind, it wouldn't be the same without Az. But Turk could always go with him, couldn't he?

No, said Mr Harriman. *Home is now, right here. I told you that a long time ago, Matthew. If you start doubting my word –*

No, I don't, I don't! he cried out. I believe you, everything!

He touched the Janet with the tips of his fingers; the neat, blunt nails; the clean, scrubbed hand. She was very soft, nice to touch. Why hadn't they gotten into the tub together, like he did with Mama? Why did they make him use the stall shower?

When the Janet and then the Neil had offered to help,

eager to show him how to bathe, Mr Harriman had told him what to say, putting the words right into his mouth like food.

I can do it.

It came out all at once, 'a complete sentence' the Janet had said, clapping her hands with excitement.

'I can do it,' he said now.

'Do what, sweetheart?'

'I can do it.'

Cute, huh?

Whir-whir-whir.

He reached down, letting go of Turk, who sat between them. He put his hands on the Janet's breasts, wondering how they felt.

'No, dear,' she said. She took his hands away as if he were doing something he shouldn't, something bad.

He looked up at her, waiting for Mr Harriman to put the right words into his mouth. 'Why?' he asked.

The Janet's short blond hair swayed like grass when the winds came down through the canyon and the air smelled of winter. Connie showed him, so why couldn't the Janet? She said she loved him, didn't she? Well, that was what love was, wasn't it? – the big black machine sounding like a choo-choo rushing through the darkness, Poppy playing horsie with his hairy rump going back and forth, making squishy wet sounds like Mama in the bath.

'I'm telling you, the kid's seen it all,' Mama had said, looking at him and sounding so proud he had to smile. 'Hell, he even likes to watch. Don'tcha, Bluie?'

When can I watch again? he asked Mr Harriman.

Soon, promised his friend. *But now you have to do as she asks and go with her to school.*

But what about Turk?

Turk will wait here for you, Mr Harriman replied.

But I don't want to. Don't hurt me, but I'm afraid.

Afraid? And inside his head Matt could hear Mr Harriman laughing.

Poppy used to laugh like that too, he remembered. He shivered, tightening his sphincter just in case Mr Harriman decided it was time for him to be punished. But instead of pain, a wave of unexpected pleasure washed over him. The Janet was stroking his cheeks and his hair.

'You're trembling,' she said. 'What's wrong, Matt?'

'No wrong,' he whispered.

'You're sure, now?'

He nodded, looking up at the Janet as she came slowly to her feet. How big she seemed then, big and soft and gentle.

If you don't go with her to this school, they'll get angry, Mr Harriman warned him. *And if they get angry, they might decide to send you back to the hospital.*

'No *hopittle.*' he said aloud. It was a big word and he couldn't say it very easily.

The Janet shook her head in amazement. 'We're never going to send you back to the hospital, Matt. You mustn't ever think such a thing. You're our son. We love you, sweetheart. That's why it's important you go to school and learn as much as you can, because the more you know, the less afraid you'll be.'

Is that true?

Perhaps, Mr Harriman grudgingly conceded. *Besides, there are other reasons, Matthew.*

What?

You like Gillian, don't you?

The girl with the red hair and freckles came to play with him nearly every day. Yes, he liked her so much he wanted to love her.

At this school of theirs there'll be many more like her, dozens to choose from.

And I can have them, anyone I want?

You can have all of them, Matthew, every last one of them.

Mr Harriman never lied, and so Matt came cautiously to his feet, reaching out to grab hold of Janet's hand.

'No hurt,' he whispered.

'No hurt,' she replied.

The Langley School for Learning Disabilities was located in West Hollywood, several blocks east of Beverly Hills. It was part of an area known as the West Side, encompassing those affluent communities which stretched along the hillsides and rustic canyons north of Sunset Boulevard, and the flatlands directly to the south. Although the Kaufmans lived somewhat to the east in the Hollywood Hills, it took relatively little time to get to West Hollywood.

All the way down Sunset and then Santa Monica Boulevard, Matt hadn't said a word, his nose pressed to the glass as he stared out the window. Sensing his anxiety, Janet had tried to be as supportive as she could, assuring him that once he got used to school, he'd like it so much he wouldn't want to miss a single day.

But now, when she got out of the car, he stayed put, reluctant to follow.

'You have to learn to trust me, Matt. I wouldn't do anything that was bad for you. Besides, you're going to get very hot just sitting there in the car.'

September was usually LA's warmest month, and this year wasn't an exception. With the windows rolled up and the air conditioner going full blast, she hadn't realized how hot it was.

Janet went around to the passenger side and opened the door. Matt remained where he was, panting the way Turk did, with his mough open and his tongue hanging out.

Perhaps it was naive to think a miracle would happen, and in no time at all the boy would be just like any other child his age. Realizing that she had to learn when to stop pushing, that Matt could only progress at his own rate,

Janet forced herself not to be impatient with him. Earlier, when he had touched her, she hadn't wanted to push his hands away. A baby touched its mother's breasts, and though Matt was probably ten or eleven years old, he was still very much like an infant, exploring his immediate surroundings and dependent upon sensory feedback to learn what the world was like. Touch was a very important way of establishing rapport, giving him the security he desperately needed. So Janet reached out and took hold of his hands, rubbing them gently against her cheek.

The boy looked at her intently, something in his stare making her feel momentarily uneasy. Even though he began to smile, his eyes were still ice-cold. But then he held onto her hand and let himself be led from the car and into the building.

Alison Danziger didn't have red hair, and she wasn't soft and plump. Her eyes were as dark and bright as a bird's, and when she walked there was something birdlike too about the way she swung her arms and legs. Each step she took was accompanied by a little jerk, reminding Matt of the dippers which used to feed along the stream after the rains, moving like windup toys as they darted about, this way and that. Everything Miss Danziger did was filled with energy and purpose, and when she spoke her voice rang out in the classroom, commanding attention.

Having been shown to his seat after the Janet left, promising to pick him up at the end of the day, Matt studied her as if she were a new kind of animal. Here was a Jess who didn't look at him as if he were someone to be pitied, a freak, as the white-coated orderlies had called him at the hospital. Instead, she acted as if he were just like the other children in the room, neither better nor worse than any of them. There were fifteen of them altogether, not including himself, nine girls and six boys who all looked about his own age or slightly older.

'This is Matt Kaufman,' Miss Danziger had told the class.

'Who gives a shit?' someone had whispered.

When he whirled around to see who it was, a fat boy who was bigger than any of the other two-legged game he and Az had brought down, stuck his tongue out and began to laugh.

If Mr Harriman hadn't warned him to stay where he was and not say anything, he would have ripped the fat boy's tongue out so easily no one could have stopped him. But Mr Harriman wasn't going to let him do anything the Jesses might think was bad. So Matt just looked away, making believe the fat boy hadn't said a word.

Then Miss Danziger began to take lots of jerky steps, moving from one child to the next. Each had a different name, except for two Jons, and Matt wondered how he'd ever remember who was who. A Jess was a Jess. What difference did it make if one was called Sara and another Sean? They had different names and faces, but they still smelled very much alike. Some had more flowers on their skin than others, but all of them carried the man-smell, a stench he still hadn't gotten completely used to, even though it was now his smell too.

When Miss Danziger had told him everyone's name, she explained that the other boys and girls in the class were just like he was in that they all needed special help with their schooling. Some, like a girl at the back of the room, couldn't sit still for very long. Others had the same kind of difficulty speaking as he did. One boy read better than anyone else but still couldn't write his name.

'But there aren't any problems we can't overcome if we help each other and work together,' she said.

Matt listened to her with one ear and listened to Mr

Harriman with the other. Miss Danziger didn't have much meat on her bones, but like the Janet she still had breasts poking up from behind her blouse. Would they feel as soft if he touched them? he wondered. Should he ask to do it, or should he just go up to her and put his hands there, the way he did with the Janet?

He was changing every day, he knew. Thoughts he'd never had before were suddenly popping up in his head out of nowhere, so that he sometimes wasn't sure if it was his doing or Mr Harriman's. A few nights before, as he lay in bed with his eyes wide open and Turk keeping guard at the foot of the bed, he had heard lots of whispered sounds coming from the room next to his, where the Janet and the Neil went each night when it was time for them to go to sleep.

He'd listened carefully, eagerly too. For a moment he almost believed he was back with Az, emerging at dusk from their lair to prowl the valley in search of game. He recalled how Az would always be the first to leave the safety of the den, reading the air for danger. Only when she felt certain all was well would she turn her head back, motioning for him to follow.

It was like that a few nights before as he listened to the soft creaky sounds coming from the Kaufmans' den. What were they doing? he had wondered. Were they talking or feeding? Did the Neil like to play horsie as much as Poppy? He wanted to creep out of his room and see for himself, but Mr Harriman told him to stay where he was, the door was locked anyway. How did Mr Harriman know all these things? Matt couldn't figure it out, and every time he asked, his friend pretended not to hear him.

But now he was hearing everything, every single word. *There will never be another like you,* Mr Harriman told him. *You're special because you have me, and I've taught you how to survive. The thoughts that come into your head are your thoughts now, Matthew, not only mine.*

He watched Miss Danziger and decided he wanted her the way he wanted the lady with red hair. At night the Connie came to him in his dreams, stalking him the way he and Az used to stalk prey. He would wait for the man with the beard and the loud angry voice to tell him what to do, for Mama to say he was a good boy and because he was so good they were going to make a movie, won't that be fun.

Thinking of the movie and the lady with red hair and Tommy and the whir-whir-whir always made his doodle get so hard it began to hurt like it did when the ladies in white washed him at the hospital. Mr Harriman never lied. Love was pain, just as he said. But last week Mr Harriman had taught him what to do to stop the pain, and though he thought it was white blood coming out, it wasn't. It was something else, something good that stopped the hurting, Mr Harriman explained.

Now he wanted to do it again. As he watched Miss Danziger he could feel the hard burning pain getting more and more intense. He pressed his hand against his doodle, but when he touched himself the pain only got worse. He rubbed harder, trying to get the pain to go away.

Maybe if he touched Miss Danziger the way he'd touched the Connie, the white blood would spurt out and then everything would be okay. But then the fat boy who was sitting behind him began to giggle. Then the boy next to him giggled too and then someone else and then someone after that.

'Matt's playing with himself, Miss Danziger.'

'He's being nasty, Miss Danziger.'

Soon almost everyone in the class was giggling and pointing his finger and yelling, 'Nasty, nasty, nasty.'

Miss Danziger, who was so like a bird he wondered if

she could sing like one too, took her jerky little steps down the aisle to his desk. Matt looked up into her hard bright eyes, and, hoping Mr Harriman would be pleased, he reached out and grabbed her hand. He wanted her to touch him to stop the burning, but she pulled away as if she were burning too and his touch were making her hurt.

'We don't do that here, Matt,' she said, speaking slowly and calmly like any other Jess, not like a bird at all.

'He ain't got nothin' there anyway,' said the fat boy.

'That'll be quite enough, Jeffrey,' Miss Danziger told him. Then she turned her bright dark eyes on Matt, and though he thought she was angry, she began to smile, so he knew she must be pretending to be nice.

Ask her, whispered Mr Harriman, giggling in his head like Jeffrey the fat boy, who probably couldn't do anything with his doodle even if he tried.

What?

Why it's not nice.

'Why?' he said, as loudly and clearly as he could.

Miss Danziger's breasts jiggled behind her creamy-white blouse. She took a quick little step back, and he wondered if somehow he was frightening her. If he was he was glad. He and Az had been the strongest, smartest creatures in the valley. Why shouldn't it still be like that now?

'Because there are certain things we never do in public, Matt, that's why,' she finally told him.

Jeffrey the fat boy giggled louder than anyone. 'You don't make doody on the street, do you, dummy?'

Everyone thought that was so funny they all started to laugh. But Matt didn't laugh and he didn't even smile. He turned around and stared at Jeffrey so hard that the blood rushed out of the fat boy's face. Then Jeffrey began to stammer, just the way he'd stammer if Matt got his way and ripped out his tongue.

Yes, do it, show the little prick how strong you are, cackled Mr Harriman.

His friend was having a wonderful time, laughing and snickering and telling Matt it was okay, do what he wanted, he was strong and he knew more than all these stupid Jesses put together.

'No one asked for your opinion, Jeffrey,' said Miss Danziger.

'No one asked for your opinion, Jeffrey,' he heard himself saying. It was more words than he'd ever spoken, and as the teacher looked down at him in surprise, Matt turned around in his seat and reached back, grabbing the fat boy by the ear.

Jeffrey began to squeal like animals did when you had them in your mouth and your jaws snapped shut, crushing their spine. He squealed and squealed, and so Matt kept tearing at his ear, smiling to see his tormentor in so much pain.

'Stop it! Let go of him, Matt! Stop it now!' shouted Miss Danziger. She tried to separate them, tugging at Matt's hand to get him to let go.

But Matt growled that she was daring to take away his game. The fat boy was his. He would do whatever he wanted to him, and no one, not the Danziger nor the Janet nor anyone else, could stop him. He was already on his feet now, and Jeffrey was screaming and blood was coming out of his ear in a bright red trickle.

The tongue, tear his tongue out, the fat shit! Mr Harriman was shouting.

The voice of his friend, the 'mister' without a face he'd met in the desert years before, was so loud now that Matt couldn't hear anything else. He let go of Jeffrey's ear, but instead of returning to his seat he used both hands to tear the boy's mouth open.

'Stop it! You're hurting him, Matt!' the Danziger was

screaming. She had her hands like talons hooked over his shoulders, trying to get him to let go.

The burning and the burning and the fire and it hurt.

'Feel it, you little bastard!' he sang as he ripped the fat boy's mouth open and reached inside, trying to grab hold of his thick, slippery tongue.

But Miss Danziger was a very strong bird. Just when he was digging his fingers into Jeffrey's tongue, and Jeffrey's face was so red and the blood was still dripping down from his ear and getting the side of his neck all wet and sticky, Miss Danziger pulled him back so that he lost his balance.

He landed flat on his rump, momentarily stunned by the fall. Snarling to keep the fat boy away, though the Jeffrey was blubbering and making no effort to attack, Matt dragged himself back along the floor.

Hurry, say this, instructed Mr Harriman, giving him the words he needed to make things right again.

He looked up at the Danziger, her cheeks flushed and her breasts going up and down, up and down, like water sloshing against the sides of the bath.

'He started,' Matt said as he tried to catch his breath. 'He made fun.'

'My ear, I'm deaf,' the fat boy was howling now that Matt had let go.

'When will you learn to stop teasing, Jeffrey?' the teacher said with an angry look in her sharp dark eyes. But she still had enough anger left over to share some of it with Matt. 'And as for you,' she went on, 'you have to learn to control yourself, Matthew. You can't go around hitting people just because they call you names.'

Later, when the Janet came to pick him up and she and the Danziger spent a long time talking together where Matt couldn't hear them, the little girl who couldn't sit still came over to him and bobbed her head up and down like the toys he'd seen in the back of cars.

'I'm glad you did it,' the girl said. 'I hate him too. He's mean and he picks on me.'

But Matt wasn't all that satisfied. What good was a little blood if he hadn't made a proper kill? Despite everything Az had taught him, he'd let the prey slip through his fingers. But next time . . . next time the Jeffrey wouldn't be so lucky.

10

The Hollywood Hills, Los Altos Drive,
Wednesday, 10 November 1982

'Right, it's the twenty-fifth this year. I miss you, too,' Janet was saying. 'Fine. You're going to be amazed, Andy. He's doing beautifully.'

Matt saw the way she glanced at him as he sat on a bar stool in the kitchen, listening to her talking on the telephone to 'Uncle Andy'. He smiled, reaching down to stroke Turk behind the ears.

He'd been at the Langley School for two months now, and though Jeffrey the fat boy occasionally taunted him, Mr Harriman hadn't given permission again for him to attack.

We scared them, the Danziger in particular, his friend had explained. *We can't do that again, not for a while, anyway. We have to play by their rules, Matthew, or else they might start thinking that you weren't well.*

I'm well. I'm fine. Janet told Neil I'm as strong as an ox. What's an ox?

Like a big cow with horns, very powerful. But that's not the well I mean. I mean mentally well, emotionally stable.

I don't understand.

I don't want them to think you're crazy.

Matt couldn't help but laugh out loud when he heard Mr Harriman say that. Crazy was for the little Jesses at the hospital who did nothing but sit on the floor and rock back and forth, or bang their heads against the wall until they made themselves bleed. Crazy was tearing at your skin, or setting fire to yourself, which he'd seen at the hospital too, when one of the patients had gotten hold of a book of matches, determined to burn himself alive.

Now, *that* was crazy, hating yourself so much you wanted to die. But he wasn't crazy at all. He wanted to live, and so he'd gotten very good at pretending and doing things according to the rules the Jesses set down for him. Some were very easy to follow, like when Janet and Neil asked him to make his bed and keep his room in order. There was nothing the matter with that and so he did it without even asking why.

But there were other rules that were much trickier. The rule about touching yourself between the legs didn't make sense to him, but he followed it all the same, because Mr Harriman told him they'd get very angry if he disobeyed. Besides, if they knew about the white blood they might start worrying about things they shouldn't, and Mr Harriman didn't want them thinking he was anything but a normal little boy.

Then there were the eating rules, and the standing-up-straight rules, and the special stretching exercises that hurt his legs so bad sometimes he wanted to cry but wouldn't give them the satisfaction of shedding a single tear. Tears were for Az, when she died, and for Mama too, he guessed. But not because his body hurt from standing upright.

A bus now took him to and from school. When he came home Janet, who liked it when he called her Mommy, would be working in her study, which was a little room lined with books on shelves. She was writing more books to go up on the shelves, and she told him that this was her work, just like Daddy taught school and that was his work, too.

But she hardly ever stayed very long in the study once the bus dropped him off in front of the house and Turk would come racing down the driveway, so glad to see him and Mr Harriman that he didn't know what to do first. Mommy would put the cover on her typewriter and play ball with the two of them in the backyard. Or else she'd help him with his schoolwork, which he didn't like, but that was another rule he had to follow if he wasn't going to be told he was crazy and sent back to the hospital.

'That was your Uncle Andy,' she said when she got off the phone. 'He and his friend Mike are coming up for Thanksgiving. Won't that be fun?'

'What's Thanksgibing?'

'*Giving*,' Janet corrected, and she smiled patiently like she always did when he asked questions.

In fact, he sensed that she liked it when he wanted to know things, having told him once it was like a great big jigsaw puzzle (and he'd asked what that was too), putting together all the pieces so that when he'd solved the puzzle the world would make a lot more sense to him than it did now.

So she explained what the holiday meant, and the big turkey dinner she was going to prepare. Ina and Gillian were coming too, and Matt would have a chance to show everyone how well he was doing.

'In school?'

'Yes, and also how well you're doing at home.'

He got down from the stool and started out of the kitchen. 'Gillie's coming,' he said, having heard her walking up the drive.

Janet shook her head in amazement. 'I wish my ears were as good.'

'Why?'

She smiled. 'You hear things long before I do.'

'It's portant,' he said.

'*Im*portant,' she called after him.

* * *

It was Neil who remarked how adaptive the human species was, how easily it adjusted to changes in its environment.

'Meaning Matt?' Janet asked as she got ready for bed.

'Meaning us.' He was sitting at the foot of the bed, flicking channels with the remote commander. Finally he turned off the set and lay back, stretching his arms above his head. 'I weighed myself the other day. Still holding in there. Guess I better join a gym, though, don't you think?'

'Nope.' Janet curled up beside him and tickled his stomach. 'I think you're fine just the way you are, Neil.'

'Sure, now?'

'Positive.'

'Happy?'

'Very.'

'Then the book's going well, isn't it?'

Janet nodded, and he could tell she wasn't just trying to convince herself. Living with a writer was probably a lot harder than living with a teacher. Although he took his job home with him in the form of tests to grade and lessons to plan, he didn't carry it around on his shoulders twenty-four hours a day. But when Janet was involved in a project, it seemed as if the book became as much a part of her as her arms or legs. She couldn't let go of it even when she finished working and turned off her typewriter. It was always there, like a voice whispering in her ear. Sometimes during a conversation she'd even stop in the middle of a sentence and excuse herself to grab a piece of scrap paper.

'What are you doing?' he would say, even though he knew.

'Thought of something,' she'd reply.

He would find these little pieces of paper all over the house, some forgotten and others undoubtedly put to use. Usually they consisted of just a sentence or two, or a particularly intriguing image that had come into her head and which she didn't want to forget. Or else he'd come across bits of obscure arcana, such as: 'Have Ralph come early,' or 'Joy's joke about the bookends.'

Neil sat up and began to unbutton his shirt. She has a career, and what do I have? he couldn't help but think. She has something to look forward to every morning, and I have a bunch of overachievers already working on their first million.

One of his students had made a small killing dealing in rare comic books. Another restored antique cars for a hefty profit. A third had parlayed his bar mitzvah money into two tract houses in the San Fernando Valley. Last Neil had heard, the boy was about to turn them over at something like a hundred and fifty percent return on his investment.

Here she is, well on her way to a brilliant future. And what do you have to show for your life, Kaufman? A teaching certificate and a gold-embossed letter of rejection from medical school.

He stared at the blank TV screen, then looked back at his wife. Did Janet have any idea how miserable he sometimes was, how he felt his life was going nowhere and at such a fast clip he couldn't do anything to change it? No, probably not. After all, she had her books, and if there was one genuine anesthetic against the world's ills, it was creativity.

'What happens to him, the kid in the book? How do you have him surviving?' He wasn't all that interested, but he didn't want to sit there feeling sorry for himself.

'On his own. Like Robinson Crusoe.'

'Not suckled by a she-wolf?'

'No she-wolves in this novel, kiddo,' she said with a laugh. 'It's strictly survival of the fittest, learning by trial and error. I had to do all this research on wilderness survival. How to construct shelters, and what plants are edible and what aren't. That kind of thing. But now the boy's about to be discovered by civilization.'

'And its discontents.'

'Of course.'

'What's his name?'

'Az,' she said, sounding very proud of herself.

'What's that mean?'

Janet shrugged. 'I honestly don't know. It just came to me. Sounds very primal, don't you think? Az the Ur-boy. I think it works very well.'

'Funny kind of name. But if you like it – ' He stepped out of his pants and went over to the closet to hang them up. That their lives had changed so dramatically and in so short a period of time amazed him, but not nearly as much as the depth of affection he felt for the boy. But one thing still bothered him. Where exactly had the youngster come from? Often he found himself on the verge of asking Matt who he really was, if he had any memories of his past.

'Haven't you ever wondered where Matt came from, even before he got lost?'

'Or abandoned,' Janet made a point of saying.

He saw by her expression that the subject troubled her, but it was something he just couldn't let go of.

'Don't you think we should try to find out who his parents are?' he went on.

Janet looked at him reproachfully. 'We're his parents. And besides, the state made every effort to locate his family, and they came up with nothing. If they left him out in the desert to die, they're the last people we want him to meet.'

'I know that, honey. But aren't you curious who took care of him there?'

'I'm sure he just took care of himself.'

'That's why we saw him running on all fours, right? That's why he snarled like an animal?'

'He snarled because he'd forgotten how to talk and he was afraid. He ran on all fours because he was reverting to the crawling stage of infancy.'

Her glib explanation was so unlike her he couldn't help shaking his head. She was deluding herself, but why? Was she so afraid a stranger would show up at their door and demand they return the boy?

He followed her into the bathroom, watching her as she began to brush her teeth. 'There's no reason to be angry, you know.'

'Who said anything about being angry?'

But her tone of voice belied her words. As she tried to step past him he caught her around the waist and pulled her toward him. For a moment Neil had the distinct impression she was about to slap him. No doubt he was projecting, sorry now for bringing up a subject Janet still had trouble dealing with. Because instead of hitting him across the face, she suddenly relaxed, not the least resistant when he leaned over and kissed her.

'Just want you to know how much I love you,' he whispered. His fingers fumbled with her nightgown, trying to undo it.

'Not here,' she said.

'Why not?'

'I get cramps in my legs standing up.' With a girlish laugh she eased free of his embrace and scampered back into the bedroom.

Neil hurried after her, glad that marriage hadn't dulled the pleasure he derived from being with his wife. When they made love he forgot his problems and his dissatisfactions. He was back in college again, his voice cracking as he called her from the frat house and introduced himself.

Remember me, the guy who accidentally spilled beer all over your sweater last week? I was hoping you'd give me a chance to make it up to you.

How thoughtful. You mean you're going to let me spill a can of beer on you? That'd be great.

Thinking of that now, and the first time they'd made

love months later, he pulled her on top of him, kissing her eyes while her lashes fluttered lightly against his lips.

'You're delicious,' he whispered. 'I could eat you up, you're so beautiful.'

'I bet your mother used to say that.'

He grinned. 'True. She'd take my lips between her fingers and give them a squeeze. "I could eat you up, *shane kup*." She loved to tell me that.'

They rolled over onto their sides, looking at each other for a long, silent moment. Neil's hand went down between her legs, and Janet closed her eyes and sighed contentedly.

In the room next to theirs Matt sat up in bed, listening intently. 'Eat you up,' he'd heard the Neil say. So they were feeding, and keeping it a secret from him. But why? Turk go up from where he lay stretched out on the floor and padded over to the side of the bed. He put his head against the mattress, yellow eyes staring up at Matt.

They're feeding, Turk. They must have caught something and now they're eating it and not sharing.

He listened again, but they weren't making feeding sounds anymore. Janet was sighing and sighing, and Neil was groaning like someone was hurting him. Their bed creaked, then creaked again. Horsie, was that what they were doing? Poppy used to like to play horsie all the time, and not just in his den. Once, when Poppy and Mama thought he was asleep and he came out of his room to get a glass of water, he found them playing horsie in the kitchen.

Mama was shaking all over and groaning like Neil in the next room. She clung to Poppy so tightly he wondered if they were stuck together and couldn't get free. Poppy laughed and jiggled and laughed some more. They hadn't seen him hiding by the door. They didn't know he was watching. It had to be horsie because it looked like they were riding each other, Mama with her back against the wall and her legs around Poppy's waist, Poppy holding her steady with his pants around his ankles while he rode the bucking horse and neighed and whinnied just like ponies on TV.

That was before the stick-pain, before Poppy sang his angry hurting song. Hiding in the shadows by the doorway, Blue had watched the same way he watched cartoons, taking everything in with wide and delighted eyes. Maybe if he was good they'd let him play horsie too, he'd thought at the time. Now he thought of that again, but he knew the Kaufmans would never consent to such a thing.

Horsie was just for the two of them, not to be shared. It was for behind locked doors. But if he could play horsie with Janet, he knew it would be more fun than anything he'd ever done before. He'd already tried it with the Gillie, but she pushed him away and called him a silly.

'You're not supposed to play doctor at your age,' she had said.

Play doctor? What did that mean? He was afraid to ask, because Mr Harriman told him she might tell her mother, and then the Ina who was even meatier than Jeffrey the fat boy would tell the Kaufmans and they'd get angry. So now when he played with Gillie he never tried to touch her, even though he wanted to play horsie so he could spurt more of the white blood.

The sounds grew even louder now. He couldn't sit there in bed listening and not do anything. He had to see it for himself. So he crept out of bed, excited though for reasons he couldn't put into words. Why was it fun to watch horsie? He didn't really know, but that didn't stop him.

Warning Turk to stay put, Matt tiptoed out of his room and into the hall. The door to their den was closed, but now he could hear them even more clearly than before. Janet was whimpering, making little whistly sounds. Neil grunted in reply, and something went thudding against the bed so that the creaking springs seemed to be telling him a story, if only he knew their language.

What is it? he asked.

He needed words almost as much as he needed food. But Mr Harriman must have been asleep, because he didn't answer. The silence inside his head frightened him for a moment, like being all alone in the desert after the Jess left him with Mama in the dark. But then the fear passed and he edged closer to the door, putting his ear against it so that he could hear everything the Kaufmans were saying.

'Oh, sweetheart, I love you so,' Janet whispered.

Love was pain. Therefore she wanted to hurt Neil.

'I love you too,' the Neil said with a harsh rattly sound, as if he were running and couldn't catch his breath.

So he was hurting her and she was hurting him and that was love. But if it hurt so much, then why did it feel good when the white blood spurted?

Why, he asked Mr Harriman.

His friend slept on and on and didn't answer.

Matt would just have to find out the answers for himself. He put his fingers around the doorknob and turned it as quietly as he could. If the door was locked he'd have to go back to his room and try again, another night when they were hungry and eager to give each other pain. But the door wasn't locked.

The door was now open a finger's width, so that he didn't have to strain in order to hear what the Kaufmans were doing in their room. They sounded just like Mama and Poppy when they played horsie, and Matt knew that's what it was even before he pushed the door open a little more and peeked inside.

There was the Neil, showing his back and rump, the Janet's legs sticking out from under him. The two of them were groaning and jiggling like they were going to keep shaking each other until the love-pain spurted out like blood from a wound.

Whir-whir-whir, he thought, and he even looked around the room, half expecting to see the man with the bushy beard standing behind his big black machine, telling the Kaufmans what to do just the way he did when Mama took him to the room with the pipes to play the movie game. But there was no one else in the room, and no hot burning lights making everything look so white and shiny it was hard to keep your eyes open.

Janet had her hands on Neil's shoulders. Matt couldn't see her face, couldn't see the Neil's face, either. But he could hear them, every single word and nonword, all the funny grunty sounds they made, the jiggles and the creaks and the whispers that passed between them like when Az used to chew the food for him and give it back, especially when he was little and cried a lot because Mama was gone and wouldn't come back.

He reached down, pressing his hand to the front of his pajamas which he hated but had to wear because he wasn't little anymore. The hardness was starting to hurt, and he rubbed his fingers back and forth, never once taking his eyes off the bed. The game was probably almost over. They were bouncing up and down and back and forth, moving faster and faster like Mama and Poppy always did just before they climbed off each other.

Then the Neil threw himself forward and Matt could see the Janet's missing thing all wet and glisteny and filled like he was filled with the stick-pain.

Love and pain, he kept thinking. But he liked this pain now that Poppy wasn't there to hurt him. He liked it so much that he wanted to do the thing Mr Harriman had taught him, the thing that made the white blood. But just when he thought it would happen, and just when Mommy and Daddy ('cause that's what they wanted him to call them) suddenly cried out to end the game, the Janet saw him.

The moment their eyes met she didn't react the way other animals did, trying to escape into the thornies where he and Az couldn't follow. Instead, she cried out so loudly that Matt jumped back, having never heard her make a sound like that before. Turk was suddenly right beside him, teeth bared and ears laid back. If he hadn't grabbed the dog's collar when he did, Turk would have leaped onto the bed and attacked.

'Jesus,' he heard the Daddy swear.

And the Mom said, 'For God's sake, cover yourself, Neil.'

Matt turned and ran, dragging Turk along with him because the dog was certain he was still in danger and wanted to protect him. He rushed into his room and closed the door, pulling the race-car up over his head so that he was safe in the warm close dark.

Was it wrong what I did? he asked Mr Harriman.

Before his friend could answer, Matt heard the Daddy knocking on the door. Then Neil turned the knob and let himself in. Turk snarled so savagely that even Matt was afraid.

Tell him to lie down before the Daddy gets angry.

Mr Harriman still wasn't talking, but he must have been wide awake because a moment later Turk did just that. The retriever flattened himself against the floor, and though he continued to growl from the back of his throat, he made no move to attack.

'It's all right, Matt. You can come out now. I'm not going to hurt you.'

Was he lying? If he was, Matt could always get Turk to defend him. So he took his chances and crept out from under the cave he'd made of the bedspread.

Neil sat down on the bed. 'It's okay, I know you didn't mean any harm. That's what I want to talk to you about.'

Pretending and more pretending, Matt thought, not liking it when the Neil reached out and gently stroked his cheek. He was probably getting ready to do the stick-pain, and Matt pushed himself away, edging back along the bed.

'Don't be afraid of me, son. I'm your father and I love you. I just want to explain, that's all.'

'What?'

'About what you did, and why it's wrong, why it's not nice to spy on people.'

Now where's the little spy?

The burning and the burning . . .

Love was pain. Spying was pain. The Neil wasn't naked like Poppy or wet and sticky. But he was naked under his robe and he smelled like Poppy did after playing horsie, musky and sweaty and something else like white blood. Matt crawled farther away along the bed, ready to run out of the room the moment the Neil who wanted to be called Daddy but he was only pretending that too did anything to hurt him.

'Hey, slugger, it's okay, it's okay,' Neil kept saying. 'You didn't know, and that's all right. But next time if our door's closed, all you have to do is knock first if you want to come in.'

'Why?'

Neil smiled. His teeth weren't sharp but they were big.

Because they don't want you watching them when they're fucking.

Mr Harriman was awake now, and Matt smiled and felt safe again.

'Because when your mom and I are alone in our room . . . that is, when we're . . .' Neil stopped and looked back at the door. 'Janet,' he called out, 'I'm not good at this kind of thing. What should I tell him?'

'You're a biology teacher, aren't you? Then tell him the truth, for Christ's sake,' she yelled back.

She sounded angry, but no so angry that she came into the room to slap him like Mama sometimes did if she said he was bad or just stop bugging me already, you're a pain in the ass.

Pain in the ass, pain in the ass.

I won't let him, I won't, I won't, he thought. He glanced at Turk, glad to see the big yellow dog wasn't lying there half asleep, thinking everything was all right again.

'When two people love each other, like your mom and I, they express their love by . . . Miss Danziger hasn't gone into any of this yet, has she? No, I guess not.'

Mr Harriman began to giggle inside his head. Matt wondered what his friend found so funny. Maybe the Neil had made a joke he couldn't understand. Maybe that was it.

'When two people love each other,' Neil tried again, 'they show that love by . . . anyway, slugger, it's just not nice to come barging in like that. It's impolite.'

'Barging in?' He'd never heard the word before.

'Just to walk right in without knocking or anything. That's all I'm saying. If our door's closed there's a reason.'

'What?'

'Jesus, we're on some merry-go-round, aren't we?' the Neil said, half to himself. 'Let me put it this way, then. If you see our door's closed and you need us for anything, just knock first. Simple as that.'

Here was a new rule to add to all the others. But this one he didn't like at all. It was fun to watch them playing horsie. Next time he'd have to be more careful, so that the Janet wouldn't see what he was doing. That way he'd be able to watch them from beginning to end, from when they started feeding together until they began to give each other the love-pain. Then, when the Neil made his white blood spurt out, he would make his spurt out too. He would be part of the pain that way, giving it back to them as he'd never been able to do with Poppy.

Pain in the ass, pain in the ass.

'Now do you understand?' Neil asked.

Matt nodded.

Neil leaned over and kissed him on the forehead. His touch didn't burn, though Matt thought it might. 'It's called privacy, Matt, that's all.'

No, it's not, he thought. It's called fucking.

Now the Mommy came in her nightie, with the smell of flowers fresh on her skin and her hair brushed back, still damp with sweat where it met her forehead.

Turk knew the Mommy didn't mean any harm, because the retriever stayed where he was, lying on his belly by the foot of the bed. The dog watched the Janet, alert to her every move. But he didn't show his teeth or make a single angry sound. Matt knew it was the Neil who was the dangerous one. Even without Turk there to protect him, he'd still have no trouble bringing down the Mommy. Maybe she was strong, but she wasn't nearly as strong as he. No, it was the Neil he had to watch out for, because the Neil and the Poppy were Jesses, with thick doodles and angry hurting songs.

'Are you still awake, sweetheart?' Janet whispered as she came into his room, knocking first because that was the new rule none of them were ever going to forget.

Sweetheart, he thought, remembering the word the way he remembered tastes and smells. She called the Neil that too, he recalled, right in the middle of horsie. Was it a special horsie word? If it was, what would happen if he said it to her now? Would she throw her nightie up the way Connie did, showing him her missing thing?

'Sweetheart,' he called out to her. It had a nice juicy sound to it. He said it again and giggled, waiting for her to laugh and lift her nightie.

Cute, huh?

Was it mimicry or did he understand? Janet wasn't certain, but she smiled all the same. 'Daddy said he had a little trouble explaining things,' she began.

'What?'

The boy's pale blue eyes shone as if lit from behind. With only the night light on beside his bed, she had the distinct impression they were glowing. She looked away and tried to compose her thoughts. Why did she have to get stuck with the tough stuff? Neil taught kids the facts of life all the time. So why did he have such a hard time explaining it to Matt?

But now she couldn't do it, either. The more the child looked at her, the more uncomfortable she became. He seemed to be waiting for something to happen, but what that something was she had no way of knowing.

'You know what "polite" means, don't you, Matt?'

'Yes, sweetheart.'

Matt giggled, showing her his broken teeth. He'd already been examined by a dentist, and in a few weeks the job of restoration would get under way. His mouth was remarkably healthy, the dentist had told her, but the chipped and broken teeth would have to be either filed or capped, depending upon the extent of the damage. Now the irregularities gave his smile a disconcertingly savage expression, and Janet looked away, not wanting him to think she was staring.

'Respecting each other's privacy is a very important thing, Matt. For instance, if you were sleeping, we wouldn't just come barging into your room. It wouldn't be polite, or fair. It's just like taking things that don't belong to us. We don't do that because it's not right.'

'Yes, sweetheart.' His laughter had an eerie ring to it, like something he'd memorized, not knowing when it was appropriate to use and when it wasn't.

'"Sweetheart" is a nice word, isn't it? It's a tender word, Matt. It's filled with love. Daddy and I love you very dearly, and that's why when you have any questions, you mustn't ever be afraid to ask.'

In response, Matt reached up and put his hand on her breast. He raised his eyes, staring at her inquisitively, almost as if he were defying her to stop him. Then he began to move his fingers back and forth, so slowly and delicately that if she hadn't looked down she wouldn't even have realized what he was doing.

The boy was exhibiting a natural curiosity, that was all. And so Janet held his hand there for a moment, wondering what he was thinking.

'I love you, Mommy.'

'I love you too, Matt.'

'It feels good. You're soft.'

She smiled, gently stroking his fingers.

'Do you remember the car?' he asked.

'What car, Matt?'

'I was asleep, remember?'

What was he talking about? She started to let go of his hand, but suddenly his fingers tightened around her wrist.

'The car, the car,' he said, raising his voice '"Mommy, Mommy, Mommy!" Don't you remember?'

She shook her head. But when she pulled her hand free and tried to get him to lie down, he reached out again, holding her breast so tightly it began to hurt.

'The car going round and round. "Mommy, Mommy, Mommy!"' he said in a shrill, anguished voice.

'What car, Matt?'

'The car, the brown car!' he cried out. His hands clutched at her breasts, something desperate and scared in the way he needed to touch her. 'The breeway, Mommy. On the breeway, 'member?'

When he finally let go of her she edged back, holding Matt's small, boyish hands firmly in hers. Behind them, their wavering shadows were thrown up along the wall like boogeymen from her childhood.

The breeway? What was he trying to tell her? What brown car was he talking about?

'Breeway. Hopittle.'

'Hospital,' she heard herself automatically correcting.

'Don't you 'member, Mommy? I went away. But I loved you so much I came back. On the breeway, the sandy go breeway.'

Matt threw his hands over her shoulders, pressing his lips against her neck. Janet held the child tightly in her arms, feeling the way he shuddered.

The breeway, the sandy go breeway . . . no, it couldn't possibly. It wasn't . . . it couldn't be. He was alive in her arms, but it couldn't be.

Sandy go breeway.

Breeway freeway.

Sandy go freeway.

San Diego Freeway.

The car that had cut them off, the tan Audi that she was driving, Matt waking up and crying, 'Mommy, Mommy, Mommy!' as they whirled around like a carousel going out of control.

Why was she crying? She mustn't cry. The past was as dead as yesterday's news. Everyone said that, and it was true. You had to live in the now, the today. Escaping into yesterday was as dangerous as . . . as a car cutting them off on the freeway, the baby waking up and crying out for her, the doctor saying I'm sorry, the casket slowly lowered into the ground.

Was this why he was here, why they'd managed to get

through all the bureaucratic red tape, why Turk had first brought Matt to her brother's house? He was kissing her now, his lips sliding down along her neck while his hands cupped her breasts. She trembled and wanted to ease free. But how could she deny him the tenderness and love he'd been without for so long?

You're mine, she thought, and we'll never be separated again.

'I love you, Mommy,' he whispered, his breath warm against her ear. 'I want to be with you always. I want to be part of you, Mommy, part of you.'

She urged him to lie back, brushing the hair out of his eyes. 'You are part of me,' she said, her voice thick with emotion.

'Horsie,' the boy murmured. He seemed to be drifting, already half asleep.

'It's late, Matt. You have school tomorrow, sweetheart. Go to sleep now.'

When she got to her feet he looked up at her and smiled, his fingers reaching out to touch her hand.

'You'll like it,' he said.

'What?'

'Horsie.' And as she left the room she could hear him giggling, just the way children did when they watched cartoons.

There was no clear dividing line between what was real and what was imagined. Although she knew she must be dreaming, Janet couldn't remember how the dream had started, or when she'd finally fallen asleep. It seemed as if it began in bed, but when she looked over at Neil, he wasn't there, and his half of the bed didn't look slept in. She wondered if she was dreaming this, or if he'd slipped away while she was asleep, careful to make up the bed before he left.

She wanted to call out to him but couldn't get her lips to work. It was as if she'd forgotten what speech was all about, and her tongue flapped inside her mouth like a bird trapped in a cage, beating its wings and trying to get out.

Breeway freeway.

When she sat up in bed her head smashed into a windshield and the walls of the room shattered like a pane of broken glass. If it was a dream, then why couldn't she just shake her head and convince herself to wake up? Surely Neil was somewhere in the house. Maybe he was in the kitchen, raiding the fridge.

She jumped out of bed and found herself racing down the hallway into the living room. But when she got there it wasn't anything like she remembered. Instead, she found herself in a large, brightly lit room, with water or heating pipes – she couldn't tell exactly – crisscrossing the ceiling.

Where was she?

Breeway, sandy go breeway, I love you, Mommy.

The doors were closed behind her. The hallway had vanished, and with it the living room, the house on Los Altos Drive, everything she knew and could recognize as being part of the real and waking world. In its place was a room she had never seen before, with an enormous mattress lying in the middle of the floor.

Movie lights were arranged nearby, burning so brightly she wasn't able to see what lay beyond them. She looked away, momentarily blinded by the glare and thinking it was like hundreds of flashbulbs all going off at once. It was then that she heard the machine, and when she whirled around to see what it was, a heavyset man with a beard that grew right up to his cheekbones looked at her and shook his head in disgust.

'What took you so long?' He was standing beside a motion-picture camera, the motor turned on so that she could hear it whirring. 'We've been standing around jerking ourselves off while you take your sweetass time getting here.'

What was she supposed to tell him? She didn't know what the man was talking about. She didn't even know who he was, and so she just stood there, afraid to move.

'He's waiting,' said the man with the beard and the loud, authoritative voice. He gestured in the direction of the bed.

She turned her head back. Despite the harsh, unrelenting glare, she could see someone's outline beneath the bed-covers.

'Who is it?' she asked.

The man with the beard threw his head back and began to laugh. 'Who the fuck do you think?' He moved behind the camera, while beneath the bedding the figure stirred, stretching its arms and legs as if awakening from a dream.

With a last hesitant glance at the man behind the camera, she stepped forward and slowly approached the bed. A moment later, as she heard the whir of the camera, a voice began to whisper in her ear.

'Mommy, is that you? Don't leave me, I'm afraid.' The child pushed the sheets down and sat up, beckoning her to come closer. 'Breeway,' he said, and he licked his lips with the tip of his tongue. 'Sandy go breeway, Mommy. I want to be part of you, Mommy.'

He was the most beautiful child she had ever seen, with luminous blue eyes and delicate features. 'You are part of me,' she said. She knelt beside him, cupping his face in her hands.

'Horsie,' he whispered.

'Ride her good and hard, kid,' said the man with the beard.

The boy took her hand in his, but when she saw what he wanted her to do she pulled away. This was all wrong, a dream that didn't make sense. How could she even imagine such a thing, the boy kicking the bedcovers off, licking his lips and laughing as she looked down at him in disbelief?

She wanted to run and never look back, refusing to acknowledge what she knew was ugly and perverted. But he was much stronger than she realized. Even as she tried to twist free he had her pinned to the bed, hovering over her and smiling with his chipped and broken teeth.

This couldn't possibly be happening. He was just a little boy, ten or eleven years old. How could he be so much stronger than she? And why wasn't she screaming now and trying to put up a fight? Why did she want him to kiss her, to reach down between her legs, guiding himself into place with a single quick and agile thrust?

She cried out as loudly as she could and it all began to change, falling apart before her eyes. It wasn't Matt anymore. Snakes hissed and lashed at the air. Flesh fell from his cheeks, revealing white sun-bleached bone. Where once there had been eyes there were now empty sockets. Her screams began to choke her and she couldn't breathe.

'Mommy, Mommy, Mommy,' the feverish voice groaned in her ear.

Whir-whir-whir . . .

Neil turned over in bed and kissed her lightly on the cheek. 'Love you,' he murmured.

The lights went out one by one until the darkness was absolute. But even then Janet lay awake, struggling to keep her eyes open, terrified of what might happen if she fell asleep.

11

Los Altos Drive, Thursday, 25 November 1982

THANKSBIGING.

Thanks for what? Matt didn't know, but it was getting harder and harder to pretend. The rules the Jesses wanted him to follow had become as confining as the clothes they made him wear. There was a rule for this and a rule for that, and hovering over all of them was the biggest rule of all. *Morality*. It was the Neil who tried to explain to him what that meant. But no matter how many times he went over it, morality didn't make any sense.

If morality was for everyone, not just Jesses, then how could anyone eat? If every creature followed morality, every creature would surely go hungry. Even now he could smell the meat being cooked in the kitchen. The fat bird they called a turkey had been killed so they could feed. Was that morality?

The Jesses made up lots of rules, all right, but their rules were tricks, and morality was the biggest trick of all. Even the sound of it sickened him, the way it got stuck between your teeth like a piece of gristle so you couldn't swallow, hard as you tried.

Miss Danziger had rules, and Neil had rules, and Janet and Ina and Gillie and everyone else he had met. Even Jeffrey the fat boy (so much good juicy meat there going to waste, he always thought) made up rules whenever he felt like it, so that one day he would come to school and be nice and another day the rule would be meanness. Teasing and eating were the rules he liked best of all. Sharing was another form of morality, but the fat boy never shared.

When he thought no one was looking – but Matt always looked, licking his lips and thinking of the day fat Jeffrey would be his – sweet gooey things would come out of his desk and disappear into his mouth.

Yum yum yum, said the fat boy, my rules are the best rules of all.

What are we waiting for? he would ask Mr Harriman. If we wait much longer I'll forget everything Az taught me. Then I *will* be a Jess, and there won't be anything I can do about it, either.

It was easier to talk in his head than on his lips. Words not spoken were fast and sure. Whole sentences flew out of his thoughts like words on a page in a book. If Miss Danziger asked him to get up before the class and read, each word was like a boulder or a thicket of green thornies – *cactus* was the Jess word, but cactus didn't sound like the pain you felt if you ran into a bunch of thornies. He would have to stumble over them, one word at a time, pausing to catch his breath between each and every jumble of letters. But when he spoke to Mr Harriman the words moved through his head as swiftly as he and Az racing through the twilight in pursuit of game.

Now he had Turk to race with, but only in the yard. Outside the house there was yet another rule to follow. TURK MUST BE ON A LEASH. He saw it in big letters because both the Neil and the Janet always made a point of telling him that, saying that there were cars on the road, and they didn't want Turk to get hit.

They were in the backyard now, a green made-up space with short crunchy grass and flowering plants. In the valley there were flowers, but no one had arranged them in neat little rows. In the valley there was grass too, and after the rains it grew as thick as fur.

Once, when game was scarce, Az had taken him up into the mountains. Here there were meadows where grass grew so high no one could see them when they moved. But it was also very cold, and each time they got close to game they got close to Jesses, who lived in little cabins in the woods, feeding from cans they threw into the bushes once they were empty.

Back in the valley Jesses rarely came, and when hunting was good it was the best place of all. He thought of that now and would have shed tears if tears would have brought Az back.

But even in this neat made-up space with the table with the unbrella and the chairs and the bicycle the Neil was trying to teach him how to ride – metal always carried a man-smell no matter how hard you tried to rub it away – game would occasionally come, especially early in the morning when Jesses were still asleep in their made-up dens.

From his bedroom window he was able to see prey emerging hesitantly from among the trees. Quail came with their fluffy chirping chicks, rats with long scaly tails and nervous snouts, and another time a deer – they were the tastiest game of all – stood in the middle of the yard and raised her black nose in the air, sniffing for Jesses and fleeing with her tail held high when he started to let himself out of the window. Coyotes came too, a small one with three legs and half of a fourth like a coyote he once had seen in a trap, and another much larger who stood almost as tall as Turk. He looked at them through the glass and they looked at him.

What are they thinking? he had asked Mr Harriman.

They want to know who you are, Matthew, so that if you should ever need them, they won't mistake you for someone else.

But why would I need them?

Mr Harriman had refused to tell him, and now he turned his attention to the clipped made-up bushes that ringed the yard. A ground squirrel with a soft flicking tail and curious eyes scampered out into the open, freezing when it caught his scent.

Janet had planted a bed of fruit – strawberries, the little red things were called – at one end of the garden. Squirrels and roof rats and jays and mockingbirds all liked to feed on the berries, and this ground squirrel was just as hungry as all the others. A berry that was still green and tart disappeared into its mouth. It sat up on its hind legs and peered cautiously about, the yellowish-gray fur along its belly catching Matt's eye.

When the squirrel froze, he froze. When the squirrel moved, he moved.

'Stay,' he whispered to Turk.

The dog didn't know anything about hunting. For him, game came in a can, just like it did for Jesses. But Turk was very good at rules and obeying. So as soon as Matt told him to stay where he was, the retriever froze the way the ground squirrel froze, watching Matt as he slowly made his way across the yard.

He knew he couldn't run the squirrel down. It was too small and fast, would disappear into the ivy long before he caught up to it. But he could lure the animal to him if only he remembered what Az had taught him. *Patience* was the Jess word for it, though when he had hunted in the past it wasn't patience he thought of so much as the empty space in his belly, the need to be cleverer and stronger than any of the animals he and Az liked to feed on.

So as the squirrel fed, filling its cheek pouches with one berry after another, he began to click his tongue, motionless as he crouched on the springy green grass. The furry little creature raised its head, its eyes as dark and shiny as pebbles on the bottom of a stream.

His tongue kept clicking against the roof of his mouth. Curious, the ground squirrel scampered out of the strawberry patch and began to head toward him. Matt could smell it now, a fresh, untainted scent. Back in the house, Ina and Janet and Gillian were tending to the turkey, but roast meat wasn't the same as fresh. Fresh had an alive taste, still warm with the blood Miss Danziger had tried to tell the class about.

Blood, he had learned, pulsed through channels called arteries and veins. When jaws snapped shut and teeth clamped tight, veins and arteries broke apart like green twigs, spurting red blood as fast as the heart could pump it. He wanted that alive taste more than anything now, and he clicked his tongue over and over again in order to draw the squirrel even closer.

What a foolish little creature it was. Did it think he wanted it to perch on his shoulder like a parrot he'd seen in a picture? (A *pet*, the Jesses called such things.) Maybe it thought he had food, because now he extended his hand, scratching at the grass and snapping his fingers lightly together.

The squirrel raised itself up so that it seemed to be sitting on its rump. It turned its head from side to side, then darted forward again. The smell tickled Matt's nose. His mouth was filling up with saliva and he knew there was no longer any need for *patience*.

With a sudden forward thrust of his shoulders, Matt pounced, both hands capturing the squirrel and pushing it down into the grass. The squirming rodent began to make frightened noises, twisting its head back as it tried to get at his hand. He'd been bitten by a squirrel before, and because he knew how painful it could be, he held the animal carefully behind the neck, squeezing its plump furry body while he bent over it, mouth opened wide.

He could easily have torn its head right off its body, but that wasn't how he'd been taught. Instead, with a sudden crushing pressure his jaws tightened around the upper part of the squirrel's neck. He could even smell its breath then, could see itchies jumping through the soft flecked fur.

The squirrel's fat little body vibrated against his teeth. It stiffened and a tremor passed through it, just as the first rush of blood spurted over Matt's tongue. He tore at the fur, drenching his mouth with the salty alive taste as he tried to get at the meat. Behind him a swirling rush of flowers blew through the air.

'Matt?' the Gillie called to him as she came out of the house.

If she saw what he'd done it would be a terrible broken rule. The Kaufmans would be angry, but Mr Harriman would be the angriest of all, and with anger came pain, not the love-pain but the stick-pain.

He hurriedly wiped his mouth with the back of his hand, trying to get the blood off his fingers by rubbing them against the grass. He couldn't leave the squirrel there with blood still dribbling in little spurts from its torn throat. So when he turned around to face the Gillie he kept the fresh kill behind his back, signaling Turk with his eyes.

With a suspicious glance at Gillian, the yellow dog trotted obediently across the yard. Matt backed away, still holding the squirrel out of sight.

'What've you got there, Matt?' the Gillie said in that teasing, coaxing voice she liked to use when they played together.

'Nothin',' he said, while Turk sniffed at the bloodstains on the grass, and Mr Harriman told the dog to get behind him and take the squirrel in his mouth.

'Come on, Mattie, lemme see.' She grabbed him by the shoulders and spun him around.

There was nothing in his hands, just the sticky traces of blood. Gillian didn't realize what it was, and by then Turk was heading off in the opposite direction, where he could dispose of the squirrel without anyone the wiser.

Uncle Andy and Uncle Mike arrived from Palm Springs soon after this, and Janet came out of the house and told him to wash up for dinner. They all sat together in the dining room. The Janet was at one end of the long table and the Neil at the other. Uncle Andy and Uncle Mike sat next to each other, while he sat across from them. Plump Ina was on one side of him, and the red-haired Gillie on the other.

There were so many smells and sounds in the dining room that it scared him a little. He looked down at his empty plate, thinking of the squirrel he hadn't been able to feed on and wondering why Jesses always cooked things first, roasting them in fire instead of just eating them as soon as they were killed.

Finally they put the game on the table. Although it was cooked it didn't smell bad at all. In fact, it smelled so good that when the Neil put some on his plate he forgot all about using his fork and just grabbed it between his fingers and started to eat.

'Matthew,' said the Mommy in a voice filled with unspoken rules.

He saw the way Andy looked at Mike, these two tall Jesses who hunted together in the desert where Turk had taken him after Az was killed. Did they mean for him to share his food with them? No, it couldn't be that, because the Neil was already heaping meat onto their plates, and now lots of bowls of dead green leaves and roots were being passed around the table.

He picked up his fork. The metal was cold against his skin, the spikes at the end sharp as thorns.

Use it, Mr Harriman instructed. *We have to prove to them how well you've learned your lessons.*

He used the fork, forcing himself to curl his fingers tightly around the length of metal so that it didn't tip back and forth in his hand.

'How are you doing, Matt?' the Mike asked. He was dark-haired like the Daddy, but thinner and with the mark of the sun on his face like his friend Andy.

The turkey was dry and stringy, like meat he and Az would bury in a cache if they'd had enough and wanted to save some for later.

'Matt's doing real well,' the Janet spoke up. 'Aren't you, sweetheart?'

'Yes, sweetheart,' he said with his mouth filled with turkey meat.

Next to him, Gillian giggled.

'He's already up to a second-grade reading level,' Janet said proudly. She glanced at Matt. 'After dinner, maybe you'll show Uncle Andy how well you're doing. He can write his name now too. Can't you, Matt?'

He looked up and nodded. There were too many things to eat. Words got in the way of feeding.

'That's marvelous,' said the Ina, who was putting the food into her mouth almost as fast as he was.

He looked up again and smiled. 'B-L-U-E,' he said, reciting each letter in turn.

'What's blue?' said Janet.

'What?' he asked.

'B-L-U-E spells blue.'

'Matt,' he said.

Mr Harriman was making angry hissing sounds in his head.

What did I do? he asked.

You're talking too much, Matthew.

But they like it when I talk.

I wouldn't want to hurt you if I can help it, Matthew.

But they wanted to know if I could spell my name.

Your name is Matthew, my little friend. You forget that again and I won't be able to stop myself.

Something hard and probing poked its way between his

buttocks. Feeling the sudden sharp jab of Mr Harriman's displeasure, he squirmed in his seat, promising to be good and that he wouldn't do anything to make his friend angry.

Everyone at the table seemed to be looking at him then.

'You all right?' said the Daddy.

He forced himself to nod, even though the thing that felt like a finger was still there, ready to be joined by another if he misbehaved.

'You want more turkey, slugger?'

'Yes.' Then he remembered and quickly added, 'Please.'

The Janet's smile was so big he could have tucked himself inside it. He was doing good again and the finger went away and everything was going to be okay.

But then Uncle Andy reached into the pocket of his blue coat with the shiny gold buttons and pulled out a piece of paper with lots of little black dots and squiggles written all over it. Newspaper. It was something cut from a *Times*, like the Daddy read every morning at breakfast.

'Take a look at this,' Andy Hilliard said, handing the article to his brother-in-law. 'I figured you guys might be interested.'

Matt watched the Daddy reading, not even moving his lips.

'What is it?' Janet asked.

'Interesting,' said Neil. He handed the clipping back to Andy.

'What's interesting?' Janet said.

Uncle Andy looked at him as if he had the answer. What answer? Matt wondered. And for what question?

'Seems they found the remains of a rather large animal not far from our house,' Andy said. 'Some kids were out on dirt bikes when they came across it. The remains were sent up here to be identified, and the curator of mammals at the LA Zoo determined it was a wolf. Not an unusually large coyote, as was originally thought.'

'So?' said Neil. 'I mean, what's the point?'

'The point is, there hasn't been a wolf reported in California since 1924. They're extinct here, in Nevada too.'

'Could've escaped from a zoo,' Janet suggested.

'Could've, but the police don't have any reports on missing animals. They figure it might have wandered up from Mexico. There's still a small population of native wolves down there.'

'I still don't – ' Janet started to say.

'Remember that murder out in Morongo Valley we were telling you about?' Andy reminded her. 'They think this particular animal might have been responsible.' He glanced at Matt. 'Do you know what a wolf is, champ?'

Before he could answer, Janet interrupted. 'I still don't see what this has to do with anything, Andy.'

'I didn't finish, Jan. Interestingly enough, when they examined this carcass or whatever was left, they removed a bullet. Well, that got them thinking. There are only a few places in town where you can purchase cartridges, and as it turned out, only two stores carried that particular brand of ammunition. It took a couple of weeks, but sure enough they managed to locate the guy who fired the shot.'

'The plot thickens, Ina said with a laugh. 'Can you pass the cranberry sauce, Matt? And I think I'll have just one more roll.'

Matt did as he was asked, but now he had eyes only for Uncle Andy, who kept looking at him curiously, as if expecting him to say something. *Cartridge* he didn't understand, but *bullet* and *shot* he did. The shot was the sound the bullet made when it killed Az, the day they snuck into the trailer camp because men were looking for them in the valley and they had to escape.

'I don't like this story,' Janet said emphatically. She started to get up from the table, when Neil motioned her to stay put.

The Mommy was getting scared. He could smell it on her, and every second it got stronger. But what was frightening her?

'He's only trying to finish up the story, hon,' Neil replied. 'So what happened, Andy?'

'They tracked the guy down, all right. Lives over in some tacky trailer park about a mile or so from where we are. Had quite a story to tell too.'

We must be very careful, Matthew. This Jess is as bad as Poppy. He wants to hurt us, just the way his friends hurt Az.

Friends?

He knew the man who killed Az. They hunted together. He must have told the man to pull the trigger. Now he wants to send us away, back to the hospital.

But why? I'm good. I pretend good, don't I?

Yes, but he hates you. He means to trick us. I know his thoughts, and I know he's evil. He'll try to take us away from here.

'I checked my calendar, and according to the guy from the trailer camp, he shot the wolf – he called it a coyote, of course – that same weekend you visited us last spring. But he said something else that – '

'Matt, what's wrong?' Janet said in alarm.

Everyone was looking at him now, and from under the table Turk began to growl.

Mr Harriman never lied. Uncle Andy was bad. Uncle Andy hated him and he hated Az. Mr Harriman had made him promise never to tell anyone they were friends. If the Jesses knew they were together they would lock him away like at the hospital, and never let him out again.

But now the Andy with the sun on his face was going to make sure they locked him away, forever and ever. Even Mr Harriman, who knew so many things and was smarter than all the Jesses put together, wouldn't be able to stop them.

He stiffened in his seat, peering across the table through narrowed, angry eyes. Turk was right beside him now, waiting to be told what to do. Mr Harriman would speak for him, Mr Harriman who knew more words than anyone.

'You all right, slugger?' Neil asked.

The Daddy started to get up from the table, when Matt threw his head back, closed his eyes, and began to howl, just like Az had taught him. The wailing rose up in the air like smoke, echoing faintly. He hated the Andy the way he hated the Jess who killed Mama, so many warm and cold and rainy times ago.

'My God,' the Ina said, 'how the hell does he make that sound?'

Matt opened his eyes and saw their world, the Jess world, like something glimpsed underwater, wavering this way and that with the current.

'Faggot,' he hissed, making the word Mr Harriman gave him. 'Faggot! Cocksucker!'

'Jesus,' someone said, and then the Neil said, 'Come, we're going outside for some air.'

Matt saw him out of the corner of his eyes. As the Daddy came toward him, he snarled and threw himself half off his seat, tearing at the fleshy part of Neil's hand.

The Daddy stumbled back with a frightened cry.

'Matt!' the Janet was shouting over and over again. 'Matt, apologize this instant. He doesn't know what he's saying. He's upset.'

'I'll say,' Gillian giggled.

'Faggot,' he said again. 'The faggot hates me.' It was his lips, his tongue, his voice. But it was Mr Harriman's too, Mr Harriman who knew evil when he saw it, who would protect him even better than Az had.

'I don't hate you at all,' the Andy replied in a dry, bloodless voice.

Matt could smell his fear, just as he could still smell

Janet's. It was a good smell, sharp and pungent, a smell that told him he could bring the Andy down as easily as any other two-legged game he'd taken in the past.

'You'd fuck me if you could, you faggot!' he shrieked, the words tumbling free of his lips. 'You'd stick it up my ass and fuck me, you filthy cocksucker!'

The Neil suddenly attacked, grabbing him by the shoulders and shaking him violently back and forth in his seat. 'Stop it!' he cried out. 'No one hates you, for Christ's sake.'

'Suckit, suckit,' he whispered. His lips were very dry. He licked them with the tip of his tongue while Mr Harriman's words pounded against the back of his head.

The Neil was dragging him outside and he wasn't putting up a fight. He tripped and the Neil hauled him to his feet, shouting at Turk to stay where he was, everything would be all right.

'Hates me, hates me,' he whispered. His head hurt the way it used to if he was bad and Mr Harriman punished him.

When they got outside he pulled his hand free and dropped down onto all fours, confused by all the excitement. The made-up space was closing in on him. The Jesses would come and hurt him. The Andy would hurt him and the Mike would hurt him, too. They'd killed Az and Mama, and now they wanted to kill him. But he wasn't crazy. Crazy was wanting to die, and dying was sleeping and never waking up, or the blood flowing out and never stopping.

'Listen to me, Matt, listen to me,' the Neil told him. 'We love you and we're going to help you. Andy doesn't want to hurt you. No one does.'

Lies and tricks. He's Poppy with another face!

The burning and the burning and the fire and it hurt.

Don't let him hurt me, Mama! Don't let him hurt me like this!

Mama cried and lay still. Jess got up naked like Poppy and looked at him pretending to be asleep. 'I didn't mean nothin', honest,' Jess had said.

'I didn't mean nothin'. Honest, Daddy.' He threw his arms over the Daddy's neck and began to make sounds like dripping tears. 'It was just that Mister – '

He stopped, biting off the word like a piece of meat. Mr Harriman would do the stick-pain if he said anything more. He clamped his buttocks together and began to whimper, terrified of the pain.

The Janet was with him now, she and the Neil holding him in their arms. Their anxious voices were like insects droning on and on in the warm autumn sunlight, whispering and saying it was all right, kissing him, everything would be okay, it was just too many people for him all at once and it wasn't fair.

'I'm sorry, Uncle Andy,' he said later, when they dried his eyes and led him back inside. 'I said bad words. I won't say them again.'

He returned to his seat, and when no one was looking the Gillie reached under the table and squeezed his hand. He smelled the fear of wanting on her skin and began to smile, knowing he wouldn't have to wait much longer before she was his.

That was what Mr Harriman promised, and Mr Harriman never lied.

When the boy was out of earshot, having gone into the living room with Gillian Stanton to watch the Thanksgiving parade on television, Andy turned to his sister and shook his head. 'The man in Palm Springs, the guy from the trailer camp, said there was a boy who ran on all fours, that the boy and the wolf were both together when he fired the shot.'

Janet glared at him angrily. 'And that's what you've come all this way to tell me, is that it? You scared the child half to death, Andrew, and for what? To prove a point? We all know something terrible happened to him out in the desert. But you're not going to get me to believe he was looked after by a wolf. And what does it matter anyway, now that it's over?'

'But a woman was killed, Jan.'

'Eaten,' Mike said under his breath.

'My God, I just can't believe the two of you,' she replied. 'Matt's not a savage. He's a thinking, feeling human being. His teacher's amazed at the progress he's making. He reads and he can talk and he's adjusting, every day he's adjusting better than the day before.'

'But you heard him yourself, Jan. Where the hell do you think he picked up words like that?'

'I have no idea. Kids at school . . . I don't know. But ever since we've shown interest in the child, you've been opposed to our plans. And why aren't you saying anything, Neil? Don't tell me you agree with him?'

Ina Stanton got up from the table and began to clear the dishes. Janet made a move to help her, but she waved the offer aside. 'Leave it, the exercise'll do me good.'

When the swinging doors closed behind her, there was momentary silence at the table. Turk came back into the dining room, and though Andy had been told the dog was very protective of his nephew – And how can I call him that when I know something's terribly wrong here? he asked himself – Turk went right over to him and laid his head against his lap, looking at Andy searchingly with his golden eyes.

'At least you've made one friend,' his sister muttered.

'Come on, Jan, give me a break. If I can't be honest and air my feelings – '

'No, you give me a break,' she interrupted. 'When Neil

and I need your support, you end up giving us the very opposite. Why is that, Andrew?'

He glanced at Turk. The dog's eyes were now half closed, his tail making slow sweeps at the air. 'You really don't want to know, Jan, so why ask?' He turned to Mike, saying it was time they started back, they still had a long drive ahead of them.

'But I do want to know,' she insisted.

He hoped Neil might say something to make peace between the two of them. But his brother-in-law looked just as disturbed as Janet.

'I'm worried about you,' he finally admitted.

'Worried?' she exclaimed. There was a hysterical edge to her voice, but now wasn't the time to bring that to her attention. 'But why? I've never been better. I'm alive again, don't you see? Neil and I . . . and now Matt . . . we're a family, Andy.'

'You were a family before Matt.' He pushed his chair back and got to his feet, smoothing out the wrinkles in his trousers. Turk waited for a final pat before going back into the living room.

Neil made a last-minute effort to patch things up before they left. But though Janet smiled and kissed him goodbye, kissing Mike too and saying she hoped to see them again very soon, Andy knew that somehow he'd overstepped his bounds. Despite the attempt his sister made to be pleasant, she wasn't ready to forgive him.

'I love you, Jan,' he said as she walked them to the car. 'You forget that and I'll murder you, sis.' He forced himself to laugh, but Janet didn't even smile.

As he began to back out of the driveway, he could see the boy watching him from the window. Matthew wasn't smiling, either. He just stared and stared, a little boy with the face of an angel. And the eyes of a hunted animal.

* * *

'Everything about that kid gives me the creeps,' Mike said a moment later. 'How the hell did he know about us, Andy?'

'That we're gay? Maybe he heard them talking.'

'But they wouldn't say those kind of things, would they?'

Andy glanced at him and smiled. 'Never can tell.'

'The voice of the cynic is heard in the land.' Mike reached over and patted Andy on the arm. 'I don't know why you're letting yourself get so worked up about this, kiddo. If Janet's being overly protective I think it's understandable, at least from her point of view. Why in the world she and Neil were so hot to adopt the kid is their problem, not ours. And frankly, I don't think it's our business to pass judgment.'

The narrow canyon road zigzagged on its way down to Franklin Avenue. It was already getting dark, and with cars parked on either side, Andy tried to stay as far to the right as he could. People zoomed up these roads as if they were one-way streets. You put a nick in a Mercedes and before you knew it, it ended up costing you five or six hundred bucks, not to mention the hassle of renting another car while it was in the shop.

'Forgetting what the boy said, the words he used,' Mike went on, 'what I'd like to know is why he was so threatened by that newspaper article. Do you really think he's the same kid that guy saw running out of the trailer park?'

'His description fits Matt perfectly – the way his hair covered half his face, the calluses, the whole bit. It's the same kid, all right. Whether or not he was involved in what happened over in Morongo Valley is another story altogether.'

'The little fucker's precocious, though, ain't he? When I was his age I thought people screwed through their bellybuttons.'

A Porsche roared by, narrowly missing the edge of his bumper.

'But you gotta give your sister credit,' Mike continued.

'The kid's made terrific progress since we saw him last. I would never even have recognized him . . . hey, Andy, watch out!' he suddenly shouted.

Turk was standing in the middle of the road, wagging his tail.

Andy put his foot on the brake and pumped the horn with the heel of his hand. But the dog just stood his ground.

'Don't, you'll hit him!' Mike cried out. He grabbed the wheel, and as Andy tried to push him aside the car swerved out of Turk's path.

Andy was still trying to regain control of the wheel when a tree reared up before them and his foot jamed against the brake. Why weren't they stopping in time? Why were they still moving, faster and faster, as if something were pushing them? He tried to brace himself for the impact, but it was all hapening too quickly.

'Christ, I didn't mean . . .' Mike said.

He wanted to tell Mike not to worry, they were going to be all right. But his head went through the windshield, and where there had been words just a moment before there was only blood, rapidly filling his throat.

'Faggot, cocksucker,' a voice whispered in his ear.

Andy Hilliard didn't hear anything after that.

12

The Langley School, Friday, 24 December 1982

The Mommy was very unhappy, but the Daddy said they had to be patient with her. 'It was a terrible tragedy,' the Daddy tried to explain. 'It's going to take time for your mom to get over it, slugger. So we both have to be very understanding of her feelings.'

There were new words in his vocabulary, not the ugly words Mommy begged him never to say again the way he'd said the day Uncle Andy and Uncle Mike came for Thanksgiving, but words like *funeral* and *casket* and *service*. These new words were sad, dark words, at least when Janet or Neil said them. But he wasn't sad at all. It was Andy who wanted Az killed, who wanted to have him put away in a place where no one would find him again, like a den with the entrance blocked up so it was always without sun, cold and black.

When he heard them using those sad, dark words he was glad and Mr Harriman was glad, his friend giving him another new word to use. *Deserved*. They *deserved* what happened to them, and he smiled and snuggled up to Turk, who was such a good dog even if he wasn't as good as Az. Turk obeyed. If he'd had to, Turk would have died to save him from the Andy and the Mike. But he hadn't died. He *deserved* to live, and so he'd come back to the house, pretending never to have left.

Cars with red lights going round and round, and men dressed all in blue like the men who'd hurt him in the desert, came up the road and parked in the driveway. Mommy cried and cried, and even the Daddy cried too.

Shed a couple of tears for the faggots, Mr Harriman had said. *They wanted to use you just like Poppy did. That's why they got what they deserved.*

A whole page of boxes on the calendar in the kitchen was almost used up and still the Mommy went around with red leaking eyes, thinking of the two faggots Turk had brought down with Mr Harriman's help. What was a faggot, anyway? He didn't know, but the word was a word like *morality*, harsh and grating against his lips.

Each day when he came home from school he put an X through a box on the calendar, wondering if it would be different when all the boxes were used up. There were only a few more left, and he was getting very impatient. How much longer would he have to pretend? He wanted the Gillie but couldn't have her yet. He wanted the Janet too, but knew that would have to wait until her eyes stopped leaking. So he thought more and more of Miss Danziger with her little bird-like steps and her hard bright eyes that seemed to see right inside you. Maybe she saw Mr Harriman too, though she never said. He never smelled the fear of wanting on her, either, the way he did with the Gillie. Was that because she was stronger than he was, or because she didn't like him? Every time he looked at her she looked right back, so sure of herself it made him want her even more.

When can I have her? he kept asking Mr Harriman.

It was always soon and more soon, we have to be careful, Matthew, so that when we do take her, no one will be able to stop us.

If he pushed too hard about it, Mr Harriman's rage would explode with the same force that had sent Andy and Mike hurtling through the windshield. With rage came pain, and pain was a truth Matt had no difficulty understanding.

Behind him, Jeffrey the fat boy sang, 'God rest you

merry, gentlemen, let nothing you dismay . . .' while at the same time the girl who sat in the back who hated Jeffrey and jumped up and down a lot, waving her arms in the air whenever Miss Danziger wasn't looking at her, sang, 'Lizzie Borden took an axe and gave her mother forty whacks – '

Whack-whack-whack. Whir-whir-whir.

' – and when she saw what she had done, she gave her father forty-one!'

Too bad the little girl in the back didn't have breasts. She was as smooth there as he was, even though her thing was missing.

Then Miss Danziger went from desk to desk and wished everyone a merry Christmas and a happy Chanukah and said that she was very proud of them, every last one. It was time to get on the bus for *vacation*. That was another new word that meant no school and staying at home like he'd wanted to do in the very beginning, before the Janet made him come here. He took all his things out of his desk like digging up food from a hole, and put them into the sack the Neil had given him to wear over his shoulders.

He wasn't on the bus but a few minutes when Mr Harriman suddenly got very excited and told him to get off, it was finally time.

Time for what?

Don't I always keep my promises, Matthew? Then do as you're told and don't ask questions.

Mr Harriman told him what to say to the bus driver so the man would pull over to the curb and let him out.

'I left a *liberry* book in my desk,' he explained. 'I'll call my mommy and she'll come and pick me up.'

'You're sure, now?' asked the driver.

His head bobbed up and down. 'It's a big book with pictures. It's portant.'

'*Im*portant,' the driver told him, and he stopped at the next corner and opened the doors.

Yes, we've been good for too long, haven't we, Matthew? Mr Harriman said as he ran down the street in the direction of school. *I'm as tired of pretending as you are. But now we won't have to pretend any longer. Whir-whir-whir, my little friend.*

'Whack-whack-whack,' he said with a laugh.

No one saw him slip back inside the building that was all quiet now and getting ready for vacation. The halls were as empty as the desert when the sun was at its highest, and not even insects broke the fierce burning silence.

What if she's already gone on vacation?

She's still there, Matthew, waiting for you.

Mr Harriman was always right. The Danziger was at her desk when he came into the room, not knocking because he knew she wasn't playing horsie . . . not yet, anyway.

She was surprised to see him, and she said, 'Anything wrong, Matt? You're going to miss your bus.'

They had to be very careful now. The Danziger was sharp-eyed as a hawk. She could read words even when you didn't say them.

'I left something.'

He went over to his desk, wondering if she believed him. She was looking at him so hard that for a moment he forgot all about Mr Harriman and thought he was alone again, forced to decide things for himself. But then his friend began to giggle, and bright little pictures like dots of dancing light exploded behind his eyes. The camera's constant whirring was like a heartbeat. If the man with the beard had giggled, Matt knew he would have sounded just like Mr Harriman.

He slipped the book bag off his shoulders and pretended to stuff something inside it.

'How are you going to get home?' asked Miss Danziger.

Matt shrugged. 'I can walk. I like walking. I used to walk and run all the time.'

The teacher looked at him with interest. 'Oh?' she said, and he could see the inside of her mouth, all wet and pink and glistening. 'When was that?'

He moved closer, and now her smell was even stronger, covering him like a blanket to hide under in the dark. 'Before.'

'Where?'

'You're pretty. You're a pretty bird. I like you.'

'I like you too, Matt. But it's getting late. Maybe we should call you a cab.'

Why couldn't he smell the fear of wanting? She stepped back, stumbling a little when she caught her heel on the edge of her desk. She was frightened now, and he was glad. She'd never given off that pungent odor before, but now it was everywhere at once, and when he breathed, he drew her mounting terror deep inside his lungs. She was such a pretty bird, soft as a quail chick. Her breasts moved behind her sweater. He would hold them in both hands and smell the fear of wanting.

Do it now, hurry! cried out Mr Harriman. *She wants it, I can tell. Do it, just like they did it to you.*

Matt reached out, putting one hand on her sweater. So soft, he thought. Even though her eyes were dark and hard, her breasts were white and soft. He wanted to put his hand under the sweater, eager to touch her, skin to skin. But again she stumbled back, and the fear-smell was so strong now it masked every other odor in the room.

'You'll be late getting home. I wouldn't want your mother to worry.'

But the Mommy wasn't worrying. It was the Danziger who worried, taking sharp little breaths when he smiled and put his other hand on her sweater. All ten fingers were touching her now, rubbing back and forth until she grabbed his hands and pushed them down.

'You know we don't do that here,' she said.

'Why? It's skin.'

She didn't understand. As she took another step back she looked at him the same way Uncle Andy had when he said the bad words.

'It's not polite, Matt. We don't touch people just because we want to. We have to get permission first.'

The bitch is itching for it. Smell how much she wants it, Matthew. Give it to her before she starts to scream.

He felt the burning and the hardness and heard Mama crying. Love and pain. Poppy took off his strap. Whack-whack-whack. The leather burned like fire. He squirmed against Poppy's lap, and every time he squirmed he felt the hardness getting worse and worse like fire on the stove.

The burning and the burning . . .

He couldn't help himself. Mr Harriman wanted the Danziger and he wanted her too. But how was it done? How did horsie start?

'Go home, Matthew,' the teacher said in her sharpest, angriest voice.

Tell her to fuck herself, the ugly bitch.

But the Danziger wasn't ugly and he wanted to touch her more than ever. Skin to skin, like rubbing hands. He reached for her breasts again, only now she was so angry she slapped his hands aside and started walking to the door.

'You hurt me,' he said.

No one had hit him since the hospital, but maybe that was part of horsie. Yes, it was beginning to make sense now. First you fed together, passing food from mouth to mouth. Then you moved faster and faster, hurting each other until you shook all over and the love-pain spurted out.

'You're not being nice, Matthew. I told you already that we don't do those kind of things.'

'I do them,' he whispered. He rushed toward her, wanting to cover her mouth with his hand before she started to scream.

Behind him the door opened and he froze like a rabbit caught in the glare of headlights. Jess in the truck. Mama sleeping. A big strong feller like you shouldn't be afraid of the dark.

But I am afraid!

'I was afraid I'd missed you, Alison.'

He turned around. A Jess they called Mr Montgomery who taught down the hall was standing in the doorway, smiling his stupid Jess smile.

'No, I was just leaving.'

The Danziger sounded relieved. She hurriedly grabbed her things off the desk and took her little birdlike steps all the way to the door. Then she stopped and looked back at him. Her cheeks were flushed, and fear still came off her like sweat from running after game.

'Maybe you can give Matt here a lift,' she said. 'He missed his bus.'

'Sure,' said Montgomery. He was a short, stocky Jess with lots of curly hair that touched the tops of his shoulders, making a big fuzzy circle like a mane around his face. 'No problem.'

Matt followed them out of the classroom, the Danziger hurrying on ahead as if she couldn't get away from him fast enough. When the Montgomery put his hand on his shoulder, he pushed it aside.

'We don't touch people 'cause we want to,' he said in a high, mincing Danziger voice, like a bird that knew how to talk. 'We have to get permission first.'

Mr Montgomery looked at him as if he couldn't believe his ears. 'Sure, Matt, whatever you say,' the teacher murmured.

The Montgomery started down the hall. Matt followed

after him, walking through the trail of Miss Danziger's fear. The sharp, biting scent reminded him of stepping-stones leading across a stream. If only the Montgomery hadn't come barging into the room, if only he'd thought to lock the door, he could have hopped from one stone to the next, catching Miss Danziger before she had a chance to escape. But now she was gone and *vacation* was a long, long word, lots of boxes on the calendar and lots of time to wait.

The dream of the room with the pipes, the man with the beard, the bed and the camera and the figure hidden beneath the sheets, came with increasing frequency. Sometimes Janet awakened from the nightmare with a soundless cry. Sometimes she slept right through it, the dream always ending when the boy began to slip away from her, his features melting and dissolving like wax running down the side of a candle.

On the nights she was spared this recurring vision, she invariably dreamed of her brother. Occasionally she saw Andy as a child, and they would be playing together just as they did when she was a little girl. But usually he looked as if he'd just left her house, and it was still Thanksgiving. But always he would try to tell her something, and always the words got garbled and she couldn't make them out. As she struggled to understand what he was saying, Andy would gesture with growing desperation, his mouth opened so wide she knew he was shouting, even though she couldn't hear him.

When she was awake, she thought of him, as well, particularly the harsh words they'd exchanged before he left. There were no witnesses to the accident, and even the police expressed surprise that it had resulted in two fatalities. No doubt he'd intended to brake, they surmised, hitting the accelerator by mistake. That was the only explanation they could think of which would account for the force of the impact.

Although she tried to immerse herself in her work, it was impossible to concentrate, to lose herself in a world of her own devising. So for the time being the boy she had named Az remained suspended in time, yet to fulfill his fictional destiny.

'We've got to get you out of the house,' Ina told her as they sat in the kitchen, each clutching a mug of coffee. They hadn't spoken in several minutes, but now her neighbor broke the uneasy silence. 'Here it is almost Christmas already and where's your spirit, Janet? It's been nearly a month now. You have to get on with the business of living.'

'Have you ever lost a brother?' she said bitterly. When Ina didn't answer, a look of embarrassment passing quickly across her face, she added, 'I'm sorry, but please don't sit here and tell me it's time to stop mourning.'

'But it is time. You can't help him now. But you can still help Neil and Matt. They need you.'

'And I need Andy!' she cried out.

She wasn't dreaming, and yet it was still a nightmare all the same. She remembered that when the police drove up to the house she and Ina were clearing the dishes and putting the leftovers away. Such a cozy domestic scene. The bitter aftertaste of her argument with her brother would soon go away, and she promised herself to give him a ring in a few days, see if they could come to some kind of understanding. But death denied her the happy ending she always saved for her novels.

The sound of a car pulling into the driveway startled her out of her memories. Janet stiffened, wrapping her arms around herself, thinking it was the police and hearing the somber words they had spoken. But it was only Matt, who walked right past her when she went to open the door for him. Sullen and tight-lipped, he barely acknowledged either her or Turk, and a moment later she heard his door slam.

Why hadn't he taken the bus, the way he always did?

'I missed it,' he told her when she knocked on his door. 'A teacher took me home.'

'You okay?'

'I'm on vacation.'

If he meant that to be a joke, it didn't sound like one.

Back in the kitchen Ina still wasn't ready to call it quits. 'You need a night out,' she insisted. 'Why don't the three of us have dinner together? There's a great new Thai restaurant just opened on Sunset. Chicken and coconut soup, mee krob – '

'What is this, be kind to Janet day?'

'Nope, it's be kind to Ina and Neil day. Besides, we deserve it, don't you think?'

Janet nodded, knowing that Ina meant well, that her neighbor was only trying to be helpful. But she hadn't made any arrangements for a baby-sitter, and since it was Christmas Eve, it was highly doubtful she'd be able to line up anyone on such short notice.

'Even with Turk standing guard?' Ina asked.

'I still wouldn't feel comfortable.'

'There's always Gillian,' suggested Ina. 'I don't think she's made any plans. She can come over and the two of them can watch TV. What do you say?'

It seemed a strange way to spend Christmas Eve. But since she wasn't celebrating this year, having declared a moratorium on the entire holiday season, what did it matter?

'I want to say no.'

'But you're going to say yes, aren't you?' Ina replied.

Janet didn't have the strength to argue. 'Guess I've been outvoted.'

Ina grinned triumphantly. 'By at least forty pounds.

If Neil hadn't stayed after school to attend the faculty Christmas party, Alison Danziger would never have gotten hold of him.

'If I've caught you at a bad time, I apologize. But it's imperative I see you, Mr Kaufman.'

'Is Matt all right?' he asked, suddenly frightened that something had happened to his son. 'He's okay, isn't he?'

'The boy's fine, Mr Kaufman. I'm the one who's . . . I have to talk to you. I just can't go into it on the phone.'

His fears temporarily allayed, he said, 'May I ask what this is all about? I mean, I know it must have something to do with Matt – '

Danziger cut him short. 'I'm at the top of Beverly Glen, maybe ten minutes away. Can't we please do this in person?'

One of the other teachers stuck a glass of wine in his hand, urging him to drink up. 'Do what?' he asked, turning away so his friend would know the call was important.

'Talk about Matthew!'

What the hell was she shouting about? It was Christmas Eve. What did she want from him anyway?

'Okay, okay.' He was annoyed now, and not afraid to let her know it. 'Gimme your address. I've had one glass of wine too many, so . . .'

'That's all right. I'll make a pot of coffee.'

Later, he couldn't even remember how he got there, or how he found his way to her apartment. She lived in one of the new condo complexes that straddled the top of Beverly Glen Canyon – *When you're thinking of rustic elegance, think of us!* – overlooking Beverly Hills on one side and the Valley on the other. Everywhere he looked neat little overpriced tract houses were set down like pieces on a

Monopoly board, and here and there Christmas lights shone through the twilight.

A pinecone wreath with plaid ribbons hung from Alison Danziger's front door. He leaned against the doorbell, hoping the coffee was ready. There were cops out everywhere – he counted three patrol cars just coming up Beverly Glen – and the last thing he wanted was to be cited for driving under the influence.

If Janet had opened the door he probably would have fallen right into her arms. But when Matt's teacher undid the locks he straightened up and tried to tell himself to act his age, Christmas or no Christmas.

'Please,' the young woman said, and she even took hold of his elbow and led him inside.

Neil had met her during Open School Week. He'd been favorably impressed, for she struck him as a no-nonsense kind of person who took her work very seriously. And judging from the progress Matt had made over the last few months, he had no doubts about her abilities.

'I'm sure you find this all very unusual,' Miss Danziger said as she showed him into the living room.

'It definitely falls under the "very unusual", yes.' He tried to grin, then abruptly changed his mind, deciding a smile would only make him look as drunk as he felt. 'But if that coffee's ready . . .'

It was, and after she poured him a cup she sat across from him, eyes on her tweed-skirted lap. 'What I have to say may not be very pleasant to hear, Mr Kaufman.'

'Oh, it's gonna be one of those kind of days. Well, cheers.' He raised the coffee to his lips, and when she didn't return his smile something clenched at the back of his throat. Pull your head together, he told himself, because it looks like we're in for rough sailing.

He settled uneasily in his seat, waiting for the lecture to begin.

But it wasn't a lecture she gave so much as a blow-by-blow of everything that had taken place just an hour or two before. 'As you can tell, I'm pretty shaken up about it,' she concluded, 'and I assure you that's not like me at all. I'm not the hysterical type, Mr Kaufman.'

Could've fooled me, he thought.

He kept that to himself, knowing he wouldn't accomplish anything by being hostile. 'Now, let me get this straight, Miss Danziger. You say the boy attacked you?'

'Not attacked. *Tried* to.'

'Tried to what? He's only ten or eleven years old.'

'And big for his age.'

'So?'

'I've had sufficient training to recognize aggressive behavior when I see it. If my colleague hadn't come in when he did – '

Neil eyed her with growing disbelief. 'You're not serious, are you? I mean, come on, this is ridiculous. Even if that's what was on the boy's mind, and I'm far from convinced it was, he's not even capable of it, biologically speaking.' He was fast losing his buzz, and though he wanted to laugh, there was something about the way the teacher reacted to this information that killed any urge he had to take her story lightly.

'Whether the boy's already reached puberty isn't the point. It's the attempt he made that I'm talking about, not the act itself.'

Neil glanced around the living room, hoping to get a clue to what the woman was like. He had a feeling she was a hysterical virgin, given to seeing rapists loitering on every street corner. Probably if he breathed too heavily she'd accuse him of making advances.

'So he touched your breasts. Christ, I wanted to touch my teacher's boobs when I was his age too. The boy's been through hell and back again, Miss Danziger. One of the reasons we enrolled him at Langley was because you people are specially trained to deal with a youngster like Matt. To expect him to be completely socialized in just a couple of months is not only unrealistic, it's unfair.'

'It's also unfair that I know next to nothing about your son's past history. If I'm to do a competent job, Mr Kaufman, I have to know what I'm up against.'

'You're up against a little boy who was left for dead in the middle of the goddamn Mojave Desert!'

The teacher came to her feet and walked to the picture window with its view of 'rustic canyon elegance'. Behind her, lights twinkled in meaningless patterns, signaling nothing but a temporary stalemate. When she finally turned back to him her lips were set, and she seemed more sure of herself than ever.

'Those are the facts. Whether I could have overpowered the child – if it were necessary, and we'll never know that, will we? – has nothing to do with why I wanted to see you. I think it would be best for all concerned if you saw to it that Matt was thoroughly tested before school resumes in January.'

'Tested?' he exclaimed. 'What kind of testing are you talking about? He was tested at Eisenhower Medical. He was tested at San Andreas State. He's had more effing tests than any six kids put together.'

Danziger eyed him coolly, refusing to lose her composure. 'I'm talking about a thorough psychological workup. It's very possible Matt might be – ' Here she hesitated, as if afraid to say what she was really thinking.

'Go on, tell me. You've just about accused a ten-year-old of wanting to have carnal knowledge of you, so at this point I wouldn't be fazed if you called him Jack the Ripper.'

'Matt may be schizophrenic for all we know.'

'Jesus, now I've heard everything.'

'Obviously you don't know much about schizophrenia. And while I don't pretend to be an expert, I'm able to see Matthew with considerably more objectivity than you are. When I was a graduate student, Mr Kaufman, one of my professors took us on a field trip to San Andreas State.'

He started to groan, but that didn't stop her from continuing.

'Not a very pleasant place, I agree, but quite typical of most state-run institutions. But that isn't the point. We were given an opportunity to meet with several of the patients and observe them close-hand. One of them was a little ten-year-old girl, the sweetest, most lovable child you can ever imagine. Only this sweet little angel was severely disturbed, so disturbed in fact that one night she managed to murder her parents. A kitchen knife, I believe. And if that weren't enough, her killing spree didn't end until she'd also taken the life of her baby brother. So please don't tell me that just because Matt's a child he's incapable of violence.'

He wasn't going to lose his temper. After all, he was a professional too, a fellow teacher. But he sure as hell wasn't going just to sit here while she rattled off a list of horror stories, each one guaranteed to be more gruesome than the next.

'Thank you for a wonderful Christmas present, Miss Danziger. You've made my day . . . maybe even my week.'

Neil got up to leave, and still she stood there looking grim and totally in control of her emotions. Let her shed a goddamn tear, he thought, and maybe we'd have something to talk about.

'If you think it gives me pleasure to tell you these things, you're sadly mistaken. I hoped to do Matthew a service by asking to see you. If you want to play overprotective father, that's one thing. But if you have any sense of responsibility to your son, you'll see to it that he's examined by a competent psychiatrist.'

And afterward we'll see to it that he's taught by a competent teacher. But he didn't say that, much as he would have liked to. As threatened as he was by what the woman had told him, he couldn't help but recognize the sincerity of her motives. It hadn't been easy for her to discuss these things, just as it wasn't easy for him to accept them.

Neil heard himself sigh, but it did nothing to alleviate his anxiety. 'I'll take care of it, soon as we can line someone up. But if you'd feel more comfortable having Matt removed from your class – '

'Why don't we talk about that after he's been tested?' The teacher raised her lips in a faint smile. 'Please understand one thing, Mr Kaufman. I like your son. I like him a great deal. That's why I'm as concerned about him as you are.'

Concerned about him or frightened of him? Neil wondered. It seemed to be six of one and half a dozen of the other.

Despite all that he'd had to drink, he was suddenly very sober.

13

It was only after he'd given himself a little time to digest what Alison Danziger had told him that Neil began to feel as if he'd been had. Although he knew very little – probably next to nothing, he had to admit – about schizophrenia, he did know that the psychiatrists at San Andreas State would never have recommended the boy's release had any of them had the slightest suspicion that was the root of his problems.

After all, an entire medical review board had gone over the youngster's case in excruciating detail. And not once had the word *schizophrenia* been mentioned. If it had, he was certain they would have turned down the application for adoption without thinking twice about it.

No, schizophrenia wasn't the problem, but maybe an overactive imagination might be the answer. Matt exhibited a good healthy curiosity, and despite his current preoccupation with sex and the parts of the male and female body, it still wasn't something to lose sleep over. Even Janet had admitted that he wanted to touch her. He'd probably never known a mother's kindness, and now it was nothing more than a necessary stage he was going through in his development.

The more he thought about all of this, the angrier he became. The woman had a goddamn nerve to sit there on her high horse and tell him he had a sicko on his hands. If she was so threatened by a ten-year-old, he hated to think what would happen if someone her own age tried to put the make on her.

Schizophrenic my ass, he thought.

But in the back of his mind there remained just the smallest kernel of doubt, doubt that wasn't helped any when he thought of what had happened at Thanksgiving. So, even if he was ninety-nine percent certain there was nothing wrong with the boy, he promised himself to talk to Janet about it, and see if they could arrange for a shrink to put the last of his uncertainties to rest.

By the time he got home he found her dressed and ready to go out, looking better than she had in weeks. Before he had a chance to ask her what was going on and why she'd decided to give in to a little Christmas cheer, Matt raced down the hall and threw himself into his arms.

'I missed you, Daddy,' he said, hugging Neil tightly. 'Where were you?'

'At school, slugger. How's my big boy, behaving yourself?'

Matt nodded solemnly. 'I'm always good, Daddy.'

Neil went into the bedroom to change, Janet going over the plans she and Ina – 'Mostly Ina,' she confessed – had made for the evening. But as glad as he was to see her feeling better, there were still Alison Danziger's remarks rattling around in his head.

'Who's gonna baby-sit?' he asked.

'Gillian. She's promised to teach him how to play Monopoly.'

No, he wouldn't tell her about his meeting with the teacher, not right this minute anyway. She was in too good a mood, and after all that she'd been through in the last month, he didn't want to say anything that might give her cause to be unhappy.

'Why don't we get takeout?' he suggested instead. 'I can go down the hill and pick up some Chinese.'

Janet made a face. 'We've had Chinese three times this week. And anything we make is better – '

'I know, I know,' he said with a laugh. 'We can cook

anything better than they can. But there's always pizza. Or I could go down and pick up the Thai food and bring it back.'

'I just feel like getting out, Neil. It's been weeks now. And Gillian's perfectly capable of taking care of Matt. You know how well they get along.'

Knowing when he was outvoted, Neil went into the bathroom to take two aspirin. He had the makings of a vicious hangover.

'Now, don't open the door for strangers, Gillian.'

'Yes, Mother.'

'And make sure to lock up after we're gone.'

'Yes, Mrs Kaufman.'

'And put the chain on while you're at it.'

'I won't forget, Mr Kaufman.'

'There's plenty of pop in the fridge. And you'll find a bag of potato chips in the pantry. There are pretzels there too, I'm pretty sure. And if you guys get hungry, there's some Häagen Dazs in the freezer.'

'They won't get hungry, Janet. They just had dinner,' said the Neil. He held the door open while soft plump Ina from next door and the Janet who smelled of flowers that came from a little bottle in the bathroom marched past him, their heels going clip-clop-clip in the chilly night air.

'Bring back an egg roll, Mother,' Gillie called after her.

'They don't serve egg rolls at Thai restaurants.'

'Then something else – I'm starved.'

Plump Ina made a funny face. She looked like she was wearing a blanket with her head sticking out at the top, so big and meaty that he and Az would have been able to eat off her for days and days.

When the door finally closed and the Jesses all drove away, and the Gillie put the chain on the door and made sure it was locked, he smiled his secret smile and followed her into the kitchen. She said she was 'starved, absolutely famished', and ripped open the bag of potato chips and went 'yum yum yum', just like Jeffry the fat boy.

'You want some wine?' asked the Gillie. She had a secret smile too, and now she showed it to him before she opened the refrigerator and took out the big green bottle of wine. 'You won't tell them, will you?'

He shook his head.

'Promise?'

Mr Harriman always kept his promises, and so did he.

''Cause my mother would really get pissed off at me if she knew. You want some?'

He shook his head, even harder than before.

After she poured herself a big glass, and he thought of getting out the ketchup (the Mommy was always saying, 'What do you do, drink that stuff?' and he did and she never knew) and pouring himself a big glass of it, too, they went back into the living room.

The game that was called Monopoly was set up on the floor in front of the TV. Turk was lying on the couch, watching them through half-closed eyes. Good dogs didn't get up on the furniture. That was a rule.

But rules, Mr Harriman had told him, were made to be broken.

'That's good stuff,' Gillian said after she took a sip of the wine. She looked very pleased with herself, and when he kept staring at her she glanced down at her shirt that had a picture of a big red tongue sticking out of a big red mouth and the words ROLLING STONES written across the top. 'I didn't spill any on myself, did I?' she asked.

He barely heard her. Behind the big red tongue her flesh was warm and soft. He wanted to touch her, skin to skin. Only this time no one would come *barging in* to stop him from doing what he *deserved*.

'You sit down over there,' she said. She crossed her legs and got comfortable, waiting for him to join her.

But even though he did as she asked, he had no intention of sitting there for very long. The game he wanted to play was called horsie, not Monopoly.

'Boy, you got big eyes tonight.' The Gillie shook her head like she was annoyed at him, then started arranging the Monopoly money in piles, each one of a different color.

'What's it mean, "big eyes"?'

'The way you keep staring, Mattie. Hasn't anyone ever told you it's rude to stare like that?'

'No. If something looks pretty I want to see all of it.'

'Jeez,' she said under her breath, 'you're weird, all right.'

'Weird?'

'Forget it, Matt. Now, these are the rules.'

She went on and on, but he didn't hear her. He was too busy watching the big red tongue. She took another sip of the wine, and inside her shirt her breasts moved up and down like she had two little furry animals sticking to her chest.

He reached across the Monopoly board, but the moment he touched her she knocked his hand aside.

'Don't be fresh. You're too young for that kind of stuff anyway.' She looked annoyed again, but then her freckles darkened and then she turned away, almost as if she were afraid to look into his *big eyes*.

Abruptly he got to his feet. Turk started to get off the couch, but he motioned the big yellow dog to stay where he was.

'Where're you going?' Gillian called after him.

'Kitchen.'

To get something to eat, because first you pass the food from mouth to mouth before the shaking starts. Then the jiggles and the groaning and that's how it's done because I've seen it all with my own big eyes.

He giggled to himself and found the bag of potato chips Gillian had left behind. Potato chips were greasy and made your skin shine wherever you touched them. They were salty too, but salty he liked, and he stuffed as many into his mouth as he could, chewing them up but making sure not to swallow.

When he came back into the living room half the wine in Gillie's glass was gone. She was leaning back with her palms flat on the carpet, the little pointy things at the end sticking up against her shirt with the fat red tongue.

Cockteaser, Mr Harriman called her.

He didn't have time to ask what that meant, because the Gillie said, 'What've you got in your mouth?'

A secret.

He wanted to laugh, but if he laughed he'd swallow the potato chips, and that wasn't how you passed food from mouth to mouth. Az did it for him in the long-time-ago. The Kaufmans did it too, feeding together before they shook each other into the love-pain. Now it was the Gillie's turn, and he walked over to her and pushed his face real close to hers and opened his mouth.

She was supposed to open her mouth too. That was how it was done when he was little, because his teeth weren't big and strong like the ones Az had. But now she scooted back along the floor.

'Gross,' she kept saying, wiping her lips again and again with the back of her hand. 'I'm gonna barf, that's so gross, showing me all the food in your mouth.'

If she didn't want to feed she didn't want to play horsie. He swallowed the chewed-up potato chips and wondered what he'd done wrong.

But now she was giggling, and maybe that was the wine. She took her giggles and her glass into the kitchen, and when she came back she was still laughing and the glass was filled all the way to the top.

'Cheers, m'dears,' she said, raising her glass. She took a big long swallow, and when she put the glass down her gray coyote-fur eyes were nice and shiny, glisteny too like the inside of a mouth or a missing thing. 'Ready to play?'

He nodded, but instead of taking his place in front of the Monopoly board, he got down on his hands and knees and crawled over to her.

'What are you doing *now*?' she said, pressing her lips together so they got all thin and tight.

Instead of answering, he raised himself up until he was sitting on his knees and the backs of his legs, just like a gopher sticking out of a hole. Then he leaned forward, grabbing hold of her breasts with both hands.

The Gillian pulled away as if he were burning her. 'I told you not to get fresh.'

'I was only touching.'

'I don't give a shit what you call it, Matthew. Fresh is fresh!'

'But it feels good.'

'Not to me it doesn't.'

'But Mr Harriman said – ' not realizing he wasn't supposed to mention his friend's name until it was too late.

A sharp stabbing pain made him jerk back. This wasn't part of horsie. You couldn't play horsie by yourself. It was the love-pain he wanted, not the stick-pain.

'Mister who?' she said.

'No one,' he replied before the pain started again. 'I just wanted to touch 'cause it's nice. You let other people touch, so why can't I?'

The girl's eyes narrowed suspiciously. 'Who told you that?'

No one except Mr Harriman. But he couldn't tell her that he knew about the boys at school who touched her and played horsie, or the funny cigarettes she smoked that smelled like the ones Poppy used to like, or any of the other secrets his friend had told him.

'Well? Who told you, Matthew?'

'No one. Can't I just see once? I won't tell, I promise.'

Gillian made another one of her faces and shook her head. But now Mr Harriman was as excited about playing the game as he was. His friend told him just to push her down on the floor and put his hands under her shirt.

What if she screams?

No one's going to hear her, anyway. And besides, as far as she's concerned you're just a little boy.

Again he smiled his secret smile. Then, before Gillian Stanton knew what had happened, he had her down on the floor, both hands pawing at her T-shirt.

'Matthew, let go of me!' she cried out. But at the same time he could smell the fear of wanting and knew that she was only saying words, not feelings. 'Okay, okay, take a look. But if you ever blab about this to anyone – '

Blab?

She wants it to be a secret, the little slut.

'I won't tell, honest.'

He pushed her shirt up as far as it would go, thinking of the Connie with red hair and already wondering if the Gillie would let him do the same things to her. Her breasts were white and smooth, and he could see the little blue veins that looked like worms right below the surface of her skin. The pointy things at the end were wrinkled like fingertips after the bath. He wanted to touch them to see if they'd move, but she shoved his hand away.

'Satisfied?' She pulled her shirt down, unrolling the big red tongue.

As soon as he saw the words ROLLING STONES, he shook his head. 'No.'

'Well, you should be, because that's all you're gonna get.'

Gillian started to her feet, but he reached out again and pushed her down, covering her mouth with his hand the moment she began to shout. He didn't know what she was trying to say, but he didn't care. Mr Harriman was in charge of things now. Even if the Gillie hadn't given *permission*, they could still play horsie because Mr Harriman said no one would stop him now that they were alone.

So he began to shake her, throwing her back and forth on the floor because shaking and jiggling were all part of the game. Her reddish hair flew from side to side, tickling his cheeks and smelling of flowers and grass. He laughed and thought it was fun, so much fun he didn't ever want to stop. But the Gillie was still trying to get away from him, her gray coyote eyes all wide and staring, angry too. He couldn't smell the fear of wanting anymore, but Mr Harriman said it didn't matter, cunts were all the same, they wanted it even when they said they didn't. She struggled to cry out, but he kept his hand over her mouth, not the least bit interested in hearing what she had to say.

Mr Harriman was telling him just what to do. Mr Harriman had promised him the Gillie and now he wasn't going to stop, no matter what. But it was hard keeping her down on the floor and feeling skin to skin, both at the same time. Her shoulders kept thumping against the carpet, and now Turk came over, whining softly and wagging his tail.

'Horsie,' he explained, wondering if Turk wanted to play too.

When he started tugging at the zipper of her jeans, Gillian tried to bite his hand. That made him very angry, and it made Mr Harriman very angry too. So he let go of her mouth and slapped her across the face, as hard as he could. For a second he thought she was going to let her eyes leak. Instead, she raised her hand and slapped him back, calling him a little shit and dragging herself back along the floor.

He liked this new game. He liked it a lot. Horsie was even more fun than Mr Harriman had promised. He didn't want it to end just because she did, and so he stood up and smiled his secret smile that wasn't a secret anymore. Then he unbuttoned his flannel shirt because Mr Harriman said you didn't play horsie with your clothes on.

'What are you, crazy?' she said.

Crazy was wanting to die and go to heaven. He wanted to live.

'You are crazy,' she said. 'You're the craziest little kid I ever met.'

'Suckit,' he whispered. Even though he didn't know what the word meant it was still a horsie word and so he said it again, louder than the first time.

'Screw you, Matthew!' the girl shouted.

Again she raised her hand to slap him, but he caught her around the wrist and twisted her arm up behind her back.

'You're hurting me,' she whimpered. Now the smell of fear, sharp and biting, began to leak out of her skin like the tears that were now leaking out of her gray, frightened eyes.

He was glad she was in pain, because that was part of horsie.

With his one free hand he started to take her jeans off. When she tried to stop him he let go of her arm and threw her down so hard that she bounced along the floor, whimpering and letting her eyes leak even more than before.

'Matthew, please.' The Gillie was pleading now, and her eyes were eyes of fear, like an animal just before you bite down hard and the blood spurts.

'I want horsie,' he said. He pushed his jeans down to his ankles and kicked them off.

'Jesus,' she said, 'you're out of your mind, you know that? If your folks ever found – '

She was saying too many things and he didn't want to hear any more. Horsie wasn't words. It was pain. You shook and joggled and shook some more to get the white blood to spurt. He was already so hard it was hurting like fire on the stove. But the moment he pulled off his underpants she began to scream.

Gillian started running to the door, and he laughed and laughed because he knew she wasn't going to get away, not with Turk and Mr Harriman there to help him play the game. Besides, he *deserved* to play. He'd followed all their rules. He knew everything there was to know about *morality* and *patience* and words like that.

Turk leaped straight up in the air, knocking the girl sideways as she tried to undo the chain across the front door. There she was, sitting in a heap on the floor while the tears ran down her cheeks like water dripping off leaves after it rained.

Take her back into the living room, Mr Harriman said.

Then what?

His friend showed him a picture in his mind, and the picture was of the Janet and the Neil. Matt liked what he saw and knew that was just what he was going to do too. So he grabbed the whimpering Gillie's hand and began to drag her along the floor, back into the living room. Even though she was whining and making all sorts of scared sounds she wasn't strong enough to pull free.

'But I've only done it once,' she finally said when he pushed her down onto her back and stood over her, showing her his doodle and so excited about playing horsie he couldn't stop himself from laughing. 'And I'm not taking anything. And you're only a little kid, for Christ's sake, Matthew!'

Words and more words. That's all the Jesses liked to do

was talk talk talk. He was tired of hearing her yapping like a coyote. Her zipper was open, and so he bent down and undid the top snap and started pulling, hard as he could. He'd seen enough of her breasts and wrinkled red things at the ends and now he wanted to see the rest of her, especially the part with the red fur. Connie showed him, so why wouldn't she?

'This is silly, Matthew.'

If it was silly why was she staring at his doodle and making big eyes?

'Come on, please, stop it. I won't tell. You're a little kid. Leave me alone, Matthew. Come on, just leave me alone.'

On and on it went, babbling word after word while he pulled her blue jeans down and then her underpants that were tighter than his, and smooth and shiny. But now that they didn't have their clothes on and he could see her missing thing he suddenly stopped. He knew how to make the white blood when he was alone. But how did you do it with someone else?

Again Mr Harriman showed him the picture, and the picture was like at school where the Danziger was teaching him to read. Only now there weren't any words under the picture like in his books. But Mr Harriman told him that if he copied the picture just the way he saw it, he'd know how to play horsie as good as anyone else.

The Gillie was still crying and saying it wasn't fair. She'd only done it twice before and she was going to tell on him if he tried to hurt her. Mr Harriman called her a lying cunt and said she was itching for it, just like the Danziger.

'It's just not fair!' she screamed.

Was that a new rule? He didn't know and he didn't care. Before she could scream a second time he fell down on top of her because that was what the picture showed. Then he began to rub back and forth, holding her hands down on the carpet and shaking her as hard as he could.

But that still wasn't horsie.

Again Mr Harriman made the picture explode behind his eyes. Yes, now he understood. It was just the way Poppy did it, just the way he'd seen the Neil and the Tommy do it, too. But before he had a chance to do what the picture showed he suddenly slipped forward like going underwater only he wasn't wet.

It was like a mouth without teeth, and he cried out because he was afraid and surprised, and because it felt so good he wanted it this way all the time. Even the Gillie cried out, and the new smell she gave off was pungent and musky, an eager, willing smell as she put her hands on his shoulders and pushed upward, swallowing him completely.

But what was he supposed to do next?

'Okay, but slowly,' the Gillian was saying.

They were skin to skin and sweaty. She wiggled under him and pushed up again. But as soon as she began to squeeze her missing thing he couldn't help himself. Now it was his turn, and as he heard himself making sounds like all the other Jesses he'd watched playing horsie he knew the love-pain was about to start.

'Shit, not so fast,' said Gillian.

Wasn't fast good? You had to be fast to bring down game, so why shouldn't you be just as fast for horsie? Instead of asking, he fell against her and began to shake all over like he did when he was alone in his room and only Turk was there to watch him. The white blood spurted and spurted, and he kept shaking and shaking, so he knew he was doing it right because shaking was part of horsie.

Even Gillian was shaking and making whistly sounds like a big soft bird, calling in the darkness. Her heartbeat was almost as loud as his, and though they were still trembling he was ready to play all over again.

But now Mr Harriman told him to do it the other way because that's what the bitch deserved.

What other way?

His friend made a picture for him. He saw Jess in the motel room. He saw Mama on her stomach with her face in the pillows. Jess was saying, 'Now you be good, little girl, and do what you're told.' He was supposed to be asleep, but he was only pretending. He thought it was a game and Mama was playing like she played with Poppy. 'Oh, yeah, that's good, that's real good,' said Jess, and he played horsie harder than anyone Matt had ever seen.

Is that what you want me to do?

Don't you want her to know the stick-pain, Matthew?

Whir-whir-whir. Whack-whack-whack.

Then do it before she gets away.

The Gillie was just lying there with wet pieces of hair sticking to her forehead. Her eyes were closed like she was dreaming. Maybe it was a dream. Maybe he'd wake up one day and they'd be at Grandma's, and his name would be Blue again. But where would Mr Harriman be if none of this was real?

'Boy, if they ever knew.' Gillian's eyes were still closed, but now she giggled, and Mr Harriman giggled too.

He tried to stand up, but the wet, glistening mouth still held him in place. He was hard again and the burning was starting. He wasn't a Jess even if he looked like one, acted like one too sometimes. He was special and different because Mr Harriman said so. Now it was time to punish the Jesses for being mean and lying and killing Az and Mama.

Horsie made him hungry, but Mr Harriman said there would be plenty of time to feed after he played the game a second time.

'Turn over,' he said. Out of the corner of his eye he saw Turk watching them, showing the tip of his red doodle,

Mr Harriman must have made pictures for Turk, just the way he made pictures for him.

Gillian opened her eyes and smiled. She looked sleepy and satisfied, and she even stretched her arms above her head and yawned.

'Turn over,' he said. 'Please.'

'What for?'

'I wanna see.'

'Don't be ridiculous,' she said, treating him like a little boy again. 'We'd better clean ourselves up before they get back.'

She started to get up from the floor when he knocked her down and twisted her over onto her stomach. He couldn't hear what she was saying, because he was pushing her face into the carpet and Mr Harriman was making pictures again, bright bright pictures like lights on poles.

The burning and the burning and the fire and it hurt.

Don't let him hurt me, Mama! Don't let him hurt me like this!

'Feel it!' he sang. 'Just the way we like it!' he sang.

The Gillie screamed into the carpet. Mr Harriman laughed and laughed. Matt sang his angry hurting song that Poppy had taught him in the long-time-ago. Now he was laughing too, so loud he couldn't hear the Gillie anymore. This was even more fun than the other way. She was really playing horsie good, shaking and bucking on the floor while he tried to get inside her to make the stick-pain. What was good for Poppy was good for him. Mr Harriman had promised, and now the promise was coming true.

When it swallowed him, drier than her missing thing but tighter, he put his hands across her forehead and pulled her head back so he could hear her. She was screaming so loudly now that Turk began to bark. If he pulled her head all the way back would she stop? Mr Harriman said she was making too much noise and they'd better shut her up before a neighbor complained or called the police.

So he pulled back as hard as he could until he heard something that was just like a twig snapping. She suddenly made a sound like there was water in her mouth. Was it the wine? He didn't know, but Mr Harriman said it wasn't worth worrying about, just pull her head back before someone hears. So he pulled and pulled and more twigs snapped and she stopped fighting him and got very quiet.

When he finally let go her head dropped down onto the carpet. Then he rode the horsie, as hard and as fast as he could. Only now it wasn't as much fun as before because the Gillie didn't want to play. She just lay there like Mama after Jess rode her, refusing to say anything.

But Mr Harriman said it didn't matter, the bitch was only getting what she *deserved.*

14

It was nearly midnight by the time they got back from the restaurant. When they left for dinner, Neil hadn't been in any great shape to drive, and so Ina had taken them in her car. 'It's probably ice-cold by now,' she said, motioning to the doggy bag Janet held on her lap.

'I'll put it in the microwave,' Janet said as they pulled into the drive.

Neil was the first to get out, the house keys jingling in his pocket as he followed the brick pathway that led to the front door. He was feeling much better now, not because of the wine they had with dinner (he only had one glass, anyway), but because Janet seemed to be coming out of her depression. And besides everything else it was Christmas, or would be in just another few minutes. Even though she said she didn't want a tree this year, he'd gone out and bought presents for her and Matt. He even had gifts for Ina and Gillian, and wondered if now was the time to give them or if he should wait until the morning.

He rang the bell, then fished the keys out of his pocket.

'What say we do a big brunch tomorrow?' Ina suggested.

'Sounds great,' Janet said.

He rang the bell again, wondering what was taking Gillian so long to get to the door. Impatient now, he turned the key in the lock, but the chain was still in place and the door held fast.

'They're probably both dead to the world,' he muttered. He rang the bell again, jabbing at it with his finger while it squawked inside the house.

Behind him, Janet shivered. 'It's cold. Feels like winter,' she said.

'That place was a real find, don't you think?' Ina remarked. Then she raised her voice and called out. 'Gillian, get your ass in gear, honey, and open the door. We're freezing our maracas off.'

Why wasn't Turk barking like he always did when someone rang the bell? And why weren't there any lights on? he wondered. All he could see was a sliver of entryway, just a slice of shadow and nothing more.

'They probably fell asleep in front of the TV,' he said. 'I'll go around to the back, get in through the kitchen.'

'Gillian Stanton, open up the goddamn door already!' Ina shouted at the top of her voice.

He expected to hear footsteps, an irritated 'All right already, I'm coming, Mother.' Instead, Ina's words were greeted with silence, and by then he was hurrying around to the back.

Instead of staying by the door and waiting for him to undo the chain, the two women followed after him. When they left earlier that evening, all the lights were on. But now the house was completely dark, and even the courtesy lights at the end of the driveway were out.

What the hell was going on, anyway? It wasn't Halloween.

'Neil!'

When he turned around to see what was wrong, Janet was pointing to a window at the side of the house, where the guest bath was located.

'What is it?'

'Oh, my God!' Ina suddenly cried out. 'Gillian!'

The window was broken, one of the panes pushed in from the outside.

Ina was already running down the path, and by the time he and Janet caught up to her she was pounding on the kitchen door, screaming Gillian's name over and over again.

'Everything's gonna be all right,' he heard himself say. It was as if someone else were doing the talking for him, Neil the teacher as opposed to Neil the father. He unlocked the kitchen door and now it was his turn to raise his voice, shouting for Matt while he reached inside and fumbled for the light switch.

His hand went up to his mouth, and he stepped back, not letting either of them inside.

'What's wrong? What's happened to them?' Ina demanded.

Janet just looked at him, and the color drained from her cheeks, leaving her with a sickly pallor. She stood there clutching Ina while she waited for him to tell them everything was going to be all right.

But it wasn't all right. It wasn't all right at all.

'Call the police,' he said, barely able to speak.

'Oh, Jesus, what is it, what's happened?' Ina moaned.

'I don't know yet,' he replied, amazed that he was still able to sound rational. 'Go to your house, Ina, and call the police. You and Janet stay there until they come.'

'But, Neil, I don't want you to – '

'Please, Janet, just do as I say.'

He waited for them to back off, Ina suddenly looking half her size. Faced with the enormity of what might have happened, he stood there trembling as Janet helped Ina down the path. Only when they were no longer in sight did he dare to open the door again.

Under the harsh fluorescent glare of the kitchen lights the blood didn't look real. It seemed more like paint, a muddy, brownish shade splattered across the walls and floor. He thought of the Manson slayings, but the blood that had dripped down along the front of the refrigerator didn't spell out a word so much as an emotion.

It was something far worse than terror. This couldn't be his house. It had to be a mistake, a place he'd read about in the morning paper.

'Matt? Gillian?' It came out a whisper, his throat so dry and scratchy he couldn't even raise enough saliva to swallow.

Something squished beneath his feet. He was walking across blood that was already tacky like half-dried paint. When he reached the swinging doors he stopped, not sure if he should go on. What if the intruder who'd gotten in through the window was still in the house? Shouldn't he just stay where he was until the police arrived?

'We already called the cops!' he shouted, finding his voice again.

Then he raised his foot and kicked the shutter doors open. All he caught was a glimpse of the darkened dining room before they swung back again.

'Matt? Gillian? Turk, are you there, boy?'

Something snapped, like a wire stretched to the breaking point. What was the good of being cautious, of exercising common sense, if they were lying somewhere inside, bleeding to death? He threw his shoulder against the swinging doors and plowed right into them, the force of the impact sending him lurching several feet into the dining room. Before he could turn on a light he cried out and stumbled back, having slammed his shin into –

What?

Neil found the light switch. It was a dining chair that he'd bumped into. It was tipped over on its side, along with several others, and everywhere he looked he saw signs of a struggle.

What happened? he kept asking himself. What in the name of God happened?

There were bloodstains in the dining room too. A pool

of blood had collected alongside the table, soaking into the carpet.

The terror he felt was now compounded by panic. They were alive. Of course they were alive. They had to be. He headed for the living room, determined to find them.

Something dark and low to the ground suddenly came streaking toward him.

'Turk! It's me!' he shouted. Maybe the dog didn't recognize him in the dark, maybe that was it.

His words came seconds too late. Turk sprang, and though Neil wanted to believe the retriever was only expressing his affection, the sheer exuberance of seeing him, when he heard the animal's low-pitched growls he knew he wasn't in for a warm reception.

The dog crashed into him, sending him stumbling back across the floor. Neil raised his arms, trying to shield his face from Turk's snapping jaws.

Was the dog rabid? Was that what had happened? No, it couldn't be. Turk was up to date on all his shots. Besides, the disease didn't come on suddenly, without any prior symptoms.

He kept shouting that it was all right. But Turk continued to leap at his face as Neil tried to deflect the blows with his forearm. He backed off, and still Turk pursued him, crouching down and snarling so viciously that all Neil wanted to do was turn and run.

The retriever darted forward, sinking its teeth into the fleshy part of his calf. As he cried out in pain he felt himself falling, while behind him Janet began to shout.

What the hell was she doing here when he'd told her to stay with Ina?

He scrambled back along the floor, glad he still had his blazer on. Turk was trying to get at his arms, first one and then the other. The tip of a canine snagged on the material, hooking him like a fish. The shoulder seam began to split and he pulled back, hoping to leave the dog with an empty sleeve and not half an arm. Turk was on top of him then, and all he could think of was to cover his face.

Something moved in the corner of his vision. Turk saw it too, but by then Janet had brought the lamp down over the dog's back. Momentarily stunned by the blow, the retriever started to slink away as Neil hurriedly pulled himself to his feet.

Janet still held the lamp in both hands, clutching it like a baseball bat. Her mouth opened and closed like a fish out of water. She was trying to tell him something but couldn't get the words out. He started toward her, just wanting to hold her, wanting to assure her everything would be all right.

'Watch out!' she screamed.

Turk threw himself at his back, and as all fifty pounds of the retriever slammed into him they both went crashing to the floor, the dog snapping its jaws and tearing frantically at his coat. Neil kept rolling from side to side as if he were on fire, trying to extinguish the flames.

'I can't . . . it's . . .' he heard Janet say, only able to see her feet now, the way she moved back and forth as if she were doing the two-step. She was trying to single Turk out from the tangle of arms and legs and golden fur that kept moving across the floor, afraid of hitting Neil by mistake.

If he could only get his hands around the animal's throat, he might be able to hold on long enough to stop him. Blood was dripping down the inside of his shirt sleeve. He could barely maintain a grip, and every time he tried wrestling Turk down onto his back the dog's teeth grazed his face, so close he could smell the animal's breath.

With a vicious cry that was fully a match for any the dog was making, Janet brought the base end of the lamp down as hard as she could. Neil saw his own terrified reflection in the lamp's gleaming brass surface, then heard something so like the crack of a bat connecting with a ball it was hard to believe it was bone, Turk's skull crushed under the force of Janet's fury.

The retriever collapsed right beside him, and blood that had the consistency of syrup began to ooze out of its nostrils. Another few inches and it would have been his head that was broken like an eggshell.

'I didn't . . . I . . .'

Janet suddenly let go of the lamp. As it hit the floor he pulled himself to his feet and just held her in his arms, not saying a word. She was trembling so violently now he didn't know what to do to help her. He just kept holding her, whispering it would be all right even though he knew it wouldn't.

'Neil? Oh, please, are they gonna be okay?'

It was Ina, calling to them from the kitchen. He stepped back, drying Janet's eyes with the side of his hand. There was a long shallow cut down the middle of his palm, and blood was still seeping out of the wound.

'Have you . . . ?' Janet gave a little gasp and shook her head, trying to find the words that were dammed up inside her. 'Are they . . . ?'

'I don't know yet,' he said softly. 'Go back inside.' He motioned with his eyes to the kitchen. 'Stay there with Ina until I come back.'

'Oh, Neil, why . . .'

'Please, honey, just do as I say. The police'll be here any minute.'

With a final glance at Turk lying motionless on the floor, Janet backed out of the dining room. Neil could hear Ina weeping as he went on into the living room, turning on the overhead track lights and then the lamp near the couch.

There was blood here too, and he found himself wondering where all of it had come from. He didn't want to know, yet he still had to find out. This room looked less disturbed than the others, and as he started toward the hallway on his way to the bedrooms he stopped short and slammed his eyes shut.

'Oh, Jesus . . .'

That was all he could say as his throat constricted and then his stomach. He was weeping but his eyes were dry. He wrapped his hands around his waist and tried taking deep breaths, knowing they needed him now, more than ever. He had to be strong. He couldn't allow himself to give in to his emotions.

But how could he not?

Gillian was lying there just inside the hallway, naked except for the tattered remains of her polo shirt. She looked as if she were sleeping, one arm tucked under her head. Maybe she was still alive; maybe he'd gotten to her in time.

Neil crouched down alongside her and ever so gently turned her over onto her back. He saw the white glint of bone, the torn and ragged strips of flesh, and knew he was going to be sick. Gillian's arm was severed at the elbow, looking as if it had been ripped off by something or someone possessed of incredible strength.

Gagging, Neil stumbled into the bathroom, bending over the toilet. He tasted vomit on his lips, and the back of his throat began to burn as if he'd swallowed acid. It was Turk, he kept telling himself. It was Turk who'd gnawed on her body, Turk who'd managed to chew her arm off. But only after her death. *After.*

Neil held onto the bowl with both hands until the sickness gradually subsided. Then he hurriedly dried his mouth with the torn sleeve of his jacket and went on down the hall to Matt's room. But even before he got there he saw his son, lying in the doorway.

'No, no, no,' he kept moaning, and the word rose and

fell like waves beating at him and trying to drag him under.

Unlike Gillian, the boy was fully dressed. As Neil bent over him, turning him onto his back and pressing his head against Matt's chest, he could hear a faint but steady heartbeat. Ugly bruises encircled the child's neck, and a thin ragged line of blood had dried along the side of his face.

But he was alive. Alive! Neil wanted to cry out. Instead, he lifted Matt up in his arms and started to carry him back into the kitchen.

The manic wail of a police siren broke the silence. He saw the flashing red lights reflected in the living room windows, and when he pushed the shutter doors open the police were already there. The moment he came through the doors they raised their rifles.

'Don't! It's my husband!' Janet cried out.

'Where's Gillian? Where's my baby?' Ina began to scream.

Janet looked at him and knew the answer even before he found his voice.

'I want my baby, I want to see my baby!' Ina kept shrieking.

He knew he would still hear her frenzied sobbing long after this night was over.

Overtired. That's what Janet's mother used to tell her when she was little and couldn't fall asleep. If only she could close her eyes. If only she could wake up and know it was another nightmare, like the one she'd had for weeks now.

An ambulance had taken Matt to Cedars-Sinai Medical Center, down on Beverly and San Vicente, a second ambulance taking Ina to the same hospital, where she was immediately put under heavy sedation. The Kaufmans had followed in a squad car, sitting side by side in the back seat, holding each other's hand and unable to say anything.

Numb. That's what she felt. Overtired and numb and unable to accept what had happened. They'd only been gone a couple of hours. How could something like this have taken place? Why hadn't Turk warned them in time? Surely they would have been able to run out of the house if he'd started barking. And why had the dog attacked Neil, instead of attacking . . . who? Janet didn't know, but as she sat on the couch in Matt's hospital room she kept asking herself these questions, wondering if she'd ever know the answers.

'He's going to be all right,' Neil murmured as he sat beside her.

'I know, but Ina . . .' She didn't know what else to say. She leaned against him, wanting to cry but so stunned by what had occurred she couldn't even do something as simple and basic as that.

The door opened and the surgeon who'd seen Matt in the emergency room came in, along with a man who wore a blue polyester suit and carried a folded newspaper tucked under his arm. Janet vaguely recalled seeing him back at the house.

The doctor went over to the bed, examining the chart he'd brought in with him. He looked down at his patient, then gingerly palpated Matt's neck. At the same time, the man in the blue suit glanced at them and nodded grimly. 'What about the dog?' he suddenly said.

The surgeon turned to him and shook his head. 'Not what you'd expect.'

'Who is he?' she whispered to Neil.

'Detective. Homicide.' He got slowly to his feet, breathing like a man who'd just run a marathon. 'What do you mean by that, Doctor?'

The physician glanced at Janet. 'Does your – ?' he started to say.

'She knows what happened, yes.'

'We're not finished with all our testing, but preliminary examination by light microscopy failed to reveal evidence of the rabies virus.'

'But . . . but I saw her. What it did to . . . and the way it attacked me,' Neil stammered in disbelief.

The doctor shrugged. 'A dog can turn on its master even if it doesn't have rabies, Mr Kaufman.'

'And my son?'

'The dog didn't attack him, if that's what you mean.'

'What about the bruises around the boy's neck?' The detective spoke up. He was a thin, rumpled-looking man, and as he waited for the surgeon to reply he slapped the newspaper back and forth against his hand.

'It looks like the ecchymotic areas – ' the doctor began, when the detective cut him short.

'Can you translate that for us, Doc?' It was two in the morning, Christmas Day, but the detective looked wide awake.

The surgeon smiled patiently. 'Bruises,' he explained. 'Contusions. The ones around the youngster's neck seem to have been inflicted by a length of rope, possibly a necktie, something on that order.'

'Not someone's hands?' said the detective.

That was what Neil had first thought when he found Matt and noticed the purplish bruises around the neck. But the doctor shook his head. 'Definitely not,' he told them. 'These contusions aren't compatible with bruises that could have been inflicted by someone's hands.'

Janet asked if there were any other injuries.

'There was a scalp laceration which required suturing in the emergency room. In addition, he sustained a cerebral contusion at the time of the head injury. Skull films were normal, however, and the neurological examination was otherwise intact. But that's why the boy's still drowsy.'

The detective suddenly turned to the Kaufmans with a sheepish expression. 'Ray Torres, Homicide Division,' he said by way of belated introduction. 'I'd like to ask your son a few questions if I could.'

The surgeon reacted to this request as unhappily as they did. 'I'd rather he had a little more rest. I'm sure that in the morning – '

'Mommy?'

Janet hurried over to the bed. 'Yes, sweetheart, Mommy and Daddy are here. You're going to be all right, Matt. Everything's going to be all right, honey.'

'What about Gillie?' he said.

'Hello, Matt. How're you feeling, feller?' Detective Torres stood by the side of the bed, looking down at him with an avuncular smile.

'Who are you?' he said.

'A policeman, Matt,' explained Neil. He turned to the detective. 'Couldn't this wait until the morning?'

'I have a family too, Mr Kaufman. Hate to disappoint 'em Christmas Day.'

'I realize that. But the child's been through – '

'I'd rather get it over with now, while it's still fresh in his mind.' Torres smiled, first at Neil and then at Matt. 'Do you want to tell us what happened, son?'

'Where's Gillie?' the child asked, looking anxiously at his parents.

Janet didn't know what to tell him, and she reached down and held his hand tightly in hers. 'Gillie's gone away, Matt,' she said softly.

'Did that man take her?'

'What man?' said the detective. Now he was strictly business as he got out his notebook, then uncapped a pen and held it in readiness.

'If I tell will he come back?' asked Matt.

'No, of course not,' Neil tried to assure him. He saw the fear in his son's eyes, fear which he himself had experienced just a short while before.

'What can you tell us about him, Matt?'

The child stared uneasily at the detective. 'He won't come back, not ever?'

'No, honey, not ever,' Janet whispered.

'We were playing Monopoly, when Turk started barking. We thought it was you. But then . . . then . . .' The child's eyes got very wide and he started gasping as if he couldn't catch his breath. 'He said his name was Jess!' he suddenly cried out.

'Jess who?' asked the detective.

Matt shook his head, the bandages making a faint scratching sound against the pillowcase. 'He came in through the back.'

'Didn't Turk try to stop him, Matt?'

'Yes, Daddy, but he hit him, he hit him hard. On the head. Turk fell down and Gillie screamed.'

Janet didn't want to hear any more. She wanted to turn and run, yet she just stood there, her feet rooted to the floor.

'Then . . . then . . .' Matt stopped and swallowed hard. 'He said it was a game.'

'What kind of game, Matt?' said the detective.

'I dunno, mister. He made her take her clothes off and she was crying. I never saw her cry before.'

Neil asked him if he hadn't tried to run away, but Matt shook his head. 'I was too afraid, Daddy. He said if I called out or anything he'd hit me like he hit Turk.'

'Then what happened, Matt?'

The boy looked away. Tears welled up in his eyes and began to drip down his cheeks. 'I don't 'member good.'

'Try, Matt. It's very important,' the detective urged.

Janet glared at him angrily. 'Can't you see he's had enough?'

'So did your neighbor's kid,' Torres reminded her.

'Just a few more questions, Matt,' said Neil. 'Then we're going to let you get some sleep. And tomorrow, when we take you home, we can open our Christmas presents together.'

'But Gillie won't be there, will she?'

'But she's thinking of you, I know she is,' Janet told him.

'That's why it's important you tell us everything that happened, son.'

Matt looked up at the detective, then nodded his head. 'He hit me.'

'When?'

'He was hurting her, I think, 'cause she was crying. I tried to get him to stop and he hit me. Then he put something around my neck and pulled. Tight.'

'What did he use, Matt, do you remember?' Torres asked, taking everything down in his spiral notebook.

Matt shook his head. 'I dunno. It hurt. He pushed me into the wall. My head hurt.' A last, sluggish tear dripped down his cheek. He licked it up with the tip of his tongue, then turned his head to the side and closed his eyes.

'I want a blood test run on that dog,' Torres said as he stepped away from the bed. He stuffed his notebook back into his pocket and recapped his pen.

'What for?' Janet asked.

'It went berserk, didn't it? For all we know, a drug might've been administered.'

'Like what?'

'That's for the lab boys to figure out.' And with a final glance at their son, Detective Torres headed for the door.

15

The day after Gillian's funeral, Ina came over to say good-bye, as well as to give Janet last-minute instructions about looking after the house. She planned to spend the next several weeks in Omaha with her parents. When she returned, she was going to put the house up for sale and move to a small apartment.

She'd lost a considerable amount of weight in the last week, but somehow it wasn't becoming. Her once round face had aged badly, and she looked drawn and haggard. 'It's best if I just get away for a while,' she said. 'I haven't been able to sleep and . . .' The words trailed off with a sigh. She started to go over the list she'd prepared. There were notes on the care and feeding of her house plants, notes on forwarding the mail, notes on turning on lights.

Ina sat in the kitchen and her voice droned on and on with a bleak and lifeless intonation. Janet could only nod, saying she'd look after things, and that Ina shouldn't worry.

'Shouldn't worry?' her friend repeated with a shrill and bitter laugh. 'A maniac's still on the loose and I shouldn't worry? Just keep your doors locked when you're home alone. The son of a bitch'll come back and . . . what's the use? What's the use of anything? I feel so helpless, Janet, like I'm not even in control of my own life anymore.'

Ina buried her face in her hands and began to weep, and as Matt stood in the dining room behind the swinging doors he listened to the woman sobbing and smiled to himself. An ungainly ball of black fur lay half asleep in his arms. Just two days before the Daddy had brought him the puppy, for Matt hadn't stopped crying when they told him that Turk had gone away, and just like Gillian he wasn't coming back.

He'd named the twelve-week-old Labrador retriever Jip, because that was the name of the dog in his first reader. Mr Harriman spoke to Jip just the way he spoke to Turk. Even though he was only a puppy, Jip was learning quickly now that Mr Harriman had explained what was expected of him.

When he finally put the dog down and came into the kitchen, Ina had stopped crying, and she even pretended to smile when she saw him. He was sorry she was going away, because Mr Harriman said she deserved to be taught a lesson, and that if she stayed around, Matt was just the person to teach her.

Although he wasn't sure what Mr Harriman meant by that, he knew that his friend liked him a whole lot better than before, because he'd pretended good and told the story so well that everyone believed him. And even if plump Ina was going away so he couldn't teach her a lesson, he still had the Janet to play with, just as Mr Harriman had promised.

'I didn't know you got another dog,' Ina remarked when Jip followed him into the kitchen.

'Neil thinks it's important for him,' Janet explained.

Ina looked uneasily at the puppy. Then she dragged herself to her feet and headed for the door. Matt was sorry to see her go. As he waved good-bye he thought of all that good meat going to waste, and even let his eyes leak.

Ina was so moved by his tears that she turned away from the door and went over to kiss him. He wanted to reach up and put his hands on her breasts that were so much bigger than Gillie's, but he knew it was against the rules when the Janet was watching.

'You be good, now, Matt. I'll miss you,' Ina said.

Matt smiled and nodded his head. Mr Harriman said he was a perfect little angel and that soon he wouldn't have to pretend anything, he could do just what he pleased.

Shortly after the New Year, all that had happened at Christmas still very fresh in his mind, Neil found Detective Torres waiting for him when he left school at the end of the last period. Looking just as rumpled as when they first met, Torres slouched against the side of Neil's car, smoking a cigarette which he tossed away with a flick of his tobacco-stained fingers the moment Neil approached.

The detective smiled his sheepish grin, transferring the rolled-up newspaper he carried from one hand to the other. 'Sorry to bother you, Mr Kaufman,' he began. 'But there's a couple of things I'd like to talk over. Do you have time for a cup of coffee?'

If he said no, Torres would ask his questions anyway. So Neil got into his car and, with the detective following in an unmarked car of his own, drove to a nearby coffee shop several blocks from school.

'I've got problems, and I need your help,' Torres admitted when they were seated in a booth and a waitress had brought them coffee.

'That's what I'm here for, Detective,' Neil replied, trying to be cordial even though there was something about the man that he didn't like. Maybe it was the way Torres kept smiling, for by now the detective's grin had nothing to do with being pleasant. Or maybe it was the way he kept flicking his cigarette ash even when there wasn't any ash to flick. But whatever it was, Ray Torres made him uneasy, and it was difficult to pretend otherwise.

'We got back the lab report on your dog,' Torres revealed, slurping at his coffee.

'And?'

'Like the doc said, not what you'd expect.'

'No rabies, I know, or else I would've needed all those shots.' He felt a twinge where Turk's teeth had dug into his calf, glad that at least he'd been spared the painful series of injections.

'No drugs, either,' Torres added. 'But then again, your son didn't mention that the intruder gave anything to the dog. Still, judging from the animal's erratic behavior, I was hoping we'd find something.'

'But you didn't.'

'Nope. That's one dead end, so we go on to another.'

What was this all leading up to? Neil didn't know, but rather than sit there in the dark, he decided to ask.

'I'm just trying to piece everything together, Mr Kaufman. We dusted the area around the broken window for prints. Didn't find any.'

'The man could've worn gloves,' he offered.

'True,' Torres agreed with another of his trademark smiles, making it seem as if Neil were doing him a great favor sitting here and listening. 'Which brings me to another dead end. But I keep thinking, Ray, you gotta be missing something. Here's a guy gets into a house, sodomizes a kid – '

Neil stiffened, not sure if he'd heard correctly. He set his cup down, but his hands were shaking now and it rattled against the saucer, spilling some of the coffee over the side.

'Are you sure?' he asked.

Torres still wouldn't let go of his smile, even though it was grossly inappropriate for the subject at hand. 'Positive. We had no trouble finding traces of semen. The girl was raped and sodomized. Then her neck was broken.'

'Christ almighty,' Neil murmured. 'You didn't tell her mother, did you?'

'Contrary to popular belief, the department does exercise discretion when it's called for. So there you have it.' He slapped his hands against the table. 'No drugs to account for the dog going berserk, chewing off half the girl's arm. No prints. And a woman by the name of Alison Danziger who had some very interesting things to say.'

You son of a bitch, Neil thought. You goddamn, slimy son of a bitch.

But he wasn't going to get angry. He was going to keep smiling just like Torres.

'Name ring a bell?'

'Several.'

'Used to be your boy's teacher, if I'm not mistaken.'

'That's right.'

'Sensible woman, but of course that's only my opinion. But she thinks Matthew's emotionally disturbed. Big words for a little boy who's been through hell. A doctor . . . what was his name again? Abernathy, that's it. We had a nice little chat too. Very cooperative guy. Filled in a lot of blanks for me.'

Why was the detective toying with him? Why didn't he just come right out and say what was on his mind? When Neil asked him, deciding it was time he put his cards on the table, all he got in the way of reply was another phony grin.

'Do you want to tell me what this is all about, or are we going to sit here and pretend nothing's wrong?'

'But nothing is wrong, is it?'

'No, of course not,' Neil said hurriedly. He had the feeling the man was trying to trap him. But he knew just as much – or just as little – as the detective, so what was the big mystery? 'Look, I know you're trying to do your job. And believe me, I'm as anxious as you are that Gillian's murderer be apprehended. But you're barking up the wrong tree. My son told you everything he could possibly remember.'

'I know. And he even had a concussion to prove it.'

'My son's been thoroughly examined,' Neil said, on the verge of losing his temper now. 'The psychiatrist says he's fine.'

'Oh, so you did take Danziger's advice.'

'It wasn't advice. It was merely a suggestion.'

'Is that why you pulled him out of the Langley School, Mr Kaufman?' Before Neil could answer, Torres raised a wrinkled sleeve and waved at the waitress. 'Just a touch to warm it up,' he said when she came by with more coffee.

'I'm fine,' Neil told her. 'And I didn't pull him out of anywhere, Mr Torres,' he went on. 'The psychiatrist who examined Matt felt it was no longer necessary for him to be enrolled in a special school. And since you went to the trouble of getting in touch with Dr Abernathy, I'm sure he filled you in on Matt's background, in which case you probably know as much about what happened to my son as I do.'

Torres greeted that with momentary silence. 'Matt was the name of your first child, wasn't it?'

Neil leaned over the table, lowering his voice so that none of the other diners could hear. 'What the fuck does that have to do with anything?'

'Just a thought, Mr Kaufman, just a thought.' The detective reached over to pat him on the arm, but Neil pulled his hand away. 'No harm intended, believe me. But there is one other question. Has the boy reached puberty yet?'

'At his age?' Neil said with a nervous laugh. But it wasn't the question which bothered him as much as the reason why Torres had asked it.

'What age is that?'

'I don't know exactly. Ten, eleven, maybe even twelve. We don't have a birth certificate, you know that.'

'So he hasn't reached puberty then?'

'I honestly don't know.'

'You mean to say you've never seen him with his clothes off?'

Neil couldn't believe the man was really serious. Surely he didn't think Matt was responsible for what had happened. He was just a little kid, a child.

'If you're shy about these things . . .' Torres started to say.

'I don't have problems in that area, Torres. I just don't make it a habit to stand around when he comes out of the shower. Does that answer your question? Or would you rather I went home and asked the boy to pull down his pants, Dad wants to see what he's got?'

Torres's response to his sarcasm was another wave of his hand as he called the waitress over and asked for the check. 'Let me,' he said, reaching into his back pocket for his wallet. 'Only reason I brought it up is that Alison Danziger seemed to think he was sexually precocious.'

'And you're gonna sit there and tell me a ten-year-old kid went on a rampage, raped and murdered a girl who was his friend, then made up a cock-and-bull story about someone breaking into the house? That's some theory, Torres.'

Ray Torres shrugged. 'It's not my theory, Mr Kaufman. You're the one who just suggested it, not me.'

Neil drove east on Sunset, into the thick of rush-hour traffic. But there was so much on his mind that he was hardly aware he was only going five miles an hour. For one, why the hell had he opened his big mouth? Why hadn't he just sat there and let Torres do all the talking, instead of mouthing off like an idiot?

There were so many unanswered questions floating around in his head that he just couldn't be sure about anything. He remembered the doubt he'd felt after speaking to Matt's teacher. There it was again, only now it wasn't something he could easily dismiss, or hope that if he stopped thinking about it it might go away. It wouldn't go away, and that was the problem.

Why hadn't Matt ever told them what happened to him when he was abandoned? And what about Andy and Mike? Wasn't it just a little too coincidental that less than an hour after confronting the boy about the very same thing, they should both be involved in a fatal accident? Alison Danziger might be dismissed as a woman with a hyperactive imagination. Yet she firmly believed that Matt was about to molest her, and that the only reason he hadn't succeeded was because the other teacher had come into the room. And now Gillian.

Raped. Sodomized. Her neck broken.

No, of course not, he kept telling himself while he waited at the corner of Crescent Heights for the light to change. He's only a kid. But you were a kid once too, looking at dirty pictures in the alley and finding rubbers in Pop's dresser drawer, hidden under the pile of handkerchiefs. But I was already thirteen then, a bar mitzvah boy in my first suit with a smudge of mustache over my lip, wet dreams of Marilyn Monroe coming into my room and whispering, 'Give me a French kiss, big boy.'

Once he got on the other side of Highland the traffic thinned considerably, and soon he was driving up into the hills.

But what was it he said to Andy?

You'd stick it up my ass and fuck me . . .

So he does know, even if he is just a kid. But how? Who would tell a child such a thing? Was it Gillian? Did she tell him about Andy, or was it someone else, maybe one of the kids at school?

And what about the way he watched us, the way he just stood there in the doorway? Was he aroused to see us making love? I didn't think about that and I was so embarrassed who the hell wanted to look? But he's not a stranger. He's your son. He came back to you.

Daddy, it's Matthew. Take me home, Daddy. They hurt me here.

Sandy go breeway.

Janet had told him what Matt had said the night they found him standing by the bedroom door. But how could any sensible person believe that the child who'd come out of the desert was somehow linked to the child they'd lost nearly two years before? Reincarnation went against everything he believed, and he wasn't about to alter his convictions just because the boy seemed to have read his thoughts.

He braked for a STOP sign, then started down the narrow canyon road to the house. Several dark shadowy shapes moved just beyond the sweep of his headlights, scattering at the car's approach. He caught a glimpse of them before turning into the driveway. It wasn't surprising to see coyotes, especially up in the hills. After all, there were hundreds of them in and around LA, maybe even thousands. But to see six coyotes running together in a pack? He'd never heard of that before, and in all the years he lived in California had never seen more than two at any one time.

Instead of pulling into the garage, Neil got out of the car and walked back down to the road. He could hear the coyotes barking in the distance, but gradually their familiar high-pitched yelping faded away. Then he remembered that tomorrow was garbage-collection day, and that most people put out their trash the night before. No wonder the coyotes were out in full force. Tonight was the night when they really had a chance to gorge themselves.

Something was the matter with the Daddy tonight. His cheeks were stubbly, dark and scratchy, and his eyes looked red and tired, but that wasn't what was wrong. It was the way the Daddy stared that made Matt feel uneasy. Could the Neil read his thoughts like Mr Harriman? Did he know what Matt was thinking? And if he did know, why didn't he come right out and say it, instead of staring and staring and keeping his lips closed?

'I want to ask you a couple of things, Matt,' the Daddy said.

'What?'

He was afraid to look into the Neil's big, watchful eyes. He held his fork tightly in one hand, trying to show them how good he pretended. Jip was sitting under the table by his chair. Good dogs didn't beg for scraps, and Jip was a good dog with sharp little teeth. He wasn't big and strong like Az but he was fast, and fast was good for bringing down game.

'Do you remember how you told us what happened the night Gillian was baby-sitting?'

He nodded and looked down at his plate, hating the dead dry food called meat loaf.

Careful now, Matthew, careful, whispered Mr Harriman.

'Let him finish his dinner first, Neil,' said the Janet who loved him, and since love was pain, he loved her back.

'What's wrong, Matt?' said the Neil with his dark staring eyes.

'You mad?' he said into his plate of meat loaf.

'Why should I be mad at you?'

'You look mad.'

The Neil smiled a big smile that was all pretending.

Careful, Matthew. He means to trick us.

But the Neil didn't say anything else until the Janet took away the empty dishes and brought out ice cream, which was like sweet snow melting burning-cold on his tongue. Then he looked across the table with a serious face. He was bigger than Poppy and probably stronger too. It would be hard to defend himself against the Neil, and so now Matt was afraid.

If the Daddy wanted to give him a licking with the strap, how could he possibly stop him? And if the Daddy wanted to use the wet-angry-pain, would the Janet make him stop or would she be like Mama, crying and calling Poppy names but never helping more than that?

'I'm good!' he blurted out, scared the Neil would try to hurt him.

The Daddy looked confused and his eyes got smaller. 'No one said you weren't a good boy, Matt.'

Neil looked at the Janet, but she was confused now too, with small curious eyes. Had they found out what really happened? Did they know that he was the man named Jess, banging his head into a wall, using Turk's leash to make marks around his neck that hurt but Mr Harriman said it was important to fool them so that afterward, when they found him, the Jesses would believe his story?

'I just had a couple of questions to ask, that's all,' said the Neil.

'Like what?' he said, while Mr Harriman listened carefully, ready to tell him what to say.

'What happened in the desert, Matt, before you came to us?'

'Why?'

'Why do we want to know? Because it'll help us understand you better.'

'Are you afraid to tell us, Matt, is that it?' asked the Janet.

'No.'

Jip came out from under the table, smelling the fear he was giving off even though he didn't want them to think he was scared.

'Did someone leave you there, Matt? Was that how it started?'

He nodded.

'Who?' the Daddy asked.

'A man,' he whispered.

The Neil and the Janet looked at each other with something like excitement on their faces.

'How old were you?' Janet said.

'Little.'

'Do you remember your name?'

'Matthew David Kaufman,' he said as loud as he could, and Mr Harriman smiled and was glad he was so good at pretending.

Again the Kaufmans looked at each other, only now he couldn't tell what they were thinking.

'After the man left you in the desert, were you alone, or did you meet someone who took care of you?' said the Neil.

'Mr Harriman took care of me,' he said because that was true, wasn't it, and the more true things he said the better they'd believe.

But it was a mistake to tell the truth to these two Jesses who really wanted to hurt him. And just to make sure that he knew it was a mistake, Mr Harriman made the stick-pain, so hard and so sudden that Matt couldn't stop screaming it hurt so bad.

The Neil and the Janet jumped up from the table, and Jip began to bark because he didn't know if that was good or bad. They hovered over him, trying to help and telling lies, and the pain was worse than fire on the stove the accident when he was little touching where he shouldn't.

No, don't, please! he begged. I'll be good, I promise!

But Mr Harriman said he was tired of promises that were lies. *You were warned,* he said, *time and time again never to reveal my name.*

He wanted to touch himself there to pull it away so it wouldn't rip. But Mr Harriman wouldn't even let him do that, and the more he screamed, the worse it became.

The Janet and the Neil were shaking him now, and asking what was wrong, and pretending to want to help.

I warned you, said Mr Harriman. *You mustn't answer their questions, Matthew. They're beginning to distrust you, and that could be very dangerous for us. If they put you back into the hospital, then there's no escaping, not ever. You'll be all alone, Matthew, locked away like a wolf in a cage. You'll wallow in your own shit, and no one will come to clean you up. They'll watch through a hole in the door, and bring the man Jess to hurt you. And Poppy too. Yes, I saw him on the street one day when you took the bus to school. He thinks of you all the time, Matthew, and what he thinks is worse than the fire on the stove.*

'Matt, please, what's wrong?' the Janet was crying.

The burning and the burning and it only got worse and worse. I'll be good, Poppy, I'll be good only don't hurt me don't put it there where it hurts like fire don't!

'Don't!' he screamed. He doubled over, trying to get off the chair because maybe if he stood up he could pull it out and make the burning stop.

Poppy's angry hurting song died away. He lay on the floor with his knees drawn up to his chest and didn't care that they were touching and touching and stroking his cheeks and telling him they loved him. He didn't care because Mr Harriman said it was a lie and if he didn't obey Mr Harriman the pain would start all over again.

'Cramps,' he said, for that was the word Mr Harriman told him to use.

'Do you want to use the bathroom?' Neil asked with a look of concern that was a lie like all his other lies.

The man-smell made him want to puke. He hated them, all these Jesses who said one thing and did another. He would kill them all.

'What Mr Harriman were you talking about, Matt?'

'Neil!' shouted the Janet. 'Can't you see he's had enough? He's not feeling well.'

'You don't love me anymore!' he screamed at the top of his lungs.

He wanted to run and hide and get their stink out of his nostrils. The puppy ran with him, snapping at Janet's heels before racing with flopping ears down the hall. But the door didn't have a lock like in the hospital, and even though he slammed it as hard as he could, making a sound like an explosion, she followed right after him and wouldn't let him alone.

'Don't,' he said when she wanted to touch him.

She made a terrible sad sound, but it was a lie, it had to be. She'd hurt him like the Neil and the Poppy if he wasn't careful.

'But I love you, Matt, I love you,' the Janet cried with leaking eyes and breasts moving up and down, up and down, under her blouse. 'Don't you trust us, sweetheart?'

Sweetheart, he thought. She says horsie words but doesn't want to play the game with me.

She will, Mr Harriman whispered. He sounded happy again and made bright bright pictures flash in Matt's head.

If he covered her mouth with his hand and pushed her down on the bed, maybe he could take her like he'd taken the Gillian.

No, there are other ways, cleverer ways, my little friend who hasn't learned his lessons well. Say this . . .

The words were pictures he painted with his lips and tongue, saying, 'I'm Matthew, Mommy, Matthew.'

'I know that, darling.'

'I came back 'cause I loved you. But now he wants to take me away from you. You have to help me, Mommy. You mustn't let Daddy hurt me.'

'No one's going to hurt you, sweetheart. How can we hurt you when you're our own little boy? You're more precious to us than anything in the world.'

'Then why can't I be part of you?'

'But you are part of me,' she said.

'No, I'm not!' he shouted. He pushed her away and scooted up along the bed, sitting there with his legs crossed and his eyes as hard and angry as Poppy's. 'Part of you is like what Daddy did,' he said, challenging her to deny it.

But the challenge went unanswered, because the Janet didn't seem to understand. Her blond hair the color of dried grasses moved lightly against her cheeks. Her skin was so white and soft he wanted to touch it all over. She smelled of flowers, but he wanted her to smell of wanting.

'What do you mean, "what Daddy did"? What are you trying to tell me, honey?'

Such a soft, honey voice she had. Was she trying to trick him again? Should he tell her what he meant, or should he just keep pretending to be good?

Tell her what she wants to hear, Mr Harriman whispered in his ear. *Tell her that you know she's been dreaming of you. Tell her you've been dreaming too. Tell her about the room with the pipes, and lying in bed hard and burning, waiting for her to come to you.*

He shivered just to think of it, filling the wet softness of her missing thing, giving back to her the stick-pain Poppy had given him.

'I had a dream about us,' he said, not talking loud in case the Neil was listening, spying on the other side of the bedroom door. 'I was part of you like Daddy. We were in a big room together with pipes on the ceiling. And a thing to make movies. A machine.'

Whir-whir-whir. Whack-whack-whack.

He could smell fear now. Thick and moist like a heavy dew, sharp and biting like dawn in the mountains where he went to hunt when game was scarce. The more he looked at her, staring at her breasts and down between her legs where he couldn't see, the more fearful she became. He saw her tremble and smiled because he was so much stronger than her, and *cleverer* too.

'When did you dream about this?' The Janet's voice was all quivery like standing in the cold without clothes on like in the mountains.

'Ever since I watched you and Daddy together,' he said with Mr Harriman's prompting.

The Janet just kept shaking her head, blond hair flying from side to side.

'There was more,' he went on with a grin that showed all of his teeth the dentist person had made nice and even.

'I don't think I want to hear about it, not now anyway.' The Janet got up from the bed, the fear-smell dripping off her skin like sweat.

'Why?'

'Because it's wrong,' she said with a little explosion of air that made her lips flutter.

'How can a dream be wrong, Mommy? A dream is what we really feel, isn't it? In the dream I wait for you like now in bed. You come to me and I pull the covers down and I'm bigger than Daddy and you want it inside you. You know you do!'

'Don't ever say that!' she shouted. Her fear was anger now, and she suddenly raised her hand and slapped him across the face like Mama did when he was a pain in the ass pain in the ass.

He touched the red sore place on his cheek. 'You hurt me,' he said angrily. But the hurt made him hard and burning, just like when he squirmed against Poppy's lap like rubbing skin to skin.

'I . . . I didn't mean to,' the Janet stammered.

'You did!' he screamed at her. 'You want it, and you hurt me 'cause you're afraid. But I'm not afraid. I'm not, I'm not!'

The Neil was standing in the doorway now, and Matt would have tried to rip his throat out if only Mr Harriman said he could. He knew what the Neil was thinking. *Jealous*, that was the Jess word for the way he looked at him and shook his head.

'Go 'way,' Matt told them. 'Go 'way and leave me alone you don't love me you don't.'

'You're very wrong, Matt. Your mom and I love you more than anyone. We'd never desert you like – '

'Like who?' he said. They were all alike, these Jesses. They all thought they were so smart, but they weren't.

'Like your real parents,' Neil said softly and he looked ashamed, embarrassed too, with his eyes on the floor.

'You know nothin' about them, nothin',' he said defiantly. 'Mama loved me she did she did. Poppy didn't he said I was a little bastard only Mama loved me we played together and everything. Everything! Then . . . then . . .'

Don't say it! came the warning.

He stiffened, bracing himself for the pain. But the pain didn't come and he was glad and grateful and he said, I'll be good, really, I promise.

He buried his face in the pillows and wouldn't look up until he was sure they'd gone away. Jip whimpered like a baby and jumped up on the bed, licking his ear with his scratchy little tongue.

Jip loves me, and Mr Harriman and Mama and Az and Turk.

You have other friends too, said Mr Harriman.

Who?

Mr Harriman began to laugh and said it was a secret. He laughed and laughed and made more pictures, pictures like in the room with the pipes. Matt closed his eyes and the pictures got sharper and sharper, so real he was there in the room with her. He began to rub back and forth back and forth, not stopping until he made the white blood spurt and that was good, that was very very good. But not as good as with the Gillie. And not as good as when he'd finally have the Janet, all to himself.

16

A distant yapping, high-pitched and tremulous, echoed through the canyon. Neil went from window to window, door to door, making sure the house was locked up tight. Maybe his bank would give him a loan to install an alarm system. That way, if anyone tried to break in again, at least they'd have some kind of warning.

The putty was still tacky where the glazier had replaced the broken window. The carpets had been shampooed and the walls washed down with soap and water, but they still hadn't been able to get out all the bloodstains. Everywhere he looked he saw traces of what had happened over Christmas – a nick in an end table that hadn't been there before, a missing dining room chair to remind him of the one that had been sent out for repair, a dark spot on the carpet and several others on the wallpaper in the kitchen.

But these were things, inanimate objects. They could all be repaired or replaced or discarded, whatever. But Gillian couldn't be replaced. She was gone and she wasn't coming back. He wanted to cry, if only to get it out of his system. But the grief he felt for Ina was linked to the grief he felt for himself. If Matt was in any way responsible . . .

Neil couldn't even bear to think it through, and he went into the kitchen and put up water for instant coffee. He took out the container of milk from the fridge and opened the utensil drawer to get out a spoon. A slip of paper caught his eye, half hidden under a pile of forks.

One of Janet's book notes, he decided, wondering what

was the good of scribbling all these reminders to herself if she ended up stashing them away like buried treasure. But this note was typewritten.

Make Neil watch when you do it.

Have Ralph come early . . . Joy's joke about the bookends . . . Don't forget Marty hates haircuts . . . Let Ellen know how much he cares. Those were the kinds of notes he usually found scattered in the oddest places around the house. They were always handwritten too, never typed, because they invariably came to Janet when she wasn't at her desk. So what the hell was he supposed to make of this one?

Make Neil watch when you do it.

Do it? Do what? And since when was there a character named Neil in any of her books? He read them even more carefully than she did, and he couldn't recall ever coming across someone with his own name.

'What's this supposed to mean?' he asked when Janet came into the kitchen, already dressed for bed though it was still early. He handed her the slip of paper and she looked at it with a blank and uncomprehending stare.

'"Watch when you do it"?' she said. 'Watch what?'

'That's what I'd like to know. I didn't know there was someone named Neil in your new book.'

'There isn't.'

'But you typed the note, Janet.'

'No, I didn't,' she insisted.

The sudden whistling of the kettle made him flinch. He turned off the flame and looked back at her. 'Then who did?'

She shook her head. 'I guess it's a joke, I don't know.' She sat down at the kitchen table with a sigh. 'The doctor said he was fine, perfectly adjusted. Doing just beautifully, that's what he said,' she went on, apropos of nothing they'd been talking about.

Neil joined her at the table, absentmindedly stirring his

coffee long after the sugar was dissolved. Make me watch what? he kept wondering. And if Janet hadn't typed the note, then who had? Was it one of Gillian Stanton's little practical jokes? Because if it was, there was nothing very funny about it, considering what had happened. Or was Matt just playing at the typewriter one day? Make me watch *what* when you do it? And who's *you*?

'Something's wrong,' Janet said, half to herself. 'I think Matt should go in for more tests, Neil. He's . . .' And again she sighed, rather than tell him what was on her mind.

But he pressed the point. 'He's what, Janet? What's worrying you?'

When she looked up, her eyes were filled with so much pain and confusion he didn't know how to help her. 'How did he know about Matthew – the accident, I mean? How did he know the color of our old car, Neil, or that it happened on the San Diego Freeway, or how Matt reacted when we got hit? It's not possible. I don't think we ever mentioned Matthew's middle name, and he knew that too. Matthew David Kaufman,' she repeated, shaking her head. 'It doesn't make sense and it scares me. It didn't before because . . . because I wanted to believe. I don't know – something, anything. I just needed to be a mother again, maybe that was it.'

'And now?'

'I haven't stopped loving him, Neil. But . . . God, if I could only cry, maybe it'd be easier.'

Neil got up from the table and put his arms around her, kissing the top of her head. He tried to tell her they were all under a great deal of strain, that everything would be okay, that she had him to depend on and she shouldn't ever forget it.

'I'm so goddamn mixed up,' she whispered. She pulled a crumpled tissue out of the pocket of her housecoat and blew her nose. 'You know how much I love you, Neil, don't you?'

'Of course I know. We're stuck with each other, kiddo. For better or worse this is a lifetime proposition.'

'And honesty's part of that, isn't it?'

'Honesty, and trust, and caring. We're lovers, Janet, but just as important we're also friends.'

'Well then here goes, friend.' She laughed nervously. 'I've been having terrible dreams, Neil. Some have to do with Andy, and I guess that's understandable. But then there are other times when . . . maybe I should see a psychiatrist, because I just can't deal with it anymore.'

'Deal with what, hon?' He eased her chair away from the table and crouched down, cupping her face in his hands.

'It's Matt,' she said, keeping her voice down as if she were afraid he might be listening. 'I . . . I have . . . you love me more than anyone, don't you?'

'Hey, it's all right, Janet. Of course I love you, and if I haven't been – '

She put a finger to his lips. 'It has nothing to do with you. It's Matt. I've been having this dream, night after night, like when I used to have the nightmare about the car accident.' She began to describe it to him, speaking haltingly, as much terrified of the dream as she was by his rejection.

When she finally got it all out, sparing him none of the details, he was more disturbed than he cared to admit. 'Hell,' he said, trying to make light of it, 'we're entitled to dream whatever we please, Janet. I've had some pretty weird dreams too, far-out fantasies I never told you about.'

'But not incest.'

'But it's not incest, not really. Biologically he's not our child.'

'But I love him like our child, so it's just as bad. If I'm dreaming this, Neil, it means I must be feeling it. And he knows it too.'

Neil straightened up and looked at her with surprise. 'You told him?' he exclaimed.

'No, he told me. He's been having the same dream, Neil. First the way we heard Matthew's voice, the way he said he'd come back to us. Then remembering all the details of the accident. And now this. I don't know what's real anymore, I just don't.'

'He must've heard you talking about it.'

Janet shook her head. 'No, I haven't told anyone. But he knew, he knew all about it, and what I wanted to do and . . . Jesus, am I losing my mind or what?'

Or what? he repeated to himself. So Danziger was right, after all. He *was* precocious. But thinking about having sex and actually going through with it were two different things. Hell, I knew what it was all about long before I could do it, so why should Matt be any different? But with someone he calls Mom?

'If he needs help, then we'll make sure he gets it,' he finally told her. 'But there's nothing we can do about it tonight. I just want you to get some rest and try to put this whole thing out of your mind.'

'Easier said than done,' she murmured.

He found himself reacting to this with scorn and growing annoyance. He was losing his temper and he didn't know why. Or maybe he did. Maybe it was outrage, and the feeling that even if it were a dream, it was still a form of psychic betrayal. But that the youngster was experiencing the same fantasy – that was probably the most frightening thing of all.

'We'll survive this like we've survived everything else,' he replied, not knowing what more he could say. 'I'll have to sit down and have a talk with him, that's all.'

'No, please don't, Neil.'

'Why not?'

'He wouldn't understand. He sees you as a rival for my

affections. You're a threat, and he thinks you want to hurt him.'

'He said that?'

Janet nodded unhappily.

'Well, that's just great. That's just terrific.' A bitter lump rose in his throat. He had tried everything possible to help the boy, loving him like his own son. And what was the result? He ends up hating my guts, Neil thought. 'Maybe they were wrong, Janet, and that's what we have to start dealing with. Maybe he wasn't ready to leave the hospital. Maybe this is just too much for him.'

'Neil, you can't be serious.'

He heard the panic in her voice, but he couldn't help himself now. Their lives had been disrupted enough. Here she was thinking of screwing a goddamn ten-year-old, for Christ's sake!

'What about Gillian? What about your brother?'

'Matt had nothing to do with that.'

'How do you know?' he asked. 'Were you there?'

'He was here, right here, when Andy was killed.'

'And where was he when Gillian was attacked? Remember that murder your brother was telling us about, the one in Morongo Valley where the woman was dismembered, and something or someone fed on the corpse?'

'Stop it, Neil. I don't want to talk about this.'

'Why not? Too squeamish? Or maybe it's too close to home. Her goddamn arm was torn off, Janet, gnawed at like a fucking drumstick!'

'I said I didn't want to talk about this anymore!'

Janet got up from the table and started out of the kitchen. But he was going to get this all off his chest, just the way she'd gotten her fucked-up dream off hers. He grabbed her by the arm and spun her around, forcing her to listen.

'We're in this together, Janet. I'm not going to let you

slip away from me just because we brought some . . . some stranger into our home.'

'Is that what you think he is? He's our son, come back to us. He's our little boy, and we can't turn on him the way everyone else has. We have to help him, Neil.'

'We have to help ourselves first. I saw what happened to Gillian. And maybe, just maybe, it wasn't Turk that did it. Someone ate her, goddamnit! They fed off her, Jan, and you're just going to stand there and pretend he had nothing to do with it?'

'Of course he had nothing to do with it. I saw the marks around his neck. You can't tell me he did that himself.' Again she tried to turn away, but he held her fast.

'Look at me, Janet,' he said, shaking her until she raised her eyes.

They were ice-cold, devoid of understanding.

'He's disturbed,' Neil said, lowering his voice as he began to plead with her. 'Maybe he had nothing to do with Gillian. Maybe everything he said really happened. But can we take that chance again? Are we going to lie awake nights wondering what he's thinking, what he might be planning for us?'

'You don't dump a child like you dump a pet,' she replied. 'He's not everything you want him to be, so you're just going to throw him out on his ear, is that it? You hated him from the very beginning, didn't you? You just pretended to care about him. He knows, Neil. Oh, yes, he senses it. No wonder you frighten him so. But you know what? I won't let him frighten me, because I know how much he loves me, how much he needs me too.'

He let go of her and stepped back, knowing there was no reasoning with her. 'Fine, you do whatever you goddamn please, Janet. But don't expect me to be part of it. And don't expect me to stand by and watch him destroy our feelings for each other. Our marriage still means a helluva lot to me. I'm not going to let you walk away from it just because somebody's trying to manipulate your mind. Because that's what it is. It's not reincarnation or telepathy or any other psychic nonsense. It's manipulation, Janet. It's being aware of what's going on and taking advantage of our weaknesses. Well I'll be goddamned if I'm going to let him get away with it!'

He wanted her to fall into his arms, to beg forgiveness, to confess all her sins, real or imagined, to cling to him and reaffirm the vows they'd made to each other. But Janet did nothing of the kind. Instead, she merely turned her back on him and walked out.

Make Neil watch when you do it, he thought. Make Daddy watch while you fuck her, isn't that what you mean, Matthew?

It wasn't funny, but he had to laugh. If not, he knew he'd only start to cry.

She hadn't fought with Neil in so long, hadn't argued so bitterly and at such length, that when she left the kichen Janet felt drained by the experience. How could he be so cocksure of everything, so uncompassionate? The man she fell in love with was a big teddy bear, a softy. He would never have jumped to conclusions without first having all the facts.

Conjecture, circumstantial evidence, that's all it was. How convenient to blame everything on Matt just because the police hadn't come up with a suspect. And as for the other business, the dream which they shared, the boy's awakening sexual desire, surely there was an explanation for that too, if only they tried to be rational and take things one step at a time.

He'll see a psychiatrist for as long as it takes, she told herself. But he'll come out of all this sane and whole. And normal. Yes, just a normal little boy.

'You mean you're not asking me to sleep on the couch?' Neil said, following her into the bedroom.

'You can sleep wherever the hell you please.' She crawled into bed and pulled the covers over her head, hoping he'd get the message.

But he didn't. 'Not even ten o'clock at night and you're already escaping.' He clucked his tongue sarcastically. 'Is your real life that boring that you have to take refuge in your dreams?'

'Fuck you,' she said.

'I'd love to.'

Before she could stop him he pulled the covers down and pushed her over onto her back. He was smiling his old softy grin, and even as she tried to wriggle free he leaned over and kissed her.

'Told you I wasn't gonna give up,' he said.

'If you've come to apologize, I'm not interested.'

'Apologize?' Neil said with a laugh. 'Believe me, an apology is the last thing I had in mind. I didn't do anything wrong, Janet. I spoke my piece. If you don't want to listen to reason it's not my fault.'

'You don't give up, do you?'

His cocky grin was answer enough. But instead of continuing what he'd started, he got up and began to get ready for bed.

She lay there with her eyes closed. She heard the water running as he brushed his teeth. She heard him padding on bare feet down the hall to turn out the lights. She heard the puppy barking softly and then a door close. Finally he got into bed, and soon he was snoring the way he always did when he slept on his back. She wanted to give him an elbow in the ribs and tell him to turn over, but instead she turned away, not wishing to have anything more to do with him.

Off in the distance a siren wailed, and coyotes began to

howl in reply. A cricket started chirping just outside the window. Why couldn't everything be easy, like it was for other people? Even her work had begun to suffer. Every time she sat down at the typewriter, all she wanted to write about was the room with the pipes, and the man with the beard. She tried incorporating the dream into the body of the novel, attributing it to the boy she called Az. But no matter how many different versions she wrote, none of them fit.

Now, listening to Neil's snores, she dreaded sleep, certain that as soon as she drifted off she'd find herself in that nightmare room, where the figure beneath the sheets waited for her with outstretched arms.

At the very edge of her consciousness she thought she heard a door opening, followed by a sound that suggested footsteps. Something clicked against the floor. How funny, she thought. The hall's carpeted, so how could I possibly hear something like that? She didn't know, and she was so tired, her limbs so heavy, that she just wanted to lie there and not do anything.

Clickety-click-click, like a dog walking across a hardwood floor. So nice and warm beneath the covers, the pillow so soft, everything just the way it should be.

Clickety-click-click.

Was that another door opening? She felt so heavy, so drained of energy.

'Mommy?' came the voice, whispering through the darkness. 'We're waiting, Mommy.'

But she was so very tired. Couldn't she just lie there and pretend she didn't hear anything?

'Don't keep us waiting, Mommy. We need you. You have to help us.'

She didn't know how she found the strength to get up, but she did. The room was dark, but on the other side of the bedroom windows she caught a glimpse of movement.

It reminded her of films taken underwater, at the very bottom of the ocean floor. But there was no luminescence, nothing but a different shade of black, a different quality of darkness, to give definition to the shifting figures which moved across the yard.

'Mommy, hurry, before it's too late,' the child called to her. Such a soft, gentle little voice.

His eyes glowed in the darkness, showing her the way. Yellow eyes, how beautiful, she thought, like bright coins catching the light. She moved slowly, dragging herself along, through the inky darkness and down the hall where her footsteps made the floorboards creak.

Clickety-click-click, she heard in front of her, like fingernails tapping. A musky scent floated toward her. She thought of Neil and giggled to herself. What the teddy bear didn't know wouldn't hurt him, wasn't that the way it went?

'Where are you, sweetheart?' she whispered.

It was like moving through a tunnel, the darkness so absolute, so impenetrable, that when she put her hand up before her face she couldn't even see it. Yet far away came the glow of his beautiful yellow eyes.

Was she finally reaching the end of the tunnel? She couldn't tell, but with each hesitant step she took the musky smell got stronger. The air was damp here too, close and humid. The floor of the tunnel began to slope downward. She had to bend over in order not to lose her balance. If she fell she would tumble like Alice down the rabbit hole, with nothing to catch her when she reached the bottom.

'We love you, Mommy,' the child called to her, sounding much closer now.

Neil would understand, wouldn't he? He couldn't be angry with her. She was only doing what she had to. The boy would hold her in his arms and she'd feel safe.

'Where are you?' she said, keeping her voice down so the teddy bear wouldn't wake up and growl.

'Here . . . here . . . here . . .'

The voice echoed in her ears, bouncing off the walls of the tunnel. She couldn't tell from which direction it was coming.

'We want you to play the game with us, Mommy.'

Maybe the teddy bear would just hibernate forever and ever. Maybe he'd never wake up and she could run her hands over the boy's smooth smooth skin, touching him the way she wasn't supposed to. After all, she was entitled to her fantasies, just as the teddy bear was entitled to his.

The gold-coin eyes gave off sparks of light. She could see him now, waiting for her at the end of the tunnel. Would the bear be angry if he found out what she was doing? Would he growl and rip off her clothes and gobble her up?

'We won't ever tell him,' she said. 'It'll be our little secret, just the two of us.'

'The three of us,' replied the boy. He began to laugh, and the sounds he made were like the sounds of a flute, a strangely seductive music that made her quicken her steps.

When she finally reached him he was down on all fours, his long curved nails scratching lightly against the floor. His skin looked dusted with pollen, covered with a faint golden down. She would give herself to him because he needed her. Asleep in his den, the bear would never know. A secret, a deep, dark secret.

The boy rose eagerly to his feet, reaching out and drawing her into his embrace.

'We want you,' he whispered. His hands tore at her nightgown. 'We have to have you before the bear wakes up.'

He dragged her down to the floor, hovering over her with his yellow eyes.

'You deserve it, Mommy. It's portant.'

She reached out, trying to help him, wanting all of him, because the bear slept in his den and didn't growl. Poor teddy the big silly, not knowing how she felt. He was hard and excited, and she wanted him to be part of her.

But even as he fell against her, in a frenzy now and snarling eagerly, she was afraid the bear might wake up and hurt him.

Was that him now? She heard footsteps slowly drawing near. If it was the bear, what could she say that would make things right again?

She tried to pull free because it was wrong, it was very very wrong, and they'd punish her for her sins. But the boy wouldn't let her go. He was inside her now, part of her the way he'd always wanted.

'Horsie,' he groaned, while something moved just beyond her sight, not yet visible in the darkness.

She was afraid now, The teddy bear was angry. He'd hurt the boy with sticks and send him back to his den and she'd be all alone. Myabe if she stopped him in time . . .

'Don't,' she said, 'it's wrong.' She tried to push him away, but he rode her harder and harder, moaning with excitement and clawing at her breasts.

'Doesn't it feel good, Mommy? Mr Harriman says you deserve it, just like the Gillie. He's watching us. He likes to watch. He used to watch Mama and Poppy playing horsie all the time.'

Who was he talking about? She didn't understand, but now her fear was like something choking at her insides, strangling her with terror. She cried out, begging the boy to let her go.

'But you like it,' he said, 'I know you do.'

'No, please, it's wrong.'

'Mr Harriman doesn't think so.'

His hand came down hard over her mouth, muffling her

shouts. He was ripping into her with sharp, angry jabs, moving so quickly her skin was burning. She had to get away before the bear woke up and found her missing. He would never understand. He would hurt her with his stick and then hurt the boy, sending him back where he came from. But the more she struggled, the more excited he became.

Something moved among the shadows. She tried to see what it was. Who was Mr Harriman? Why had he brought her here, and what did he want from her?

'The blood, the white blood!' the boy cried out.

He began to shake violently, nipping at her with his teeth. With each tremor his seed uncoiled inside her while something else slithered through the darkness, rearing up before her so that there was no way she could escape.

The boy scampered back on all fours, his sex still rigid, outthrust between his legs. Help me! she screamed. Where was the bear when she needed him? Why didn't he wake up and save her?

'Ahriman,' the boy whispered reverently. He pressed his forehead to the ground, bowing in submission.

Harriman? Hairy Man? Horror Man? What was he saying? A blast of foul-smelling air fanned her cheeks. Janet tried to drag herself along the floor that wasn't wood but earth, hard-packed like the floor of a cave. If she could only find the tunnel again she might be able to awaken the bear, and he would rush out of his den and save her.

The air was slowly being poisoned with the stench of filth and decay. She screamed and screamed, but the bear kept sleeping. Why was it doing this to her? Hadn't she been good, hadn't she cared? She had tried to do everything for the boy, but now he was laughing, holding her down while something –

What? Dear God, what have I done? What is it!

– began to inch its way up along her legs.

It was wet and slippery like an afterbirth, like something that had dragged itself out of the mud. She couldn't bear to have it touch her, but the boy held her down, laughing to see her so helpless.

'Ahriman,' he said, 'don't I pretend good?'

It dragged its great creaking bulk over her legs, pinning her down to the ground, crushing her with its turgid heaving weight. There was evil here, evil so pervasive and omnipotent it touched every cell in her body, filling her with revulsion.

Janet began to shriek, the agonized cries tearing at her throat. But now it was on top of her, as hungry and eager as the boy. It tore its way into her, burrowing deeper and deeper until it reached her womb. Thick and slimy, it was part of her now, a monstrous coupling from which there was no possible escape. It would stay there and grow, feeding off her until it was strong again and ready to be reborn.

The boy kept laughing, howling now like a wolf. A matted ball of lice-infested hair covered his face, hiding his golden eyes. He laughed and laughed, telling her he liked to watch. Then he swung around, kneeling over her.

It was inside her all wet and slippery, reeking of death. It shook her again and again.

The burning and the burning . . .

Dear God in heaven, don't let it . . . don't . . .

It was too late. It had already begun to feed.

'Wake up, Janet!'

But how could she awaken if the bear was asleep in his den and the hairy man was inside her, feeding and growing stronger?

He slapped her across the face, a hard, stinging blow.

She was soaking wet, gasping for breath. The teddy bear had a face, and the face was love. Neil was holding her in his arms and shaking her.

'Make it stop, make it go away,' she groaned. Her throat was dry and scratchy. She still couldn't get enough air into her lungs.

'There's nothing here. It was a dream, a dream,' Neil said, pleading with her to believe him.

She fell back against the pillows as the room slowly came into focus.

Clickety-click-click.

'Oh, my God, it's still there!' she screamed.

'There's nothing, honey. It was a dream, a nightmare. You're awake now. Everything's going to be okay.'

Clickety-click-click, something scratching at the door, trying to get in. It wanted to have her again while the teddy bear slept on and on, hibernating in his den.

'Don't . . . don't let it,' she begged. 'Oh, Neil, don't let it in.'

'Let what?'

Clickety-click-click.

She pointed to the door, and he was on his feet before she could stop him. He flung the door open.

The puppy was so frightened to see him standing there that it squatted in the middle of the hall and began to urinate.

'As if we don't have enough problems.' Neil looked back at her, smiling patiently. 'I'll get something to clean it up.' And he went off to the kitchen to bring back a wad of paper towels.

Even as she lay there, knowing she was awake, knowing it was only a hideous nightmare, she could still feel its presence.

The hairy man, Janet thought. What in the name of God is the hairy man?

17

It had to be a dream. If not, her nightgown would have been torn. There would have been bite marks where the boy had nipped at her skin. There would have been a discharge too, torn and lacerated tissue. Janet was trying to be as clinical as possible. But the next morning, after she saw Matt off to school, pretending nothing was wrong as she smiled and waved good-bye while he boarded the bus, she stripped off her clothes and carefully examined herself in the bathroom mirror.

There was nothing in her reflection to suggest what she was certain she'd experienced. Yet the dream seemed even more real than reality itself. As she stood under the shower, letting the hot, stinging spray work the tension out of her neck and shoulders, Janet could feel it happening all over again, down to the texture of the earthen floor along which she had dragged herself, trying to escape.

Harriman or Hairy Man or Horror Man or what? She didn't know how to spell it and could only say it aloud the way she thought she heard it. But the boy had spoken of a Mr Harriman who'd taken care of him in the desert. In the dream he said the name with reverence, bowing obsequiously before it.

It. And what was *it*? She had felt something crawling over her, something which reeked of putrescence and decomposing flesh. Yet she had never actually seen it.

Any self-respecting shrink would tell me I have phallic symbols on the brain, she thought as she dried herself off. But it has to be more than that.

It was one thing to dream she was in some kind of

grotesque porno film. But it was something else altogether to conjure up an entity of such all-consuming horror that just to think of it made her shudder.

Maybe Jung had a word for it, she wondered. Maybe it was part of what he called the collective unconscious.

After she had dressed, she went into her study and dragged out a copy of *Man and His Symbols* she found on one of the shelves. If the Hairy Man was listed in the index, she wasn't spelling it correctly, because she found no appropriate reference. But there were pages devoted to phallic symbols and the role of serpents in dreams.

The one mythology text she had in her library made no mention of such a creature. Or demon. Or demigod. Or whatever it might like to call itself. But she wasn't about to give up so easily. Determined to find out exactly what it was she'd encountered – And wasn't that a ladylike way of describing being raped by a monster? she thought – she stuffed a legal pad into her shoulder bag, made sure she had a pen and her wallet, and was soon driving down from the hills, where she turned west and headed in the direction of UCLA.

After spending more than an hour combing the card catalogues, all she drew was a blank. But she still wasn't ready to call it quits. Remembering the help the library staff had given her in the past, Janet went into the reference room, where she found one of the librarians working at his desk.

The young man, casually dressed in khakis and a faded workshirt, listened attentively while she tried to explain what she was looking for.

'I don't know much about mythology myself,' he admitted, 'but you might want to check an encyclopedia. Come, I'll show you where it is.'

The Compendium of Religion and Mythological Lore filled an entire shelf, some two dozen volumes in all. The only reference to Harriman was Harriman, Jeremy C., co-author of an article on Ainu folklore. As for Hairy Man, Horror Man, and any alliterative variation in between, she found nothing. As she replaced the dog-eared volume on the shelf she thought again of Jung's collective unconscious and hauled out Volume II, ARTHUR to BUNYON.

When she saw the name in print her breath caught in her throat.

AZ (the heading read). In Zoroastrianism, the feminine demon AZ represents insatiable greed and lust. She is the embodiment of chaos and the forebear of death, destroying everything in her path until, never satisfied, she turns upon herself. So great is her appetite that, although the whole world is surrendered to her, she can never be appeased. *See also* AHRIMAN, OHRMAZD, ZOROASTRIANISM.

Ray Torres wasn't a happy man. Every time he got out the file on Gillian Stanton, he came up with a blank. He thought that maybe, just maybe, if he kept going over the facts, he might be able to solve the case. But his middle name wasn't Holmes, and without a Dr Watson to assist him, the answers he was looking for continued to elude him. It was for this reason that he drove into nearby Glendale, that same morning Janet was doing her own brand of research at UCLA.

Earlier in the week he'd dropped off the samples at Forensic Science Associates, an independent testing laboratory that did work for the county medical examiner. Now, with the morning paper folded tight beneath his arm, he paced the reception room.

The facts just didn't add up, that's what kept bugging him. Here they had a classic case of forced entry, then a crime of violence perpetrated by an unknown assailant. But where the hell was this assailant anyway? Maybe the chief pathologist at Forensic would be able to tell him.

'Detective Torres?' A young guy with long hair, his stained lab coat reaching just below the knees of his jeans, came into the waiting room and motioned him to follow.

Once he got past the door that said EMPLOYEES ONLY, it was like being inside a Gilbert chemistry set, the kind that as a kid he'd always ogled in store windows, his folks never having had the bread to buy him one. Smelled real authentic too, he thought, and he wrinkled his nose in distaste, wondering how the lab techs could put up with the stink for eight hours at a stretch.

The young guy with the long hair was the assistant director of the lab and personally assured him that he'd done all the work himself. Torres didn't know if he should be thrilled or not, except that when the kid started rattling off his twenty-five-dollar words, he knew he was in competent hands.

'Take it slow, Doc,' he said, slapping the newspaper against the nearest tabletop. 'I'm still working on my bachelor's.'

The serologist smiled patiently and showed him to a chair. 'Here's what we found,' he said. 'You brought us some blood and semen samples, that correct?'

Torres nodded.

'Okay, then. Utilizing what we call electrophoresis – '

'Electro what?'

'It's a technique to analyze the samples for their protein content,' explained the serologist. 'Anyway, using that technique we're able to determine a precise genetic profile of both the victim as well as her assailant. Now, we found three distinct blood types. One was canine in origin – '

'The kid's dog. Yeah, we figured on that.'

'The second matched samples of the victim's blood.'

'Okay. And the third?'

The young kid with the long stringy hair smiled as if

he knew a secret he just might be willing to share. 'Revealed a genetic profile identical to the semen sample.'

'So she put up a fight, didn't she?'

'He bled, if that's what you mean.'

'But how do I know it fits the kid?' he asked.

'You don't,' admitted the serologist, 'not until you bring us a sample of his blood. If it matches what we've already got, you're in business.'

'And if it doesn't I'm back where I started.'

'But at least you'd be eliminating your prime suspect. How old did you say this kid was?'

'Eleven, maybe twelve at the most,' replied Torres.

'Hell, I was gettin' it on with myself at that age. No reason he couldn't too. One question, though. Couldn't Cedars give you a sample of his blood?'

Torres frowned. 'I already asked, and what they told me ain't fit for public consumption. Against the law, know what I mean? They can't release anything without a court order. And by now whatever samples they had don't even exist.'

'Kid had a head injury, didn't he?'

'What about it?'

'You mean to say your men couldn't find the weapon?'

'Nope.'

'Well, Ray, that's about the best I can do. You get me that blood sample and I'll take care of the rest.'

Torres came unhappily to his feet. 'Question is,' he murmured, 'can I get that court order?'

'Maybe the kid's parents'll give permission without one.'

'Doubtful.'

'Why? If they're so convinced he's innocent, what are they afraid of?'

Torres smiled at the serologist, thinking how the guy spent all his time playing mad scientist with his chemicals and retorts. But though he had the technique of electrophoresis down pat, he still had a lot to learn about human nature.

The demon of demons, destroyer of the world whose ultimate defeat shall be brought about by man. But what if none of us live to see it happen? Janet asked herself as she drove home. Five hours in the stacks, dragging down dozens of dusty, battered books from the shelves, had only convinced her that whatever was happening, she still didn't know what it was.

Ahriman, she had learned, occupied a position in the Zoroastrian religion that was roughly equivalent to that of Satan. But unlike his counterpart in Christianity, Ahriman wasn't a fallen angel. Standing in opposition to the Holy Spirit, Ahriman was portrayed as the very essence of evil, and entity that chose by preference to do wrong and oppose the spirit of goodness.

According to ancient Iranian doctrines, the wolf was created by Ahriman, just one of a host of demons (Az among them) brought into existence to accomplish his work of destruction. In one of the books she consulted, Janet had come across a photograph of a third-century rock relief, a massive tableau which depicted Ohrmazd, the principle of truth and light (Ahriman's twin brother who represented God the Son), trampling on Ahriman's snake-covered head.

But what bothered her more than anything was the way her imagination had conjured up such a creature, when prior to the nightmare she hadn't known the first thing about Zoroastrianism, let alone its pantheon of gods. Yet she had heard the boy whisper its name, had felt its slimy reptilian presence as it crawled on top of her.

And why an Iranian demon, if in fact whatever had been happening was demonic in origin? No, the whole thing was much too farfetched. She wasn't about to start convincing herself the youngster was in communication with a ghost, or whatever the hell it was. Maybe if she tried to think it through, she might recall having heard someone discuss Ahriman, or perhaps she'd read about it years before. But though she racked her brains trying to remember, she couldn't come up with an explanation.

Why had she dreamed of Ahriman? That was what it seemed all to boil down to. When she got home, Janet couldn't put her research aside, and as she went next door to Ina's to collect her friend's mail and water the plants she kept thinking about what she'd read.

The moment she walked inside she felt uneasy and began to shiver even though the house wasn't cold. There was something very disturbing about being here, as if Gillian were still around.

She still found it difficult to accept the girl's death. When she caught sight of a recent snapshot Ina had taped onto the refrigerator door, she stopped short, peering at Gillian and wondering if all this weren't a dream, a complex multilayered nightmare from which she might ultimately awaken.

But it wasn't a dream. It was real and it had happened and she'd been at the funeral and seen the youngster lying in a coffin. She shook her head sadly, then decided she'd best get down to work if she was ever going to keep Ina's plants alive.

The collection of succulents in the kitchen didn't mind being dry, but the pothos in her friend's bedroom trailed limply to the floor. Janet carried it outside, along with the staghorn fern Ina had hung like a trophy in the living room. But when she went over to turn on the garden hose, she heard someone whispering on the other side of the fence that separated the two houses.

'Here, kitty, that's a good kitty.'

It was Matt, who'd probably just gotten home from

school. She turned the water on low, letting it trickle through the sphagnum moss on which the staghorn was planted. Then she went over to the fence and, standing on tiptoe, peered over the top.

How cute he looked, kneeling there on the grass while Jip frolicked nearby, rolling back and forth and kicking its long, awkward legs in the air.

'Here, kitty, kitty,' Matt called.

At the opposite end of the yard she could see a lanky gray cat slowly making its way toward him. As Matt continued to call to it, snapping his fingers and clicking his tongue, the cat warily approached until Janet was able to see it had a collar around its neck. She smiled to herself. maybe they should consider getting him a kitten. He seemed to have a wonderful way with animals, Jip already following him around just the way Turk used to do.

She heard herself sigh, then turned away. The lawn could use a good watering too, and since Ina had never gotten around to putting a timer on the sprinkler system, she turned it on by hand.

Above the sound of the running water she heard something else, something that made her freeze for a moment until she suddenly realized what it was.

Janet rushed back to the fence, but it was already too late. Matt was down on all fours, and as the cat continued to scream the boy tore at its throat until a jet of blood drenched his lips and the animal went limp in his hands. She felt her stomach recoiling, wanted to be sick, but couldn't tear her eyes away.

Instead, she continued to watch him, even as he glanced furtively about, not noticing her peering at him from behind the fence. Satisfied that no one was around, he began to feed, using his hands and his teeth to disembowel the cat with so little effort it was hard to believe he was only a little boy, and not a wolf.

Although Janet was tempted to run back to the house and surprise him in the act, she remained where she was, mesmerized by what she was watching. For a long time now, she had tried to convince herself that Matt was perfectly normal, that despite all he suffered, the privations he endured, he would come out of them with flying colors. Even when her brother tried to tell her differently, she refused to listen. And last night, when Neil too had gone on at great length about his fears and suspicions, she railed out in anger, unable to accept what he had to say.

But how could she pretend everything was all right, when all she had to do was look at Matt to see that it wasn't?

He was eating it. He was actually tearing it apart and sharing it with Jip, who snarled as savagely as a wolf pup. The two of them were devouring the cat in a frenzy.

At last she turned away, leaning against the fence and taking deep breaths. Like a documentary on television, she thought, like Jane Goodall in the wild. Kill or be killed. This was how he'd managed to survive his ordeal in the desert. She could accept that because there it really was a matter of just staying alive. But now he didn't want for anything, and yet the first chance he got he reverted to savagery.

She thought of the wolf whose remains were found near her brother's house, and the man from the trailer park who claimed to have seen a boy running on all fours, the boy and the wolf together when he fired the shot. Had a wolf actually taken care of him in the desert? Was such a thing possible?

Having read a great deal on the subject for her new book, Janet recalled that most authorities placed little credence in tales of 'wolf boys.' The few well-documented cases of feral children all seemed to conclude that the youngster in question was probably autistic, and even though the child's behavior might have appeared to be bestial, it in no way implied he was actually raised by an animal.

But Matt wasn't autistic, of that she was certain. Yet he was clearly reverting to his former state, despite all that she and Neil had tried to do for him. Yes, he would need intensive psychiatric care. He might even have to be institutionalized for a time. All these things she could accept. But something otherworldly, something supernatural? No, that just wasn't possible.

Yet how had he known about his namesake?

Sandy go breeway . . .

The phone was ringing when she unlocked the kitchen door and let herself in. 'Matt, I'm home!' she called out, trying to sound as if nothing were wrong. 'Have you done your homework yet, honey?'

'I'm playing,' she finally heard him call out just as she picked up the phone.

'Mrs Kaufman?' a man asked.

'Speaking.'

'Hope I haven't caught you at a bad time.'

The irony of his remark was so heavy-handed she decided not to dwell on it. 'Who am I talking to, please?'

'Sorry,' the man replied. 'Ray Torres, Homicide Division.'

Janet heard the plumbing begin to creak and realized Matt was probably washing himself off under the garden hose in the yard. 'Yes, what can I do for you, Mr Torres?'

'I take it your husband – '

No song and dance, she thought. If he has something to say, let him just get it over with. 'I know all about it, Mr Torres.'

The detective didn't sound the least bit put off by her sharp and impatient tone. 'In that case, I'll come right to the point.' He told her of his visit to Forensic Science Associates earlier in the day. 'I'd like your cooperation in securing a blood sample. I don't doubt the boy's innocence, but we need this kind of evidence for documentation.'

She heard herself laughing, an angry, embittered sound. 'And you expect me to believe that? You don't think he's innocent. You think that whatever happened here was all his doing. What is this, a trick or something?'

'I need that blood sample, Mrs Kaufman.'

'Then get a court order, you son of a bitch!'

She slammed the phone down and collapsed into a chair. She just couldn't take it anymore. First Andy and Mike, their deaths so senseless, so unnecessary. And then Gillian, and Matt saying one thing and Torres implying another. Then nightmares, a voice whispering to her and claiming to be her son . . .

My son died in an automobile accident, she said to herself. They tried to save him, but they couldn't. We buried him two years ago . . . or did we?

'Here I am, Mommy, nice and clean.' Matt stood in the doorway, holding out his spotless hands for her inspection.

She was afraid to look too closely and forced herself to smile. 'That's my good boy,' she said.

'What'd you do today?'

Janet sighed loudly, trying to get her thoughts in order. 'I went to the library.'

Matt peered at her curiously. 'Why?'

'I had work to do.'

'For your book about Az?'

Since when had he been going through her papers? 'Have you been reading it?' she asked, surprised to hear him mention the character's name, a name that had begun to take on ominous implications.

Matt giggled to himself. 'You know I can't read that good,' he said with a smile. 'Who was on the phone before?'

'What is this, Matt, twenty questions?'

He didn't seem to understand the reference and just stood there by the door, smiling and smiling until Janet thought his lips would crack under the strain.

'Don't you love me anymore?' he suddenly blurted out.

There was something so accusing in the way he said this that Janet was momentarily taken aback. 'Of course I love you,' she said nervously, looking away rather than continue to try to stare him down.

'I loved you last night. Don't you remember? In the dream, Mommy, we played horsie in the dream.'

'Horsie?' she said in confusion. 'What are you talking about, Matt?'

He was giggling now, laughing at her and unable to stop himself. His pale blue eyes narrowed until they admitted no light. 'Horsie,' he said again. 'Only next time we'll both be awake, just like he promised.'

'Who promised? Who are you talking about?'

Rather than answer, Matt turned away and walked off. Janet ran after him, stopping him just as he reached his room. The moment she grabbed hold of his arm, Jip began to bark, snarling at her shoe. She had a terrible urge to kick the puppy aside. But before she could even say anything, Matt snatched Jip off the floor, holding him protectively in his arms.

'Who were you talking about?' she demanded, determined to find out what was going on, once and for all. 'Mr Harriman?'

The boy eyed her silently. 'I don't know a Mr Harriman,' he finally said. His tone of voice was so dispassionate that it sounded inhuman, as if someone else were doing the talking for him.

'Don't lie to me, Matthew. Is he the one who was here the night Gillian was killed?'

'No one was here but Jess. But you better be nice to Jip, 'cause he'll bite you, he'll bite you real bad.' He stepped back and, with a scornful expression, slammed the door in her face.

'Matthew Kaufman, you come out here this instant!' she shouted.

When he didn't answer, Janet tried the doorknob. But somehow he'd managed to lock himself in.

'Unlock this door, Matthew!'

'Go 'way,' he said. 'Go 'way or you'll be sorry.'

'You're the one who's going to be sorry. Now open this door!'

Clickety-click-click.

It was probably Jip, scratching at the door and trying to get out. She tugged at the knob, but it still held fast. Where had he gotten a key? She didn't even think there was one.

'Matthew, please, I want to talk to you.'

Clickety-click-click.

'Go 'way,' he whispered. His voice was so low she had to put her ear against the jamb in order to hear him. 'Go 'way or you'll get what you deserve.'

'I deserve a little kindness, that's what!'

Again she grabbed hold of the doorknob, but now, when she turned it, the door swung back. Something flew through the air. She instinctively ducked, not knowing what to expect. It landed at her feet, a wet, sticky substance spraying across her shoes. When she looked down she began to gag. It was the disemboweled remains of the cat, its mangy gray fur matted with blood. It stared at her with glazed marble eyes, baring its teeth in a rigid and lifeless grin.

Janet stumbled back even as Matt rushed after her. Laughing now, he bent down to retrieve his prize, then swung it around by its tail before once again flinging it at her feet. Again it landed with a sickening thud, half-dried clots of blood splattering over her shoes and stockings.

'Didn't I tell you to leave me alone?' he said. 'But you didn't listen, Mommy. And now you're gonna be sorry.' He sang the words, a hideous lilting song, taunting her as she rushed down the hall.

But why am I running? she asked herself. He's just a little boy. He can't hurt me, I know he can't. He didn't hurt Gillian. It was someone else, someone named Jess or Mr Harriman. But not Matt. No, it couldn't be my son.

He was right behind her, Jip too, the two of them howling excitedly as they took up the chase. She glanced back just as Matt reached out. Both hands gripped her tightly around the waist. He tackled her like a football player, trying to throw her down to the floor.

'Leave me alone!' she screamed. She raised her hand and slapped him across the face as hard as she could.

Matt let go of her and staggered back. At the same time, the puppy darted between them, and before Janet could stop it, Jip sank his sharp milk teeth into her ankle. She kicked out again and again, trying to get it to let go. Finally she reached down, leaning against the wall for support. Tearing the puppy off her, she sent it tumbling head over heels across the living room. Jip bounced along the carpet, regained his footing, and started toward her.

'Leave her!' Matt shouted.

The puppy froze, as motionless as the cat that had been thrown at her feet. Jip began to lick himself, whining now as Janet limped into the kitchen. Blood was slowly trickling from the puncture wound in her ankle, and it was already becoming painful to walk.

Calm, Janet, just stay calm, she kept telling herself. A tantrum, that's all it is. The boy's emotionally disturbed and he's taking out his frustrations on you. But it'll be all right. Just stay calm, and everything will be fine.

Matt flung the swinging doors back and followed her into the kitchen. She wanted to take him up in her arms and shake him, trying to convince him that she and Neil were on his side, that if he turned on them now he'd have no one to look after him.

But Matt never gave her a chance to explain. 'You hurt me,' he said, his voice low and menacing. 'I don't like it when people hurt me, I don't like it at all.'

'You hurt me too.' She was blotting at the wound with damp paper towels. There wasn't much blood, but the puppy's bite was such that she could feel the pain all the way down to the bone.

'But you didn't hurt me in the dream,' Matt went on. 'No, in the dream you wanted horsie a lot, didn't you? And you got it too. 'Cause you deserved it, that's why.'

What was happening here? Why wasn't she in control? What was she afraid of? She was stronger than he was. She could run out of the house if necessary. She could call the police too, if it came down to that. Yet she remained where she was, unable to believe that her son would try to hurt her.

She took a deep breath, deciding to take an entirely different tack. 'I want you to go to your room and put that . . . that thing you found in the trash.'

'I didn't find it,' he said in the same taunting tone of voice he'd used earlier. 'I killed it, just like Az taught me.'

'How can Az teach you anything when it's just a character in a book?'

'She's not. She was good to me. She was my friend until that Jess killed her with his gun and Turk came. You think you're so smart, don't you, Janet? But you're not, 'cause you don't know the things I do. You dream of me, but now you're scared. But maybe I'll make you dream again.'

'You won't make me do anything, Matthew Kaufman. Do you hear me?' she shouted, trying to put as much conviction into her voice as she could. But now he was frightening her, and what was worse, he seemed to know it, too, as if he were capable of smelling fear the way other people smelled perfume.

'I can make you do anything,' he whispered. ''Cause that's morality. Only it's my rules now, not yours.'

The harsh, guttural voice wasn't even his anymore. Could she rush out the door before he stopped her? 'Your father's going to be home any minute,' she warned him, hoping that would be enough of a threat to get him to calm down.

But Matt just shook his head, his corn-silk hair waving back and forth like grass tossed by the wind. 'No, he won't. He has science club today. He won't be back till late.' He stepped forward, while all this time Jip was right behind him, the puppy's ears flat against its head, and its lips drawn back to show all its teeth.

'Go to your room and clean up that mess,' she ordered.

'I wanna play first.' He reached down and began to fondle himself, rubbing his hand across the front of his jeans.

Janet looked away, turning her back on him. I'll call Neil at school and have him leave right away, she decided. Because if I call the police, then Torres is bound to find out. He may be disturbed, but he's not a murderer, I know he's not.

She reached for the phone, but Matt snatched the receiver out of her hand. He flung it against the wall, smiling as he watched it bounce up and down on its long springy cord.

'I'm your mother, for God's sake!'

'Mama's dead in the desert where he left her dead. They were playing horsie and he hurt her I saw I watched.' The words tumbled from his lips, dry and lifeless, devoid of emotion. 'Dead in the desert I saw the Jess playing and I'm gonna play too 'cause I deserve it I do I'm a good boy Mama's good boy she told me so herself but Poppy hurt me the pain . . .' A bubble of saliva broke across his lips. He grabbed both her hands in his, trying to get her to touch him. 'In the dream you played horsie,' he kept reminding her.

'But it's not a dream anymore, Matthew. You don't want to hurt me, you know you don't. If you hurt me, then no one'll take care of you. They'll put you back in the hospital and you'll be all alone.'

He shook his head, refusing to believe her. 'Talk, talk, talk,' he said, clicking his teeth. 'I don't want talk, I want horsie.'

He shoved her back, head lowered like a butting goat. Janet lost her footing and tripped, trying to catch herself before she fell. She grabbed onto the edge of the butcher-block counter, but Matt pried her fingers away, laughing as she fell back onto the floor.

He was right on top of her before she could pull herself to her feet. When she tried to push him aside he captured her hands and pinned them down, straddling her and holding them in place with his knees.

'Look what we got for you, Mommy,' he said, giggling. He reached down and unzipped his fly even as she turned her head away and closed her eyes. 'Don't you wanna see, Mommy? Gillie wanted to see. She made big eyes.'

Janet tried to stay calm, but it was a losing battle. 'Let me go, Matt. You don't know what you're doing. You're hurting me.'

'So what? It's part of the game, isn't it? Now you be good, little girl, and do what you're told. That's what he said to Mama, only she didn't hear, she was asleep and never woke up.'

'I'm not asleep, Matt. I'm wide awake, and you're my son and you're hurting me. I know you don't mean to, and maybe you can't even help yourself. But you have to try, Matt, because if you hurt me, then no one's going to be here for you anymore. Daddy couldn't take care of you by himself.'

'Daddy doesn't love me anyway,' the boy spat out. 'But he likes to play like Poppy, and now I'm gonna play too.'

She felt his hands on her skirt, and as he pushed it up around her waist she said, 'Tell Mr Harriman I know all about him. I know his real name, and I know what he's trying to do to you.'

When she opened her eyes, Matt was staring at her with a look of both surprise and disbelief.

'You're lying,' he said. 'You don't know nothin' about him, nothin'.'

'Oh, yes, I do. And I know that he's trying to hurt you. He is, isn't he, Matt?'

Matt shook his head, but the expression of doubt and confusion lingered.

'You mustn't let him do this to you. You have to be strong. You have to trust me, Matt, because I love you.'

'Love?' said the boy. He tilted his head to the side and peered at her curiously. 'Love is what Poppy did when he hurt me. The stick-pain, don't let him Mama but he did. And you know what? He did it more than once too, only Mama never knew 'cause it was a secret like Mr Harriman's a secret.' He suddenly winced and reached back, touching the seat of his pants.

At that instant Janet threw herself forward, catching him off guard. He toppled back, and she clambered to her feet, limping now as she felt the pain throbbing in her ankle.

If she locked herself in the bedroom she might have

time to – what? She didn't know, but she ran out of the kitchen, throwing the shutter doors open and hurrying through the dining room and then into the hall.

'I'm gonna get you now!' he called after her, sounding like a child playing hide-and-seek. 'And when I catch you I'm gonna play horsie till you go to sleep and don't wake up!'

Janet rushed into the bedroom. She started to slam the door shut, when Jip squeezed through the opening, snapping at her as he tried to wriggle his way inside.

'You'll be sor-ry,' the boy was singing from out in the hall. He hurled himself against the door, forcing her to let go.

Feeling panic now like a noose tightening around her throat, Janet raced into the bathroom, the pain shooting up her leg each time she put weight on her ankle. She barely managed to get the door locked before he started pounding on it with his fists.

How long would the lock hold? Would she have enough time to crawl out the window before he broke in?

Trying to ignore the throbbing pain as best she could, Janet climbed up onto the marble countertop and pushed the window up as far as it would go. If she screamed, would anyone hear? Probably not, because the bathroom faced the back of the house, and her closest neighbor wasn't home during the day. But if she managed to crawl out the window she might make it to the street, where surely someone would be able to help her.

Behind her he was still banging on the door, trying to wrench it off its hinges.

There wasn't any time left, and Janet hauled herself over the top of the sill. A button on her skirt snagged against the side of the window frame, holding her there for a moment before she tore it free. It was about a five-foot drop into the row of hedges directly below.

Watch your eyes, she kept telling herself as she wiggled her way clear of the window.

She was halfway out when she heard the sound of splintering wood, followed by the boy's victorious cry as he rushed into the bathroom. She pushed forward, both hands on the edge of the sill, when he suddenly grabbed her feet, his hands snapping shut around her ankles. He began to pull her back, and though she kept lashing out and trying to kick him away, Matthew held on to her so tightly she couldn't free herself.

Screaming as loudly as she could, Janet prayed someone would hear. But her anguished cries didn't frighten the boy. If anything, they seemed to make him more determined. He continued to haul her inside like an angler reeling in his catch, slowly but steadily dragging her back through the window. She held on to the sill with all her strength, her fingers turning white as she tried to maintain her grip.

'Horsie's fun,' he was saying, giggling too as he pulled her down off the window ledge until she finally had to let go.

Her shoulder slammed against the frame. She was falling, unable to stop herself, striking her head first against the mirror which faced the sinks, and then against the marble countertop. Her hands swung out blindly as she tried to break her fall. She heard bottles crashing to the floor, and still he laughed, not content until she was down on her back, feeling pieces of broken glass digging into her skin.

He slammed his hand over her mouth, and her cries stopped abruptly. 'You liked it in the dream,' he whispered while he pushed her skirt up around her hips, then reached for the top of her panty hose. 'You liked it so much that now you're gonna have as much as you want. It'll be fun, Mommy, just like he promised. And after, you're gonna go 'way like Jess and Gillie and you won't come back 'cause you'll be asleep, dreaming of me all the time.'

He had her hands pinned down, but Janet was still able to move her fingers. She swept them back and forth along the cold tile floor. The smell of perfume from the broken bottles drenched her clothes. Maybe he couldn't smell her fear because of it. When she found what she was looking for, she tightened her fingers around the shard of glass. It cut into her palm, but she knew she had to get a good grip on it if she was ever going to stop him.

'It didn't hurt when the Neil did it, so why should it hurt now?' he said.

'Daddy makes love to me,' she gasped, hoping he wouldn't see what she was holding in her hand. 'But this isn't love, Matt. Ahriman wants you to kill me, but have you ever bothered to ask him why? Maybe he's afraid that you care about me because I care about you. Yes, maybe that's it. He can't bear the thought that someone loves you for you and wants to protect you.'

The rage in his eyes wavered like a flame. She didn't want to hurt him, not if she could help it. But there just wasn't any way out of it. Reason didn't seem to work, and he was still holding her down, making no move to release her.

'There's still time,' she said. The glass was cutting deeply into her palm. She couldn't hold on to it much longer.

'You'll tell the Neil,' he replied. 'He'll come and hurt me like Poppy did.'

'Neil isn't like Poppy. He's different. He loves you and he doesn't want to hurt you, not ever, Matt. You must believe that, because if you don't . . . then Mr Harriman's the one who ends up winning. But you don't win either way. You're the loser, Matt, because they'll lock you up again, and this time there won't be a Janet and a Neil to come and get you and take you home.'

'Is that true?' he said. But he wasn't talking to her. He was talking to Ahriman. 'I thought you said we'd go 'way after. But where could we go? Az is dead.'

'We love you!' she cried out. 'Love isn't hurting, Matt. Love is caring. Love is forever, don't you understand?'

The pressure was beginning to diminish along her arms. He wasn't sure anymore, but she still held on to the piece of glass as best she could, not wanting to use it unless she absolutely had to.

'Mr Harriman doesn't love you!' she shouted, forcing him to listen. 'He hates all of us, Matt. You're no different than we are. You're a person just like us.'

'I'm special. He said so. Different.'

'He's lying. He's trying to trick you. He doesn't love you. How can he, when you're a man? Men will destroy him in the end. That's what it says in all the books, Matt, and that's why he hates people so. Men will destroy him because he's evil, because he lies.'

He let go of her then. Shaking his head in confusion, he sat back on the floor. Janet let the shard of glass slip from her bloodied fingers. She pulled her skirt down and crawled over to him, holding him in her arms.

'I did bad. I told. Now he'll hurt me,' whispered the boy, as if he were afraid Ahriman might be listening.

'We won't let him do anything bad to you, Matt.'

'You can't stop him. No one can. He can do anything 'cause he's strong. And he's here, he's here all the time.' His blue eyes grew wide with fear, but when he realized they were alone he finally allowed himself to cry.

He was still sitting on the bathroom floor, sobbing softly and trembling in her arms, when Neil came home. Together they carried Matt into his room and put him to bed. Then Janet washed and bandaged the cut on her hand and began to tell Neil everything that had happened.

18

It was dark and terrible and he didn't ever want to open his eyes. Maybe if he pretended to be asleep, Mr Harriman wouldn't hurt him anymore. But how could he pretend when the man was inside him all the time, watching what he did, listening to everything he said and everything he thought?

You let the bitch trick you, and now you're going to suffer for your treachery. You think the stick-pain is bad, my little friend? Then wait, because I know other kinds of pain that'll make you beg for the stick, you'll think it's so much better.

But she loves me. She said so.

And you believed her, didn't you? She would've cut your heart out with that piece of glass she was holding, and yet you let her trick you. You've learned nothing, Matthew, nothing but what it is to be a Jess.

A man. A person. Jess isn't everyone. He was just one man hurting Mama.

And Poppy? Was he just one man raping a little boy? And more than once too, remember, because he said if you ever told your mama he'd get you when you were alone and he'd cut it off.

Yes, but he didn't. We went away. Mama loved me and the Janet loves me, but you don't.

He bit into the pillow, not wanting them to hear his screams.

How could it hurt so when there was nothing there? Invisible, that's what it was. Magic. A trick. There was no one there and no one tearing him open and pushing inside, and yet he felt it, the pain so terrible that it seemed to clutch at his heart, making it hard to breathe.

It came and went like that, one finger, then two, three fingers, then a fist. When it wasn't the stick-pain it was pictures flashing again and again in his head – Jess and Mama, Poppy dragging him onto his lap, Connie lifting her nightie, the man with the beard and the white-coated Jesses at the hospital, the gunshot and Az faltering, the blood dripping until everything he saw was colored red as a sunset, but burning with pain.

But you still don't believe me, do you? Mr Harriman said. *Then listen to their lies, my little friend, and judge for yourself.*

It was another picture, only now the words were there as well, so clear he could have been standing right outside the kitchen, listening to them talking about his future.

'What choice do we have?' the Neil was saying as he sat at the table, drumming his fingers nervously on the arm of his chair. 'He could've killed you, Janet. He just about admitted killing Gillian.'

'But he didn't, don't you see? I was able to get through to him, Neil. So it's not as if this . . . whatever it is, controls his every move.'

The Neil looked very doubtful, and he said, 'When I was a little kid my father used to pretend there was a man who lived under my bed named Mr Colucci. Any time I didn't want to go to sleep, he'd knock on the wall when I wasn't looking. "That you, Mr Colucci? Yes, I know Neil isn't being a good boy. Of course I'll tell him, sure." He had me convinced there was this little guy under the bed who'd do God knows what to me if I didn't go to sleep when I was supposed to. This Ahriman or Harriman or whatever the hell its name is is just the same. He's made it up, Janet. And because he's lived with this make-believe friend of his for so long now, he actually believes it's there.'

'And if it really is?' the Janet asked.

The Neil frowned and shook his head. 'If Ahriman's there, then I'm the Prince of Wales.'

'Then what are we supposed to do? Give Torres his blood sample?'

'Maybe we don't have any other choice. If we say no, he'll get a court order, if not this week, then next. And if he is guilty – '

The Janet wouldn't even let him finish. She jumped to her feet, and when she held on to the edge of the table, Matt could see the way she winced because of the bandage. 'You think they're going to let him out, say he's cured? They wouldn't allow us to put him in a private institution. It'd be another San Andreas State, probably even worse than that.'

'I'm sorry, but he can't live here, Janet. We can't take that chance. Next time he goes off the deep end – '

'Jesus Christ, Neil, he's just a little boy.'

The Janet was weeping and the Neil was holding her in his arms.

'What if we just admit him to a private hospital, not tell Torres, at least not right away?' the Janet suggested. 'If he sees the boy is no longer a danger to anyone, he might be satisfied. After all, you can't punish someone who doesn't know what he's doing.'

'We'd have to do it right away,' said the Neil. He held the Mommy at arm's length and looked long and hard into her wet, leaking eyes.

The Janet nodded. 'I can start making phone calls tomorrow morning, soon as he leaves for school.'

But no, you don't want to believe me, Matthew, do you? Mr Harriman said as he made the Kaufmans fade like TV when you turned it off and the picture got smaller and smaller until it was just a dot of light and then that went out too and everything was black. *You think you're a Jess now, but you're not. I told you you're special, different, and you are, Matthew. You're so different you'll never be able to live the way Jesses do.*

But that means I'm all alone. Az is gone, Turk; Yip's too little. It's not the valley where no one saw me and I could hide. How can I hide in the city? They'd find me and put me away in a hospital and lock the door and never let me out.

They're going to put you away tomorrow or the next day, Matthew. That's why we have to stop them. My work here isn't done.

What work? he asked.

Such terrible pictures exploded behind his eyes! Such terrible frightening horrible pictures that he couldn't bear to watch them. But when he closed his eyes they were still there.

The Poppy was coming for him, the Poppy and the Neil and the Jess. They would tear him apart. They would gobble him up until there was nothing but bones and pieces of shredded skin like an empty carcass, like the cat he'd had that afternoon. They didn't want to kill him 'cause they were hungry. They wanted to kill for the pleasure of it, 'cause they liked to hurt and give him pain. Hadn't they done that in the past? Yes, of course they had. The Daddy didn't love him even if the Janet did. And maybe Mr Harriman wasn't lying the way she said. Maybe she didn't love him, either. She said she would make telephone calls to hospitals, that they would put him in a room and lock the door. He had to stop them, didn't he?

Of course you have to stop them, said Mr Harriman. He sounded so calm, so understanding. His friend was holding him in his arms and he was safe like with Mama before the bad things happened and she went away.

And you won't ever hurt me again? he whispered.

Why should I hurt you when you're part of me? And now that I know where to find Poppy, once we finish here we can punish him for what he did.

That made him smile and feel glad. And Jess?

We'll find him too. But if we don't stop the Janet and the Neil, the men will come with white coats and sticks and take you away. And if that happens, I'll have to go away too.

You wouldn't do that to me, Mr Harriman, would you?

I don't want to be locked up forever and ever, Matthew. There's too much work to be done. I'd have to go away.

But then I'd be all alone, worse than alone without you inside my head to talk to.

Then you have to listen to me and trust me. Because if you start listening to the Janet like you did before, they'll lock you up without me.

I'll listen, I promise! he cried out. Just tell me what I have to do to make you stay.

You must obey me, my little friend. You must do just what I tell you.

I will, I will, only you mustn't go 'way and leave me all alone.

What was love if the Kaufmans were going to send him away? That wasn't love, that was the treachery of their morality. But if they were as treacherous and deceitful as all the other Jesses, why had Mr Harriman chosen them for him? Why had he sent Turk to be his protector, his guardian?

Because the Janet writes books, said Mr Harriman.

I don't understand.

Books are ideas. Ideas change people. And young people are the easiest ones to influence, because if it says so in a book, then many of them will simply believe what they read, and think that it's true. But it doesn't matter now. Just do as I say. CALL THEM!

The voice was louder than thunder. It tore through his head like a wind coming off the desert, a hot, howling wind that sucked up the air and turned everything to ash.

Matt nodded dreamily and climbed out of bed. It felt as if he were floating, his feet not even touching the floor. He moved to the window, undid the lock, and pushed it all the way open.

CALL THEM!

The voice was a scream that cut through the darkness, lighting up the night. To ignore the command would be death, the burning and the burning that would never end for all of time, for every season forever and ever. They hated him because he was different. They hated him because he was strong and knew things they could never possibly understand. He had the wolf inside him, and the devil. He had centuries of cruelty locked away in his head. But now he would call them, obeying Ahriman's command.

Matt closed his eyes and began to concentrate. They had to come or else he'd be all alone, locked away without anyone to talk to.

'Can you see them yet?' he whispered aloud.

Yes, they're coming. Soon, Matthew, they'll be here very soon.

Neither of them could sleep. They lay awake, eyes on the ceiling, holding on to each other like two children frightened of the dark.

'I still can't believe this is happening,' Janet whispered. 'But if there's no such thing as Ahriman, then what about the voice we heard, the way he claimed to be Matthew?'

'Maybe we heard ourselves, Janet. Maybe we wanted to believe so badly that – '

Neil never finished the sentence. From the direction of the kitchen they heard something shatter, like breaking glass. They both sat up in bed, listening intently. Janet held her breath, trying to convince herself it was just the wind, playing havoc with their imagination.

But no, there it was again, as if someone were throwing dishes onto the kitchen floor.

'Christ almighty, now what?' Neil got out of bed, tightening the drawstring of his pajama bottoms before starting to the door. Just as he reached for the knob he looked back at her. 'Stay near the phone,' he said.

'In case of what?'

'Hell if I know.' But then he smiled, as if to say it couldn't be very serious. 'He must be having a tantrum or something. Maybe we ran out of ketchup . . . or raw hamburger.'

He left the door ajar and started down the hall. The door to Matt's room was closed, but before he had a chance to open it he was distracted by the sounds coming from the kitchen. Someone – or something, he thought uneasily – was still throwing things onto the floor.

Maybe there really was a guy named Jess. Maybe the kid was telling the truth all along. He was suddenly much more cautious, knowing there was little he could do to defend himself against a Saturday-night special.

I should be carrying a baseball bat, Neil thought, to bash the fucker's brains in.

He tiptoed through the darkened living room, eyes on the shutter doors. He couldn't hear anything but the sound of his own breathing, the adrenaline already beginning to pump through his bloodstream. Prepared for anything, Neil kicked the doors open, then jerked to the side in order to be out of the range of gunfire. But a slug didn't come whistling through the air, boring a hole into the wall just inches above his head.

Instead, the doors swung back again, and once more there was silence.

'You picked the wrong house,' he called out. 'Hell, we can barely keep up with the mortgage.'

No answer, though he hadn't really expected to hear anyone coming back with a snappy one-liner. He reached out, pushing the doors open as quietly as he could. The switch for the overhead lights was just on the inside of the doors. But he had to walk around them in order to flick it on. That meant going into the kitchen, and thus leaving himself completely vulnerable.

Maybe we should just call the police, he thought.

'That you, Matt? You okay, slugger?'

The only thing that was doing any talking was his heart, a mad thumpety-thump as he swallowed hard and stormed into the kitchen. He rushed around the doors to switch on the lights.

Nothing, not a goddamn thing, he thought with relief. Except – Shit!

Several of the bottom panes in the kitchen door lay in pieces on the floor. It looked as if they'd been kicked in, though the door itself wasn't open, the safety chain still in place.

He went over to get a better look, picking his way gingerly through the broken glass when he realized he hadn't bothered to put on slippers. He jiggled the knob, but the door didn't swing open as he feared it might. Neil bent down to get a better look, certain that by now the would-be intruder had already made good his escape. A long reddish-gray muzzle suddenly thrust itself through one of the missing panes.

Neil scrambled back along the floor, trying to avoid the glass but more interested in steering clear of the two rows of menacing teeth that now glinted in the light.

The door began to rattle, and he caught a glimpse of something – a dog, a coyote, a wolf? – just outside the door, when again the muzzle pushed through the opening, jaws snapping futilely at the air.

Neil turned and ran just as he heard glass shattering from the other end of the house. When he switched on the yard lights he couldn't believe his eyes. He stood there petrified, not knowing what was happening or what to do.

There were some two dozen coyotes in the backyard, and even as he watched they began to hurl themselves at the sliding doors, trying to break in.

COYOTES ON RAMPAGE, he saw the imaginary headline. PROMINENT LA WRITER AND TEACHER HUBBY CAUGHT IN CANINE BACKLASH.

'Jan, you all right?' he called out. 'Janet?'

'I'm calling the police!' she finally shouted.

He glanced back at the sliding doors. They were still holding, though the coyotes continued to throw themselves against the glass, increasingly desperate to break in. He expected to hear them howling, yapping, and barking as they moved restlessly around the yard. But they weren't making a sound, and that in itself was enough to give him the chills.

Rabies, that's what it is, he kept telling himself. He hurried down the hall, pausing just long enough to remove another sliver of glass from the sole of his foot. He'd get Matt, and then they'd lock themselves in the bedroom and wait for the cops to arrive.

'Matt, you all right, son?' He threw the door open, hanging on to the knob as if it were a lifeline.

The boy was sitting up in bed, crouched on all fours. A low, menacing growl erupted from the back of his throat, rising in volume until it became a shriek of rage, so maddened and inhuman that Neil could hardly believe his ears.

Abruptly, Matt turned his head in the direction of the window. It was wide open, and now a lean, shadowy figure jumped over the sill, quickly followed by another. Neil slammed the door shut as the coyotes hit the frame and the wood splintered under the impact.

Janet was just putting down the phone when he rushed into the bedroom. He locked the door behind him, then hurried over to the dresser and began pushing it across the floor. At first she seemed reluctant to help him and even made a move to open the door before he managed to shove her aside.

'Matthew,' she was shouting, 'we have to get him before – '

'They don't want Matt, they want us!'

How could he explain what he'd seen, when he didn't even know what it was?

'Please, just give me a hand with this, Janet. There isn't time.'

Something threw itself at the door, something that wanted to tear them apart like the woman who'd been attacked in Morongo Valley. Janet was right beside him then, and together they dragged the chest of drawers in front of the door, trying to barricade themselves in.

'He was there, on all fours, in his room,' Neil said breathlessly. He looked around the bedroom, hoping to find something they could use to defend themselves. 'The window was open and he must've called them because they were right there before I could say anything.'

'But how? I mean . . . how could he be able to – ' Janet stopped and took a deep breath. 'What are we going to do, Neil? I couldn't get through to them.'

He looked at her in disbelief. 'What are you talking about?'

'I couldn't get a goddamn dial tone,' Janet said hysterically. 'The phone's out.'

'He thought of everything, didn't he?'

Before Janet could answer, a coyote leaped up against the bedroom window, striking it with its hindquarters. The glass didn't break, but it rattled so loudly that he knew if they kept it up much longer the window wouldn't withstand the strain.

'Daddy! Daddy, let me in!' Matt cried from the other side of the door. The boy's fists beat a sharp tattoo, the sounds muffled by the chest of drawers. 'Mommy, help me, they're hurting me . . . no, don't, leave me alone, don't!'

Angry snarls followed, then a scream that was filled with so much terror and pain that Neil had to clap his hands over his ears, it sounded so convincing. But if he was certain it was a ruse, just a way to get them to open the door so the coyotes could rush inside and tear them apart, Janet was just as certain that what she'd heard was actually taking place.

She was clawing at the dresser, trying to push it aside, when he grabbed her by the shoulders and threw her back.

'What are you trying to do, Neil? They're attacking him, for God's sake!'

'They're not. They're listening to him, obeying everything he says. He's fine, Janet. We're the ones in trouble now, not Matt . . . or whatever his name is.'

He could see by her expression that she still didn't believe him. She began to call to the boy, trying to get him to respond. But there was silence now, and though Neil waited to hear the sound of breaking glass, the heavy thud of bodies hitting the sliding doors, he heard nothing at all.

Moving cautiously to the window, he peered outside. The yard was empty.

'Why?' Janet was saying. 'I thought I got through to him this afternoon. I thought he trusted us.'

You can't tame a wild animal, Neil thought. You can make it jump hoops and do all sorts of tricks, but you can't domesticate it.

'He must've heard us talking in the kitchen,' he told her. 'But now we have to worry about ourselves. If we can make it to the garage we'll be all right.'

'But what if they're still out there?'

'I didn't see anything.'

'Maybe the neighbors called the police.'

'And maybe they didn't.' Neil glanced at the window. 'It's not going to hold much longer. And once they get inside – ' He left the rest unsaid, thinking of Gillian Stanton and the way her arm had been ripped off at the elbow, the flesh gnawed right down to the bone.

'Maybe he's run off,' Janet whispered.

'About all we can hope for, isn't it?'

They pushed the chest aside. Neil put his ear to the door, holding his breath and listening intently. Nothing, not a goddamn thing but his heart pumping to beat the band.

'Take the shade off the lamp,' he said.

Janet didn't have to ask why. She unplugged the lamp, wrapped the cord around the base, and then removed the shade and the bulb. 'It's only china,' she said.

'Better than nothing. And whatever you do, Jan, don't take your time deciding.'

She nodded, gripping the lamp like a club. She looked completely in control of herself now that their very survival was in jeopardy. Neil put his fingers around the knob, turning it as slowly and silently as he could. He opened the door about an inch, the light from the bedroom streaming into the hall. So far, so good. Maybe Janet was right. Maybe the boy had decided to just run off, afraid of what might happen if the police showed up. Neil opened the door a little wider.

Something streaked past him, pushing its way into the bedroom. He slammed the door shut and spun around. It was Jip, but the puppy was behaving as savagely as the coyotes. It threw itself at Janet, and though she swung the lamp, it dug its teeth into the back of her leg and hung there like a leech, unwilling to let go.

She was screaming and trying to tear it off her when he rushed across the room, lashing out with his foot. As the puppy dropped to the floor Janet hobbled back. The dog turned on him then, flinging itself into the air, its jaws narrowly grazing his forearm.

'The blanket,' Neil gasped. 'Throw it over him.' He backed off, jumping to the side when Jip darted forward, still trying to attack.

Janet yanked the blanket off the bed and heaved it into the middle of the room.

'The pillows too!' Neil yelled. He threw himself down on top of the snarling animal they'd managed to trap beneath the bedding. Any moment and Jip would tear his way free. He pressed the pillow over the puppy's struggling outline, holding it there and counting off the seconds until it finally lay motionless.

Blood streaming from the wound in her leg, Janet bent down and retrieved the lamp. Behind her a frenzied chorus of high-pitched yaps signaled the coyotes' return. One of the animals leaped against the window, striking it sideways with its flank. The glass cracked under the impact, a long jagged line running from the top of the frame all the way down to the sill.

Neil grabbed her by the hand and dragged her toward the bathroom, only to realize that, thanks to Matt, the door was already broken. Behind them the window caved in with an explosion of shattering glass.

'The closet!' Janet cried.

They piled inside, slammed the door behind them, and turned the bolt. There was nothing they could do now but stay there and wait.

Torres was thinking that his wife was going to be so pissed off at him she probably wouldn't even give him a chance to plead his case. 'That's what happens when you're married to a cop,' he heard himself say, trying to reason with her even though reason wasn't going to get him anything but a door slammed in his face. 'So what if it's our anniversary?

We can always go out tomorrow night. I just couldn't help it, honey. We found another kid out by the San Diego Freeway, strangled like the last one and . . . come on, Rosalie, give me a break. I'll take you some place fancy tomorrow, I promise.'

Slam!

He heard her fling the door shut. But maybe he wasn't giving her enough credit. Maybe she'd take it on the chin, knowing it wasn't his fault. After all, he had a job to do, and it wasn't as if he hadn't called, warning her he might be delayed. Of course, at the time he thought it would only be an hour, not four.

Torres was halfway up Laurel Canyon, with at least another thirty minutes' drive ahead of him before he got to Northridge, when a call came through. The mention of a disturbance on Los Altos Drive made him put his flasher up on the dashboard before he even had a chance to think twice about it.

If he didn't watch out he was going to cream the guy in front of him. He flipped the toggle switch that activated the siren. As his unmarked car began giving out with a series of whoops and warbles, everybody started moving over to the right to let him pass.

Torres raced up Laurel Canyon, leaving rubber as he turned right on Mulholland. It was so clear out that he could even see the mountains at the far side of the Valley.

Some night for a view, he thought. But maybe now the guys in homicide would finally stop ribbing him about wanting to nail a ten-year-old for sex assault, murder, and probably even cannibalism.

When the coyotes started crashing into the closet door, slamming against the wood one after another, Janet raised her voice, calling out to Matt. Perhaps she could still reason with him as she'd reasoned with him earlier. He might call them off, if only he'd give her a chance to try to get through to him.

But if he was listening, he wasn't saying anything, and all her pleas went unanswered.

Neil told her she was wasting her time. If he'd gone this far, he wasn't about to stop. It was then that they heard the sirens. And it was then that the boy finally began to talk.

'You wanted to send me away!' he screamed from the other side of the door. 'Mr Harriman showed me and I listened. I heard you talking 'bout hospitals. You don't love me, you never have. But we're gonna get you for being mean and lying. Mr Harriman can do things no one else can. He's not gonna let anyone hurt me anymore. They're all gonna be punished, and you're gonna be punished worst of all!'

A voice boomed out at them from a bullhorn, the amplified sounds echoing loudly through the closet.

'We're in here!' Neil shouted, hoping they could hear him.

There was a last futile effort to break the door down, followed by gunshots and an animal's frighteningly human scream.

'In here, in the bedroom!' Neil called again.

'Just stay where you are!' the electronically amplified voice responded.

They were huddled together in the farthest corner of the closet, the air heavy with the smell of mothballs. Now they came slowly to their feet, waiting to be told it was safe to unlock the door. There was another round of gunfire, doglike barks, squeals of pain, and footsteps moving swiftly across the floor.

'Christ, I never saw so many in my life,' someone was saying.

'In here!' Neil yelled.

'It's safe to come out now,' one of the officers called from the other side of the door.

When they stepped out of the closet, the first person Janet saw was Detective Torres, dressed in the same rumpled blue leisure suit he had on the night she met him at the hospital.

We'll have to call the animal regulation boys, get 'em to come out here and clean up this mess for you. What'd you do, slay the fatted calf and leave it out as bait? You got coyotes up the kazoo.'

Torres's light, bantering tone failed to elicit a smile.

'Where's my son?' she demanded. There were two dead coyotes in the bedroom, one of which had only three legs and the stump of a fourth. Fragments of glass crunched noisily beneath her feet. But she saw no sign of Matthew.

'Good question. Was he here when all this started?'

'You're damn right he was here.' Neil spoke up.

She glared at him, hoping he wouldn't say more than he had to. But why are you still trying to protect him? she asked herself. Because the voice had spoken, whispering sandy go breeway. And sandy go breeway was a lot easier to accept than some demon with a snake-covered head a bunch of Persians had dreamed up to keep the masses in tow.

'Then why don't you start telling me what happened, Mr Kaufman?' replied Torres. Before Neil could say anything, however, the detective turned to his men, ordering them to fan out and search the rest of the house.

'There's nothing to tell,' Janet insisted. 'They went berserk. Maybe they have rabies or something. It's happened before, hasn't it? Like lemmings throwing themselves into the sea, or a school of whales beaching themselves.'

'Coyotes don't run in packs of two dozen. And to the best of my knowledge, Mrs Kaufman, they've never been known to attack a man.'

Her throat was dry and scratchy. Every muscle in her

body ached, the wound along the back of her leg worst of all. She stepped past Torres with his smug, condescending expression, picking her way through the glass as she headed to the kitchen.

The kitchen door looked as if someone had set off a bomb under it. One of the police officers was dragging a dead coyote across the floor, leaving a trail of blood in its wake.

Take everything one step at a time, she kept telling herself. Get a drink of water. Wash the cut. And hope he's managed to escape. But if he should ever decide to come back . . . no, he's much too clever for that.

'Where does that lead to?' Torres crossed the kitchen, pausing before the door that opened into the garage. 'Nasty wound,' he said. 'Coyote?'

'Labrador retriever.'

He grinned, then killed the smile when he realized she hadn't intended to make a joke. 'Where's it go?' he said again, jiggling the doorknob.

'Garage,' said Neil.

Torres released the deadbolt. He tried to push the door open, only to discover that instead of being hinged, the door slid back into the wall. 'Where's the light?'

'Just a chain pull,' said Neil. 'Can you see it hanging down between the two cars?'

Torres glanced back at the officers who'd come into the kitchen. 'Any of you guys got a flashlight?'

'Right here,' one of the men replied.

The detective took out his service revolver and flicked off the safety.

'But he's not armed!' shouted Janet.

'We don't know that for sure, Mrs K,' Torres said dryly.

'Don't give me this "Mrs K" shit. You seem to be forgetting he's just a little boy.'

'A little boy who commands wild animals to do his bidding seems pretty special to me. 'Course, it could've all been a coincidence. And besides, what are you worried about? We don't even know if he's in here.'

One of the men aimed the beam of his flashlight on the dangling length of chain. Another held his thirty-eight in readiness as Torres stepped cautiously into the garage. He reached up and tugged on the chain. The bare hundred-watt bulb sent glaring shadows from one end of the garage to the other.

Don't let him hurt me, Mommy. I'll be good, I promise, only don't let him hurt me.

Janet heard the voice as clearly as if he were standing right before her. Yet the words were like a thought, unspoken.

Can you hear me, Matt? she called out, using her mind to say what she couldn't bring her lips to utter.

Mommy, help me. I'm Matthew. I'm your little boy, and they want to hurt me. But I'll be good, only don't let them do mean things to me like before. Make them go 'way, Mommy. Please, make them all go 'way and I'll be good, I promise.

'Don't hurt him!' She rushed after Torres, only to feel Neil grabbing hold of her arm and dragging her back. Even as she struggled to break free, the detective was calling out to the boy.

'I know you're in here, son. Why don't you just come out now? No one's going to hurt you, I promise.'

Lies, Jesses with their lies, lies and more lies! Why do they hate me so, Mommy? I was good, I pretended good, I was Mama's best little boy.

Wave after wave of emotion flooded her brain. She was being bombarded with all of the child's mounting terror, the fear he was experiencing now that he realized he was trapped.

'Do what he says!' she called out to him. 'He won't hurt you, Matt, I swear!'

Lies! the child's voice shrieked through her brain. *They killed Mama and Az, and now they want to kill me too. But I won't let them. Mr Harriman'll protect me. He'll make everything right again.*

Torres was still calling to the boy, urging him to come out.

'Listen to him, Matt!' she cried at the top of her voice. She tore herself away from Neil, trying to get between Torres and her son.

But by then Matt had finally come out of hiding. With a maddened scream, a sound of both fear and aggression, he bounded along on all fours, hurling himself at the detective.

'Don't shoot!' Torres shouted to his men.

The warning came seconds too late.

There was a deafening blast. For a moment the boy seemed to be suspended in mid-air. Then, as he crumpled to the floor, clutching his chest and groaning in pain, Janet too began to groan. His terror was now hers. His agony would be with her forever. She was choking on his blood. He couldn't breathe and neither could she.

The burning and the burning and the fire and it hurt . . . Don't let him hurt me, Mama! Don't let him hurt me like this!

Janet slid down to the floor, screaming now as the pain touched every cell, and Ahriman reared up before her, howling with glee.

LIES AND MORE LIES . . .

The voice slowly faded, reverberating in her ears. She felt Neil's steadying hands helping her to her feet. 'I'm sorry,' she heard Ray Torres say. 'It's over,' she heard Neil whisper.

Matthew Kaufman lay in the middle of the garage, both hands still clutching his chest. She would kiss the blood from his lips and hold him in her arms. He was Matthew David Kaufman, and he would always be a part of her, the most beautiful child she had ever seen, with luminous blue eyes and delicate features.

Part of me, she thought. No matter what they've done to you, you'll always be part of me.

Rebirth

Los Altos Drive, Tuesday, 4 October 1983

'How's she doing?'

'Beautifully. Soon as I put her in the crib she went out like a light.'

'How's my little girl?'

'Shh, you don't want to wake her, Neil.'

'And how's my big girl? How are you feeling, Janet?'

'Still a little tired. A few more days' rest and I'll be fine.'

'Still upset about the book?'

'Wouldn't you be, all that work down the drain? Automatic writing, that's what they'd probably call it. Obscenities, Neil; the whole thing was filled with filth, perversion. All the decency taken out of it. All the human values, anything that was worthwhile, uplifting, twisted into something hideous, something evil and grotesque. I never knew I had such thoughts. I never dreamed – '

'It's all right, Jan. It's over. They weren't your thoughts anyway. And you'll write lots of other books, I guarantee. The important thing is that it's all behind us.'

'And we're a family again, and that's all that counts.'

Behind the pale, translucent lids of her eyes shapes moved, swaying from side to side. She heard sounds pressing down against her ears, soft, gentle sounds of varying degrees of pitch. Did the shapes and the sounds belong together? Did the shapes make the sounds, or did the sounds make the shapes?

She couldn't open her eyes yet, and so she lay there against the softness of the crib, feeling vibrations now as the shapes moved off, thudding faintly like the heartbeat of the wet, fragrant darkness where they had floated for so long.

It was warm and safe like the inside, but dry instead of wet. And even when the shapes and sounds were gone, she would never be alone. They were together, part of each other, a link that could never be broken. He would teach her everything he knew, and when she grew strong she would do whatever the companion wished, for that was why she had been born.

The baby gurgled happily. There was still so much work to be done, but now they had all the time in the world to do it.